THIS IS NOT A TALE OF OUR OWN WORLD.

It is a world like ours in many ways, but one where dragons live in their own lands, wary of humans. One with Sorcerers, light and dark. One where Pipers can control things around them merely by playing a Song.

Yet tales of other worlds *can* reach us, sometimes. All it takes is a little magic, and the Pipers have always known something that – for us – is easy to forget:

There is magic in music.
Listen…

TO MY SON ELIAS,
WHO HEARD IT ALL FIRST

First published in the UK in 2018 by Usborne Publishing Ltd., Usborne House, 83-85 Saffron Hill, London EC1N 8RT, England. www.usborne.com

Copyright © S.A. Patrick, 2018

Cover and inside illustrations by George Ermos

Title typography by Leo Nickolls

The right of S.A. Patrick to be identified as the author of this work has been asserted by him in accordance with the Copyright, Designs and Patents Act, 1988.

The name Usborne and the devices ♀ 🎈 are Trade Marks of Usborne Publishing Ltd.

A CIP catalogue record for this book is available from the British Library.

ISBN 9781474945677   04819/2   JFMAMJJASO D/18
Printed in the UK.

A DARKNESS OF DRAGONS

S.A. PATRICK

USBORNE

every villager could imagine where the terrifying mouth was, fangs dripping, ready to sink into the flesh of anyone who got too near.

Its slow steps drew a heavy crunch from the snow underneath. From its head came a steady moaning.

And the villagers kept moving towards it.

"Go!" they called to the children as they passed them. "Run to your homes!"

There was one child left, though. One small boy, too frightened to move, standing directly in the creature's path – Hap Werner, only four years old.

"Little Hap," called the Elder. "You go home now! Go on with you!"

But Hap shook his head, rooted to the spot. The creature was getting closer to him.

With no time to waste, the Elder raised the shovel she was carrying. "I'll have you, Beast!" she cried, and ran towards the creature. The other villagers followed, wielding what weapons they had – hoes, pitchforks, brooms.

The Elder was first to reach it, and she swung her shovel hard, hitting the Ice Beast's head; the creature made a strange noise before falling to the snowy ground with a thud.

There it lay, motionless, as the villagers surrounded it, ready to hit it again if it moved even a fraction.

But where the shovel had hit its head, a few chunks

of ice and snow were now gone, revealing something underneath. The villagers stared at what they saw: a very cold, very red nose, and below that, a very human mouth.

"*Ow...*" the mouth groaned.

For a moment the villagers looked at each other in shock. Then they began to scrape away what they could of the ice and snow that clung to the stranger. With each chunk removed he was smaller, lighter, yet what they found underneath was a curious giant, the legs and arms unnaturally thick. Only when more ice was cleared did it make sense to them.

Clothes.

Layer upon layer of shirts and trousers: dozens, perhaps more. The stranger's neck was thick with a hundred scarves, the hands and head puffed out by gloves and hats. Torn strips of material were densely wrapped around the face, gaps left only for the mouth, nose and eyes.

Too heavy to carry, they dragged the unconscious stranger to the village, his legs and feet still ice-bound. In the village hall a fire was roaring, and they propped him up in a chair in front of the blazing logs, then began cutting and unravelling the layers with care. In one corner of the hall, the pile of discarded garments grew, while the unconscious stranger shrank, until all that was left was a thin figure slouched in a chair, with a long coat over his simple clothing.

It was a *boy*, his hair dark and scruffy.

"Look how young he is, he can't be more than thirteen!" said a villager. "How did he survive his journey?"

"A good question!" said the Elder. "To emerge from the forest where he did, he must have come through Andig's Pass. An icy hell this time of year."

"It's certain death for anyone crazy enough to go that way!" said the villager.

"And yet this boy made it through," said the Elder, thoughtful. "There must be more to him than meets the eye!" She reached inside the boy's coat and searched the deep pockets within. After a moment, she slowly pulled out her hand; with it came a wooden flute, the length of her forearm. Those watching gasped as they saw.

It was *not* a flute, of course. The small finger holes were far more numerous, the layout much more complex, than on any flute they had ever seen.

This was not a flute.

It was a *Pipe*.

The Elder lifted it up. "The Piper has come," she said in awe, and the people cheered. The doors of the village hall were flung open, and the news was passed on to those waiting outside. Everyone took up the call:

"The Piper has come! *The Piper has come!*"

2
THE STRANGER

When the boy finally opened his eyes, he found himself on a small bed, in a room he didn't recognize, wearing a simple nightshirt that he was certain didn't belong to him. He sat up and tried to recall how he'd got there, but nothing came. Nothing but a sense that there was something very important that he needed to remember…

"You're awake at last," came a voice. Startled, the boy turned and saw an old woman sitting in a chair in the shadows of the corner. She stood and brought the chair over to the bedside. "My name is Greta," she said. "I'm the Elder of Patterfall."

"Of where?" said the boy.

"Patterfall," said Greta, looking worried. "This village."

"I'm sorry," he said. "I don't remember much. About anything."

Greta nodded. "Perhaps that's to be expected. The stress of your journey here has robbed you of your memory."

"Will it come back?"

"I've seen this kind of thing before," said Greta. "You're not the first to have stumbled out of the forest close to death, although you're certainly the youngest. Your memory will return soon enough. Something will spark it back to life. Do you remember anything about your journey?"

He thought for a moment, but all that came was that terrible dark walk through the forest, one step after another with no end. His eyes widened. "I don't even remember my own name!"

"I think I can answer that one," said Greta. She stood and fetched a coat that was hanging on a hook on the far wall. "When we found you, you were snowbound from head to toe, and wearing layer upon layer of clothes. Underneath them all was this coat. Is it yours?"

The boy smiled when he saw it, feeling relief at remembering even such a small thing. "Yes," he said. "It is."

"Then here," said Greta. She turned back the collar of the coat, to reveal a name embroidered in neat stitches. "I suspect this is your name."

The boy read the name aloud: "Patch Brightwater."

It felt right, and with the name came another small piece of his memory. "My grandmother stitched it in my coat, so I'd not lose it."

Greta smiled. "It's very good to meet you, Patch Brightwater!" she said. "It's *more* than good. You see, I know why you came here." She reached into Patch's coat pocket and pulled out the Pipe. "You came to save us!"

Patch stared. "Me?" he said, and Greta nodded. "I'm a Piper?" He reached out slowly and took the Pipe in his hands. As he held it, more memories came back to him, precious fragments and images. Moments, he realized, from his training at Tiviscan. *Yes*, he thought, *Tiviscan Castle, the home of the Pipers' Council*. The place where those hoping to become Pipers go to learn the Piper's Art.

There was still so much missing, but as his fingers moved over the holes in the Pipe, he knew that the Songs were clear in his mind.

"I *am* a Piper," said Patch at last, and now the tears came, flowing down his cheeks and past his broad smile.

Greta gave him a kindly pat on his hand. "You're much younger than we expected, I admit…"

Patch was filled with a sudden worry – the same feeling he'd had when he'd woken, that there was something very important he still needed to remember.

"But no ordinary traveller could have made it through

12

that snow!" said Greta. "We summoned a Piper, and here you are!"

Another memory came to him then. "Wait... There was an emergency. I was in a hurry." He looked to Greta, and she nodded to encourage him. "I think...there was a trader. He had the only cart heading this way, him and his family." His eyes narrowed as he concentrated. "The road was blocked, the snow too deep. As we turned, the cart's axle snapped. The trader unhitched his horse, mounted it with his wife and child, and rode off."

"They left you?"

Patch sighed. "Who can blame them? I looked in the cart for food, and all I found was clothing – the trader's wares. At first I stayed in the shelter of the cart, and played a heating Song on my Pipe to keep me warm. But the cold became too great; my fingers grew numb and I had to stop. So I put on layer after layer of clothes, and waited for the weather to improve, but it just kept getting worse. Finally I started to walk. There's a simpler heating Song that can be whistled – lip-playing, we call it. I used that for a time, until my dry lips cracked in the chill and I was forced into silence. I kept walking, all through the night..." He thought of how *long* that terrible icy walk had seemed. *Endless.*

"And you reached us!" said Greta. "You mentioned an emergency, Patch, and that's exactly what our village has! One that will leave us all in poverty, and perhaps end our lives. As soon as we knew how dangerous things had become, we sent a messenger to Wassil, the nearest town. The messenger took the only horse strong enough to make it through the deep snow; his mission was to summon a Piper. You!"

"Tell me, Greta," said Patch. "Tell me what I've come here to do."

Greta paused, looking weighed down with worry. "In summer," she said, "the fertile valley gives us enough grain to last a year, for our cattle and our bellies and for seeding the next year's crops, with some left over that we can sell. Each winter, the roads become impassable. The village remains isolated until late spring. Our dogs and our cats deal with any vermin from the forest. But not this year. One by one, our dogs went lame, our cats grew fearful, and the food in our homes was plundered. At first we couldn't understand what was doing it. They were not seen, and they left no signs."

Patch's face grew pale. "What…what was it?"

"Rats," said Greta. "More than we've ever known. Bigger than we've ever known. Smarter than we've ever known. Anything we did, it wasn't enough. They ate no poison. They triggered no traps." Greta shook her head, visibly distressed. "Nothing we've done has stopped them. They are frightening, Patch. And now they're all in the grain storehouse in the centre of the village, but we dare not attack them. They like it there, protected from the cold, with enough food to last them a few weeks. But when that's done, they'll find all our hidden stores. They'll consume everything we have. And then—" She closed her eyes, unable to speak for a moment. "None of the villagers have been hurt by them, yet. Not one. But when the grain is gone that will surely change."

Patch stared at her in horror. "Change? What do you mean?"

"We are trapped in the village, but so are the rats. When they're hungry enough, they'll come for us! You can see why we're desperate."

"Rats…" he said, thinking. What had he been taught? "Infestations are a common thing for Pipers to deal with, be it rats, mice, cockroaches." He let his fingers move over the Pipe, and smiled as he realized they were already marking out the notes of the Song he needed. "It's strange," he said. "There's so much I don't remember, but my training comes back to me easily."

"We should have called for a Piper weeks ago," said Greta. "But some of the villagers were afraid to."

"Afraid?" said Patch. "They have nothing to fear from me!"

"They thought of what happened in Hamelyn."

Patch opened his mouth to answer, but then the memory of the Hamelyn Piper returned to him like a slap to the face.

It was the greatest shame of Pipers – ten years ago, the town of Hamelyn had been infested by rats. A Piper came, a Piper with nothing but evil in his heart; once he had got rid of the rodents he played another Song, and led the children of Hamelyn off into the night. And what had become of them? To this day, nobody knew. Even after the Hamelyn Piper had been caught and thrown into the deepest dungeon, he had never revealed the truth.

For centuries, Pipers had been trusted completely, their honour beyond question as they wandered the lands, seeking work – helping crops to grow, say, or finding the right place to dig a well. A price would be agreed, and the work would be done.

The events in Hamelyn almost destroyed that trust. Never again would a Piper be able to simply turn up and offer their services. Now, Pipers had to be officially summoned, so that people could be sure that the Pipers who came were qualified and trustworthy.

"They have no need to worry," said Patch. He pulled back the blanket that covered his lower half and swung his legs out of the bed. "There's no time to waste. My clothes?"

"The clothing you wore under your coat has been cleaned in readiness," said Greta. "But I think you need to eat and rest first, to regain your strength."

"Nonsense," he said. "Waiting just means the rats eat more of your precious grain!" The rats, Patch thought, couldn't be as bad as Greta had made out. They were scared, these villagers, and their fear had made everything seem so much worse that it really was. He would cure them of their rats, and cure them of their fear!

He tried to stand, but his legs gave way at once and he fell back onto the bed, breathless.

"You see?" said Greta. "You've been unconscious for two days. You must eat and drink, and rest some more. Only then will you have the strength to deal with those rats. Tomorrow!"

Patch knew she was right; he was only just getting his breath back, and the mention of food had made him realize how hungry he was. "Tomorrow it is," he said.

Patch ate his fill, and slept well. In the morning, after a bowl of stew for breakfast, he got dressed and spent some time exercising his fingers. Nothing more of his memory had come back yet, but he was confident about his Piping – and that was all that mattered.

Greta knocked on the door and entered. "Are you ready?" she asked.

"Almost," said Patch. "First, though, we need a plan – a way to kill the rats! Somewhere to drown them, say."

"Follow me," said Greta.

Beside the village was a river twenty feet across, a simple

wooden bridge spanning its fast-flowing water. They followed it a short way downstream until they came to a cliff edge. There, the river became a roaring waterfall.

"This is where our village gets its name."

"Patterfall?" said Patch. "I would have expected something more gentle."

"The village has been here for three hundred years," said Greta. "Back then, the river was little more than a stream. Things have changed."

"No kidding." He crept forwards to the precipice and looked over. The drop was at least a hundred feet, and the base of the waterfall was littered with jagged rocks. The falling water would dash the rats against the sharp stones, so a quick death was assured. "This will do it," he said.

When they got back, everyone had gathered around the oak tree that stood in the heart of the village. They cheered at the sight of the Piper.

Patch waved to them, and Greta led him to the front of the large grain storehouse where the rats had taken up residence.

The cheering fell away to silence as the people of the village waited for the Piper to begin.

Greta walked to the doors of the storehouse. She removed the chains that had been thrown across the doors, then placed a huge key into the lock and turned it. She looked to Patch, who nodded. Slowly, Greta pulled the doors open, returning quickly to Patch's side. All eyes watched as he studied his quarry.

Then Patch, his body completely rigid, fell backwards in a dead faint.

3

THE PIPER OF
PATTERFALL

Patch came to, the flagstones cold under his back.
He opened his eyes and saw Greta's worried face.

"Take my hand!" she whispered, supporting him as he
stood.

"Let's try that again," said Patch, but his breathing grew
more and more rapid, and his grip on Greta became ever
tighter.

He didn't want to look through the storehouse doors
again, but he had no choice.

He looked.

Rats!

Sleeping among mounds of grain and bags of seed and
sacks of corn, sleeping in groups of three and groups of ten
and – Patch shivered – groups of far *more* than ten. Brown

rats, white rats, speckled rats, long rats, short rats. One had a tail with curious markings, ringed with red hoops all down its length.

All were asleep, but nowhere, not anywhere he looked, could Patch see a rat that could be called "small", or "thin".

Some were too fat even to curl up for their sleep, looking like big furry marrows or hairy loaves of bread. The fattest of all was a great rat pumpkin that surely couldn't have moved even if it wanted to, its feet sticking straight out, high off the ground, its belly making a dent in the grain where it lay.

Not a sound came from them – except perhaps, if he'd been brave enough to step inside and listen with a careful ear, the noise of little ratty snores and burps.

Rats, content and asleep.

Huge rats.

A vast number of huge rats.

He turned to Greta and opened his mouth to speak. No words came.

"You thought I was exaggerating," she said.

Patch nodded. He took a very long breath, and let out a very long sigh.

"Is it too hard a task?" said Greta.

Patch saw hope drain from the Elder. *No*, he thought, *I won't give in.* These people needed him, and they had saved his life.

But he could hardly pretend this was a selfless act. *He* was trapped here, just as the villagers were. Yet the rats did seem oddly cosy; they were so peaceful that it was a bit of a stretch to imagine them bearing down on him with blood-drenched maws.

He shivered. His mind had already started to imagine it.

He turned and addressed Greta. "The Art of Piping," he started, but it came out squeaky. He cleared his throat and tried again. "The Art of Piping," he repeated, in the confident voice that came from reciting such a well-learned passage, "has many magics. The Song most often used for clearing pests of whatever kind is called the Dream. This magic fills the target's mind full of the wonderful things that they most desire, and makes them think those things can be found by following the music of the Pipe." He looked at the rats, his mouth suddenly dry. "There are…*more* than I expected, I admit, but you avoid thinking about the number, you see. Then it's just as if there were ten, or twenty, rather than—" He gestured towards the rodents, then reached into his coat and took out his Pipe.

The Dream, he thought, grateful that he could remember his training. His fingers were already moving against the Pipe, rehearsing the intricate patterns that would draw the rats to their doom.

He put the Pipe to his lips and began.

It started with a simple melody, six notes repeated with a little variation. Patch played this half a dozen times, then took his mouth from the pipe.

Yet the music continued. Greta's eyes were wide with astonishment. "It...it keeps *playing*—"

"Of course," said Patch. "Otherwise you couldn't add layers, and it's the layers of a Song that make it so powerful."

Now, Patch started another melody – overlapping the first, seeming to shift away from it, then towards it again. Beside him, Greta was smiling, *grinning*, at the sound.

With the second melody holding, Patch added another sequence, then another, and another. The real work was being done. There was a change in the overall sound, a change that spoke of things that *could be*.

The Dream. The Dream was forming.

Patch's fingers moved in what seemed like effortless complexity. Suddenly he frowned and stopped playing. His hands fell to his sides, the Song starting to fade. He looked at Greta, anxious.

"What's wrong?" she asked, but Patch's attention was stolen by the sound that started among the villagers. The sound of cheering and applause.

He looked from the villagers to Greta, confused. "Why are they clapping?"

"They've never heard anything like that," said Greta.

"It was… It was—" She shook her head, grasping for the word. "It was *beautiful*."

"Maybe so," said Patch. "But it didn't *work*." He nodded towards the storehouse. The rats hadn't even stirred. "I don't understand! They should be filled with the knowledge that their dreams, *all* their dreams, await them if they follow the sound!" He began to mutter to himself.

It was Greta who realized what was wrong. "Patch, look at those animals." They both looked. "Do you think they *could* find somewhere better? They are warm, and sleeping in a building full of food! Don't you think they're already in their dream?"

"Of course!" said Patch, putting a hand to his forehead. "Think, think!" he said to himself. He began to stride up and down, his Pipe clenched behind his back. "Wait!" he said at last. "There's another way. But it's a little bit –" he paused for a moment, before finishing – "a little bit *unusual*."

"Unusual" wasn't the first word that had come to Patch's mind.

When Greta had pointed out the reason for the Dream's failure, he'd hunted around in his memory for an alternative. *Maybe I can't remember enough of my training after all*, he'd thought, and that was a *terrible* thought, because part of his mind had got really very *good* at imagining how the rats would go about feasting on him if he botched this whole thing.

24

But eventually one idea *had* come, a Song that was so clear and so strong, something he *knew* would work, because he somehow knew that he was particularly good at it. Unfortunately, there was one other thing that he knew about the Song.

He knew that using it was absolutely against the laws of Piping, and had been ever since the Hamelyn Piper had played it to such devastating effect.

In short, it was *illegal*, and "illegal" was the word that he'd almost said to Greta. "Unusual" seemed a lot less alarming, so he'd gone with that instead.

He tried to recall what "illegal" meant for a Piper, and images came to him, images of very serious-looking Pipers in black-and-purple robes. *Oh, yes*, he thought. *Them*.

The Custodian Elite, they were called. If a Piper was to break the laws of Piping, the Custodian Elite would be the ones who brought them to justice.

Still, this was an emergency, and surely even the Custodian Elite would understand.

"This one is called the Dance," he said, then he raised his Pipe and started to play.

4

THE DANCE

Layer upon layer, the Dance took shape in his Pipe. At the sound of it he felt a familiar joy grow in his heart.

Soon the Song had formed. At first, the sleeping rats seemed oblivious to it. Then one of them stirred – the strange rat with the red-ringed tail. With a yawn it stood and sniffed the air, and saw Patch. Its paws came up to its mouth in a way that was strangely human, as if it was shocked. It waved frantically, shaking its head and squeaking, almost as if it was trying to warn the others.

How peculiar, Patch thought.

The strange rat clamped its paws tightly over its ears, attempting to shut out the sound – as if that would make any difference! – but after a few seconds the animal's rear paws were tapping to the rhythm, its agitation vanishing as it started to whirl and swish from side to side, caught in the Dance. All thought of escape had gone, Patch knew. The only thing it would know, from now until the moment it hit the rocks at the bottom of the waterfall, was the joy of the music.

In the centre of the storehouse floor was a small clearing, and that was where the red-ringed rat made its way. One by one, the other rats woke and followed, hopping and marching in time to the Song that Patch played. A circle of rats formed in the clearing, all on their hind legs, their little paws grasping those of the rats either side of them. As the ring completed, another larger ring started to link up outside the first.

It's working, Patch thought, thrilled and relieved in equal measure. *It's working!*

It wasn't long before ten circles of rats danced round and round, more rodents joining them every second. The circles danced one way, then turned and danced the other. The faces of the rats were happy, and gleeful squeaks could be clearly heard over the music.

The centre of the floor was almost full, so the rest of the rats formed groups in the hollows and spaces where they found themselves. The fattest rats, unable to dance, waggled their paws and heads and feet with smiling eyes and loud cheering squeaks.

All the rats were caught in the Dance now.

It's time, he thought. *Time to take the Dance outside to the river, and the waterfall!*

He backed away from the storehouse. In each of the dancing groups, the rats paired up and began skipping to the exit, with the fattest being rolled out by some of the others.

Patch glanced towards the villagers; anxiety was written on their faces. They wouldn't have to worry for much longer. He turned towards the bridge that crossed the river. From there, he would guide the rats into the water and keep them entranced until they went over the precipice. Greta was already heading to the bridge – the sight of the rats streaming out of the storehouse was enough to make anyone want to get away as quickly as they could.

Patch couldn't hurry, though. As he played, he took slow steps and kept glancing behind him, making sure his pace was right.

Hundreds of rats – thousands! – were pouring out of the doors, following Patch in a line ten rats across, spinning and jigging their way along, twenty feet behind him.

Had he been walking at normal speed he would have reached the bridge within a minute. Matching the pace of the rats, it took five times longer to get there, his fingers racing over the Pipe.

He reached the middle of the bridge and sent the rats towards the water. Line by line, the rats waded in, and each line kept dancing as they swam, forming a little circle as the strong current carried them downstream. Entire circles of rats would turn one way then another, before diving under the water, their tails and feet sticking out and moving from side to side in perfect time, before they brought their heads back up and danced on.

When a third of them were in the river, Patch looked to the waterfall's edge; so did Greta, who was now standing beside him.

"It almost seems cruel," said Greta. "Look at them, with no idea what's coming!"

Patch shook his head and took his lips from the Pipe. "They'll dance all the way down to the sharp rocks below," he said. "The whole time, they'll be happy."

"And we'll be free," said Greta, suddenly overwhelmed. "The village is saved!" She stepped forward and embraced him, then quickly stepped back again with an apologetic nod.

Patch smiled. He was almost overwhelmed, both with emotion and fatigue. It was only excitement that was keeping him on his feet, he knew. It would be a while yet before he fully recovered from his icy journey to the village, and he was still close to exhaustion.

Greta waved to the cheering crowd. Patch waved at them too, but only briefly – the Song could start to unravel if he didn't maintain its melodies. He turned back to the rats, nearly half of them now in the water.

He'd glanced so briefly at the villagers, he couldn't be blamed for not noticing one *very* important detail...

The villagers' feet had started to tap.

Almost there, Patch thought.

The frontmost rats were floating downriver and close to the point of no return, where the water quickened before hurtling into the void. The rearmost were just entering the water now.

He looked at Greta, expecting to see triumph on her face, watching the rats get ever nearer to oblivion.

Instead, Greta was staring past him, back down towards the villagers. Patch turned to follow her gaze, and gasped:

The people of the village were dancing.

Dancing in a column that was speeding towards the river, their grinning faces lit up with absolute glee.

"Oh no!" said Patch, horrified.

"What's gone wrong?" said Greta.

"The Song spilled out beyond the rats," he said. "The villagers are caught in the Dance!"

He looked to the rats near the waterfall, then back to the people. He played his Pipe, trying to add in a separation, to keep the rodents on their way and send the people back.

He quickly realized that it wasn't working.

Next option, he thought: *wait until most of the rats have gone over the falls, and bring the Dance to an end.*

But the people were so much *faster* than the rats, and many would be in the water by then. *Too risky*, he thought. There were children among the dancers. The water could sweep them to their deaths, however short a time they were in the river. Besides, could everyone even *swim*?

He added counter-rhythms that should slow the Dance down. That way, most of the rats would simply drift to their fate.

It had no effect. Closer the villagers came. Closer to the river's edge.

Greta grabbed his shoulder. "Patch! You have to do something!"

If he merely stopped playing, the Song would take too long to fade. As the first line of people stepped into the icy water, Patch knew there was only one option left.

He took the Pipe from his lips and snapped it in half.

At once the Dance died.

The grins on the faces of the villagers dropped away. Those who found themselves standing in the ice-cold river looked at their sodden legs, baffled. Panicked squeals came from the rats, who were now scrabbling their way towards the riverbank, finding purchase at the river's edge. The villagers watched as the rats helped each other and emerged from the water, scurrying back towards the village.

Patch's heart sank. He had come so close to success, but would have to start again once he'd recovered enough strength to...

The villager nearest the bridge raised a trembling arm, pointing right at Patch.

"He tried to kill us!" the villager screamed.

"Uh, no, I—" said Patch.

"He almost drowned us all!" cried another.

Greta stepped forward. "Wait!" she shouted. "That's not what happened!"

But the accusations kept mounting. Soon it seemed as if the whole village wanted his blood.

"He's like the Hamelyn Piper!" they cried. "Twisted, evil! Lock him up and throw away the key!"

"Um, Greta?" whispered Patch. "Maybe I should, uh, run away..."

She shook her head. "If you run, they'll chase you down like a mad dog! Your only chance is to reason with them."

"He's got Greta under a spell!" a villager cried.

Greta's eyes narrowed with anger. "*I'm not under any spell!*" she shouted, and the villagers fell silent at once, looking at her like children caught misbehaving by a parent. "Now all of you just calm down and listen! Angry decisions are bad ones, don't I always say?"

Nods and grumbles came from the villagers. Some agreed with Greta, but it was clear that many didn't. For Patch it was torture. Wherever he looked he saw suspicion and hate-filled eyes. It proved too much for him. Thinking this was his only opportunity to get a head start, he made a terrible mistake.

He began to run.

Over the bridge he went. The villagers were taken by surprise, but soon most were giving chase.

"Don't hurt him!" yelled Greta.

Patch hadn't yet realized the madness of his action – indeed, as he ran and found the road leading out of the village, he was hopeful. It didn't look impassable by any means! Pure white snow, flanked by trees, running straight on into the distance. He could outrun the villagers! He could keep ahead of them, and...

Suddenly the snow was too deep to run through. Too deep to *walk* through. He lost his balance and stumbled, falling face-down into white. His limbs felt impossibly heavy as he looked back to the villagers.

"Send him over the waterfall," one of them yelled, fist in the air. "See how he likes it!" It got a hearty cheer from the others.

Perhaps Greta could talk them out of it. Perhaps not.

Patch was so tired he almost didn't care.

The villagers fell suddenly silent and halted, staring past him. Patch looked at the road ahead. In the distance, the tops of the trees were shaking. The movement came nearer; the air itself was twisting, spinning.

The deep snow in the road was being hurled out to either side, as a corkscrew of white approached.

"He's summoned the Devil!" screamed one villager, running away. Some followed, terrified, but most were transfixed by the sight.

He could hear it now – a harsh whirring, almost like the buzz of wasps. And under that sound was another: rhythm and melody blending together in a Song for the wind.

When the twisting air broke through the last of the snow, Patch wasn't surprised by what he saw. Two horses, on a road that was clear of snow behind them. The riders wore the black and purple garb of the Custodian Elite.

Exhausted, he let his head fall. He half-laughed, and half-sobbed. He was safe. The villagers couldn't harm him now.

He heard the horses stop, then the crunch of boots in snow as one of the riders approached. Patch lifted his head and strained to look up. The face looming over him was young; with a shock, Patch realized it was familiar.

"Patch?" said the young man. "Patch Brightwater?"

Patch squinted at the young man's face.

I know you, he thought. *How do I know you?*

Ever since he'd woken in Patterfall, he'd known there was something very important that he needed to remember; at long last, that very important thing came back to him, and with it came everything else, all his lost memories returning at once.

"Oh no," he said. His head dropped back down to the snow.

He wasn't a Piper, not really. He'd fled from Tiviscan in disgrace before completing his training.

And now he knew just how much trouble he was in.

5

A RAT OF DISTINCTION

Patch woke from a dream.

He'd been walking hand in hand with his mother, feeling the kind of total happiness that he'd not felt in a long time. He'd only been three years old when both his parents had died, leaving him to be raised by his grandparents. He'd been left with no memories of his father at all, and only that single precious memory of his mother: holding her hand, looking up to see her smiling at him.

He was in a small room with a bare flagstone floor; there was a little window and a thin mat for a bed. It was cold. A fleece and a blanket covered him, and without it he suspected he would freeze.

He could feel a weight around his ankle – it was a manacle. Wrapping his covers around his back, he followed the chain to an iron ring on the wall. Out of the window, he could see the grain storehouse, its doors locked tight once more. He was wearing the clothes he'd fallen unconscious in, but his coat had been removed. On the floor was a tin bowl with a few hunks of stale bread, and a cup of water.

Hearing a clatter of keys, Patch turned to the door, and when it swung open he saw the face of the Elite Piper who had brought his memory rushing back. Erner Whitlock was his name; two years his senior, at fifteen. One of the three best Pipers that Patch had trained with.

"Erner," said Patch, looking at the robes Erner wore – rich purple on thick black cotton. "The Custodian Elite! The clothes suit you. I knew you'd pass your final trials."

Erner nodded. "I wish you'd been there to see it," he said. "Three of us went through the trials, and all three succeeded!"

"Who were the other two?"

"Mort and Kara. Mort is apprenticed with the Marinus Pipers in the Eastern Seas, but Kara was like me – Custodian Elite. She's gone to Skamos."

Patch could picture them both. Mort was a tall, strong lad with a love of the sea; Marinus Pipers were keenly sought by merchant ships, and needed a knack for whipping up winds and fending off pirates, which the Eastern Seas had plenty of. Kara, meanwhile, had been Erner's match in every task they'd ever done. Skamos was an important place, the only human city left on the continent known as the Dragon Territories. Peace between humans and dragons had always been fragile, but problems at Skamos had almost tipped things into war more than once. The Custodian Elite there had a crucial role in stopping that happening.

"Pirates and dragons," said Patch. "Exactly what they wanted. It's good to hear."

Erner stepped forward and gave him a sudden, brief hug. "I've missed you, Patch. We all did."

For a moment, Patch couldn't speak. The thought of all he'd left behind in Tiviscan was too much. Six months ago, just like Mort and Kara, he had known exactly what lay in his future – for him, it would be a glorious career in the Custodian Elite, bringing justice and help to those most in need. Then he'd thrown it all away, leaving Tiviscan behind, struggling to make ends meet. And now...the future wasn't something he even wanted to think about. "So," he said at last, changing the subject, "*Apprentice* Whitlock then!"

"It still sounds strange to my ears," said Erner.

An apprenticeship lasted two years, after which the title changed from "Apprentice" to "Fortis", which was the first proper rank of the Elite. Patch thought of the other figure he'd seen in the snow: "Who are you apprenticed to? What rank are they?"

"A Virtus," said Erner.

"Impressive!" said Patch – "Virtus" was the highest rank of all, and it was rare for them to take on an apprentice. "Which Virtus is it?"

Erner smiled awkwardly, and Patch could tell he was almost embarrassed to say it. "Virtus Stone."

Patch stared. "Good God, Erner. *Rundel* Stone?"

"Himself," said Erner.

The name of Rundel Stone brought two strong emotions to Patch. First, a deep sense of pride that his friend had been taken on as apprentice by such a legendary man – Stone was one of the Eight, the group of heroes who had finally captured the Hamelyn Piper.

The second emotion was utter despair, that the very same man held Patch's fate in his hands. Pity, the story went, was not a word Rundel Stone knew.

"Virtus Stone is making preparations to deal with the village's rat problem," said Erner. "While he does that, I'm to question you about…recent events."

"Hang on," said Patch. "Elite Pipers, dealing with rats?"

"With this many rats, people think of Hamelyn," said Erner. "The pride of all Pipers is at stake! We came to Patterfall because we happened to be in Wassil when the call for help was received, and the Virtus immediately volunteered. We arrived just in time to stop you being lynched. According to the villagers you burst out of the forest half-dead and with amnesia. They assumed you were the Piper they'd sent for, and you assumed the same. What were you doing in the forest?"

"I, um, just happened to be travelling nearby," said Patch. "The merchant's cart I was getting a ride on broke, and I was abandoned. The merchant hadn't known how dangerous the region was at this time of year."

"The villagers told us what happened to them, when you tried to deal with the rats."

Patch hung his head. "I broke the law," he said. "I played the Dance, yes. But I didn't mean for the people to get caught up in it!"

Erner nodded, sorrow in his eyes. "There's something else, Patch," he said. "It's the reason Rundel Stone and I were in Wassil. There was a great mystery we'd come to solve."

"Um…go on." Patch didn't like where this was going.

"A few months ago, the Pipers' Council became aware of tales of travelling musicians whose music was said to be the best anyone had ever heard. Witnesses all said the same thing: people danced like they'd never danced before. It seemed that the musicians had a mysterious Piper among them, and that the Piper had been playing the most illegal Song of them all. The Song that you played for the rats, Patch. The *Dance*. Forbidden, since Hamelyn!"

"Er…gosh," said Patch. He *really* didn't like where this was going.

"The Council grew even more concerned, because every description of this mystery Piper was different. In one place, people had seen a tall, thin woman. In another, a short, wide man. One week, old. Another week, young. The Council was scared, Patch. Scared! A Piper who played the Dance even though it was forbidden! A Piper powerful enough to change physical appearance from one day to the next! Unheard of! A dark and evil Piper, the Council assumed. *Toying* with us. So they sent Rundel Stone to hunt this villain down. And myself, of course."

Patch coughed. When he'd fled from Tiviscan, earning money for food and lodging hadn't been easy. Piping was all he knew, but as a failed student fleeing in disgrace, working as a Piper was impossible. After a week on the road, hungry and tired, he'd met a travelling band of musicians who were barely scraping a living themselves. He'd offered to play the flute for them, but they already had a flute player.

That was when he'd had the idea.

He told them of a wonderful tune he knew, a sea shanty they'd never heard before, and convinced them to try it out. While the band performed, Patch stayed hidden and played the Dance in secret, making sure the audience had the time of their lives. Tips flowed, of course, and the grateful band gave him some of the money. They asked him for another tune, and so it went on.

That was how he had spent the seven months since he'd left Tiviscan: staying with a band for a few weeks, then parting company and setting off to find another band before anyone got suspicious.

He thought of all the bands he'd been with, and of the flute players in them – a tall, thin woman; a short, wide man. Old, and young.

Meanwhile, the Council had heard rumours of an evil Piper, and the varying descriptions they got were simply those of the different flute players.

I scared the Council, he thought, amazed.

He opened his mouth to confess, and stopped. There was a pained look in Erner's eyes.

"You already know it was me," said Patch.

Erner nodded. "Changing the bands you played with was clever," he said. "It made it difficult for us to track you down, but we got word from Wassil and headed there at once. It seems you'd left the town just before we arrived."

Patch sighed. "Someone had been asking too many questions. I figured it was time to scarper, and the merchant who gave me a ride was the only one leaving that day."

"Yet fate led all of us to Patterfall," said Erner. "Virtus Stone has examined your broken Pipe, and the history of its Songs was still there to hear. I can't tell you how shocked I was to discover that it was *you* we'd been chasing all along!" He shook his head, saddened. "Why, Patch? Why would you take such a risk? Playing the Dance to deal with the rats was one thing, but playing it to entertain *people*?"

"It was the only way I could earn money, Erner. Nobody was harmed, and I didn't think anyone would find out." The look of disapproval on Erner's face was almost unbearable. "So," said Patch, "you'll take me back to Tiviscan, then. To certain imprisonment."

Erner seemed utterly deflated. "The Dance is absolutely forbidden. Ten years is the penalty." He walked over to the small window and looked out, silent for a moment. "There's some room for hope, though. The Lords who preside on your case can reduce the sentence by half – the rash actions of a trainee Piper without a malicious bone in his body."

"Five years, then," said Patch. "If pity is taken." He wondered if it might have been better if he'd died in the snow.

After Erner left, Patch lay down on his thin mat and despaired. Exhausted, he fell into an uneasy sleep. A curious sound, somewhere between scratching and rubbing, dragged him slowly back from slumber. He became aware of a gentle weight on his chest.

He opened his eyes and saw a rat.

It was the rat with the red-ringed tail, and it was looking at him.

The part of his brain that had done such a good job of imagining the rats *attacking* him went into overdrive. With a sudden yelp he sat up and backed away as far as he could, flinging the rat off him. It landed and gave him a very obvious glare, then raised a paw out to its side.

"I'm sorry! I'm sorry!" said Patch, gathering his blanket around himself. "Don't kill me!"

The rat looked to the ceiling and let out a tiny sigh, then nodded in the same direction as its paw.

"You're…you're not here to kill me?" said Patch, looking around frantically to see if the other rats were about to pour out of every crevice and devour him.

The rat shook its head and impatiently jabbed its paw towards the wall, its glare intensifying.

Patch stared at the rodent. He followed the line of its paw. On the flat stone of the wall beside him, written in chalk, were the words *Help me.*

The rat picked up a small piece of chalk from the floor and scurried over to the wall, ignoring Patch's whimper.

Patch wondered if he was still asleep, or if madness had taken him. All he could do was stare at the animal as it wrote more letters on the wall. At last it squeaked at him, and he read aloud what the rat had written.

Help me. I am the young daughter of a rich nobleman. I have been cursed by a Sorcerer into the shape of a rat. You will be well rewarded!

44

Patch looked at the rat, and the rat nodded. "Right," said Patch, and hid under his blanket. He clearly wasn't asleep, so madness seemed the only possibility.

After a few seconds he could feel the rat on top of him. He peeked out; it had its paws clasped together, pleading. "No!" he said. "You're not real!" The animal kept looking at him, forlorn and pitiful. A tiny tear formed and fell down the side of its face.

Patch felt a horrible stab of guilt. "Okay, enough!" he said. "Stop crying! I'll help." The rat gave a little jump for joy. "But why me?"

As if in answer, there was a sudden cheer from outside. Both Patch and the rat looked to the small window. Patch stood, and as he did the rat scampered up onto his shoulder. Patch walked to the window and looked out; a crowd of villagers had assembled by the oak tree, watching Virtus Stone and Erner as they approached the storehouse.

Patch turned his head to the rat. "The other rats all just went back to the storehouse?" he said. The rat nodded and slapped a paw to its forehead. "Not the smartest, are they?" said Patch, and the rat shrugged. Then the penny dropped. "*Ah!* You need protection from the Pipers, and who better to provide it than another Piper?" The rat nodded. "You'll be safe here," he said, wondering what Rundel Stone would play to get rid of the rodents. Stone had studied Patch's broken Pipe, so he probably knew the

Dream wouldn't work. Which Song would he try?

Stone took out his Pipe, and Patch could see that it was very dark in colour. There was an old rumour that Rundel Stone's Pipe was made of obsidiac, one of the rarest magical substances in the world. It was a form of obsidian – black volcanic glass – only ever found in the Dragon Territories. Stone's Pipe couldn't actually be *made* of obsidiac, of course – no piece big enough had ever been found, and even if one had been, the material was impossible to carve. But it could certainly have been coated in an obsidiac glaze, if the obsidiac was finely ground and mixed with resin. Such a glaze had once been highly prized in Pipe-making, as the resulting Pipes were immensely powerful. However, obsidiac was considered holy by dragons; as a result, the Piper's Council had banned its use in new Pipes long ago, in an effort to keep peace.

The Virtus raised his Pipe and began.

Patch listened carefully to the first notes, trying to identify the Song. He frowned. "I'm not sure what that is," he said. "The safest thing would be to wrap you in my blanket, little rat. Then, however the Song tries to compel you, you'll be unable to move and—"

He stopped talking.

The Virtus had started a rhythmic section, complex and primal. It was ringing a bell in Patch's mind. A great big worrying bell, one with *panic* written all over it.

"Oh," said Patch. "Oh no."

He had placed the rhythm. He knew the Song.

It was called the Dispersal, and it was a Song of execution – a terrifying thing, one of the most difficult Songs to perform.

Yet here was the Virtus, using it against a vast pack of rats.

The effect of Dispersal was simple. Every part of the target, every tiny *fragment*, would be utterly destroyed, the target reduced to its components – a devastating, instant unravelling that left nothing behind. Those components were widely dispersed, spread so thinly that not even a speck of blood would remain. Only dust, scattered across a thousand miles.

Patch listened in horror. The Dispersal was a highly selective Song, and the Virtus was allowing it to spread out, knowing that only his target – the rats – would be affected, without risk to the villagers. *All* rats within the bounds of the village would be killed, and perhaps for some distance beyond.

Patch had no idea if any defence was possible.

"Uhhh…" he said. "Um…" The rat put its paws over its ears so it couldn't hear, as it had done with the Dance, but Patch shook his head and it put its paws down again. "A Song isn't just heard with the ears," he said. "Every single *part* of you hears it." The rat stared at him, terrified.

Patch looked around the small room and his eyes settled on the tin bowl the bread was in. "Worth a try," he muttered. He grabbed it, tipping the bread out. "Quickly," he said to the rat. "Under the bowl!" The rat ran to him, and he turned the bowl upside down on top of it. "Keep entirely inside," he said. "And whatever you do, whatever you hear, don't come out!"

He placed his hands on the bowl and thought about what he could do. To keep the rat safe, he needed to play a counter-Song, and create a bubble of protection that surrounded the animal. He had no Pipe and would have to play it by lip, which made it harder – especially since his lips were still cracked and sore – but the bubble wouldn't need to be big.

Time was running out. Virtus Stone's Song was building. Patch could hear the chatter of the nervous villagers, as they sensed the sheer force of the music.

Here goes, he thought. With one ear on the Song outside, he began. The counter-rhythm he whistled was almost identical to the core rhythm of the Dispersal, but with a few carefully chosen added beats. Next, he whistled a modified version of the Song's secondary melody. Without a Pipe, all he could do was switch from rhythm to melody and back again, faster and faster, his lips getting ever closer to the upturned bowl.

The protective bubble began to form just in time. He

could sense it surrounding the metal of the bowl, a bubble that would guide the flow of the Song safely away, and not let it penetrate.

He tensed, knowing the moment was close. The bowl started to vibrate as the counter-Song struggled to hold together. On the floor nearby, the piece of chalk began to shake, then it rose up onto one tip, spinning. Patch felt his hair stand on end, and the chain around his ankle grew oddly warm.

The Dispersal reached a sudden crescendo and the force of it hit him, almost knocking him over. He managed to keep his hands firmly on the bowl, but he despaired as he felt his counter-Song shatter. From outside came the anguished cries of terrified villagers.

Then silence.

Shaking, Patch took his hands away from the bowl, wary of lifting it. Who knew *what* he might find there. "Hello?" he said. "Little rat?" There was a pitiful squeak. "It's okay," he said. "You're safe. You can come out now." The rat peeked out, trembling, looking at him for more reassurance. "Really," said Patch.

Outside, the shocked silence of the villagers was broken by hesitant cheers. "They've gone!" cried a voice. "Look! The rats have all gone!" The cheers grew.

The rat emerged from under the bowl and looked at Patch, a question in its eyes. Its companions were all dead,

Patch realized – turned to dust and scattered across vast distances. "Yes," said Patch. "The other rats… They've all gone."

The rat slumped.

Patch waited a moment before he spoke again. "I have two questions," he said. "First, were any of the other rats human too?" The rat shook its head, which was a huge relief. "And second," he said, lifting the piece of chalk from the floor and offering it to the rat. "What's your name?"

The rat took the chalk and wrote two words on the wall. Patch looked at them and smiled. He held out his hand, taking the rat's paw and gently shaking it. "Good to meet you, Wren Cobble," he said. "I'm Patch Brightwater."

Wren dashed up Patch's arm to his shoulder, and gave his neck a grateful hug.

6

JOURNEY TO TIVISCAN

"**H**ow old are you, Wren?" said Patch.

Wren ran down from his shoulder, and wrote *13* on the wall.

"Same as me!" he said. "And educated enough to read and write! A benefit of your wealthy family, I suppose. I was in training at Tiviscan Castle from the age of ten. It's a free education, for those with the gift of Piping. That education will come in handy now that I'll never be a real Piper—"

Wren frowned at him.

"Oh, I mean it," said Patch. "I've played an illegal Song. The Custodians will take me to Tiviscan, I'll be put on trial, and jailed for five years at the very least! As a criminal, I'll never be permitted to work as a Piper." He sighed; his gaze moved to Wren's chalk-written plea for help, and he read the last part aloud: "*You will be well rewarded!*" He turned to Wren. "I'm thankful that your parents are rich. Don't think me greedy, but when I'm released from the dungeons in five years, I'll need that reward." He gave her a weak smile, then bowed his head and closed his eyes. If he'd still been looking at her, he would have seen a curious expression cross Wren's face: a mixture of guilt and worry.

Patch opened his eyes again. "You'll have one heck of a story to tell your parents," he said. "When you get back home."

Wren shook her head and started to write again, Patch waiting patiently as she slowly drew out each letter: *Not until curse lifted.*

"I'm sure your parents—" started Patch, but Wren jabbed at the words she'd written and added an exclamation mark.

Not until curse lifted!

"Fair enough," said Patch. He could sympathize, really – his grandparents thought he was still training to become a Piper, and the idea of them finding out the truth made him feel ill. He would leave them to their happy ignorance for as long as he could. "We'll have to get help from the Custodian Elite, then. They're in the best position to know what can be done for you."

She shook her head firmly.

"Saving you from that Song is one thing, Wren," he said.

"But as a prisoner, I won't be able to do anything more to help you. You'll need the Custodians. Let me talk to them."

Wren shook her head again, and mimed a lumbering monster. Patch laughed, because he understood who she meant.

"He's *Rundel Stone*," he said. "One of the Eight who hunted down the Hamelyn Piper. There isn't a more respected Custodian in the world! He's no monster."

Wren put her hand to her chest before taking it away sharply, as if it was painful. The Cold Heart of Justice, she was saying – Stone's famous nickname.

Patch sighed. He could understand why Wren would be wary of putting herself at the man's mercy. There were plenty of stories about how Stone sometimes applied the law far too strictly, and as a rat, Wren had certainly been guilty of stealing food and scaring the villagers. "Yes, but who can blame him for his cold heart?" said Patch. "He vowed to find the children of Hamelyn and bring them home, safe and sound. Rundel Stone and the rest of the Eight did all they could: they caught the Hamelyn Piper, and brought him to Tiviscan to be imprisoned. But the children weren't found, and their fate is still unknown. Rundel Stone couldn't keep his vow. That's enough to leave anyone with a cold heart."

Wren was standing with her arms folded. She wasn't having it.

"Very well," said Patch. "We'll leave Stone out of it. I know his apprentice, Erner Whitlock. Honest and decent. You'll like him. When I get a chance to talk to him alone, I'll *have* to tell him about you, okay? There's no other choice."

After a long pause, Wren gave him a reluctant nod.

"Strange to think I'll actually *meet* Rundel Stone," said Patch. He recited the rhyme every child knew – the names of the Eight, the heroes assembled by the Piper's Council to capture the Hamelyn Piper. "Palafox, Corrigan, Kellenfas, Stone," he said. "Casimir, Hinkelman, Drevis and Throne. My grandmother has a way with stories, and she told me their adventures every night. A race against time, hunting across every nation of these lands and into the Islands of the Eastern Sea, until they finally caught the Hamelyn Piper and locked him away to rot in the dungeons of Tiviscan Castle." He paused, knowing that it was in those very dungeons that he would be spending the next five years – or maybe ten! "To be jailed by one of my heroes..."

Wren nodded, downhearted. She set down her chalk, climbed onto his shoulder again, and curled up.

Patch was glad of the company. "It's at least a week's journey to Tiviscan Castle from here by horse. Ever seen it?"

Wren shook her head.

"It's impressive," he said. "It sits on a cliff, and the dungeons extend deep into the rock. The deepest of the

dungeons is called the Dark. No natural light reaches it."
He sat on the floor, miserable. "The Hamelyn Piper is
imprisoned in the Dark, of course. At the deepest point of
the deepest dungeon. It's said that each night the prisoners
in the dungeons can hear him scream – scream until he's
hoarse and can cry out no more."

He fell silent and closed his eyes.

After a while, Wren ran down to the ground and picked
up her chalk. She wrote, but Patch was lost to his misery.
She squeaked to get his attention.

You're too young for prison, she'd written.

"I'm not," he said. "Children younger than me have
been jailed there." The Tiviscan dungeons were mainly
used for those who broke the laws of Piping, so almost all
the prisoners were Pipers themselves. Even the youngest
child, discovering their own Piping ability for the first time,
could accidentally break the law and end up in a cell.
Although, Patch knew, it would often be just for a day, to
scare them and make sure they didn't do it again. He honestly
didn't know the longest time someone his age had been
imprisoned for. Perhaps he would be setting a new record.

He could see that Wren was trying to think of something
else to write.

"Look, I know you're trying to cheer me up," he said.
"And thank you. But the only things that are important are
that you're okay, and I'm not alone."

Wren nodded. She set down her chalk and clapped her paws together to get rid of the chalk dust, coughing as a little cloud of it engulfed her.

"It'd be easier with a quill and paper," said Patch. An image of a tiny feather cut to a quill came into his mind, and he smiled. "Perhaps Erner will get you that. Although…" A thought had occurred to him. "Have you heard of Merisax hand speech?" Wren shook her head. "Merisax is a language used by mercenaries and pirates. My dream was to join the Custodian Elite, and they're required to be fluent, so I spent a lot of time learning it." Ah yes, his dream… Long since shattered. He sighed. "Anyway, with Merisax you only use your *hands* to talk. It allows for total silence in setting an ambush – you can hold a conversation without giving away your position. It's also useful in battle. Or in a loud tavern. Or any time you can't speak—" He gestured towards Wren and paused, waiting for the penny to drop. When it did, Wren's face lit up. "How about I run through some phrases, to give you a feel for it?"

She gave him a brisk nod and sat facing him, eager to begin.

"*Yes, No,*" said Patch, thumbs up, then thumbs down. "*Hurry up. Slow down. Come over here. Go away.*" With each example, he gave Wren enough time to mimic the sign he was showing her. "*Keep going. You're an idiot. Pass the rum.*" Next he made a throat-slitting motion. "*Kill,*" he said.

"Lots of variants of kill, actually. Lots. That's pirates and mercenaries for you, I suppose. *Kill quickly. Kill slowly. Kill everyone. Don't kill anyone.*" He thought for a second. "That last one's probably not used much. Let's see... *Don't do that here. I'm bleeding. You're bleeding. Please stop the bleeding. You're on fire. The ship is on fire. The ship is sinking. Oh no it's a shark. Maybe we should murder the captain.*"

Wren studiously copied each action, deep in concentration.

Patch continued. "*You smell terrible. Run away. If you do that again I'll kill you.* The eyes are important for that one," said Patch. "Otherwise it's a bit too much like *Pass the rum.* I expect that's caused a few fights in its time. Anyway, that should give you the flavour of it. What do you think?"

Yes, kill everyone, oh no it's a shark, signed Wren.

"Well," said Patch. "It's a start."

It was several hours before Erner Whitlock returned, and by then Wren had shown herself to be exceptionally quick at learning Merisax. Patch reckoned she would soon get to grips with it – something that had taken Patch months to achieve.

When the keys rattled in the door, Wren hid under Patch's blanket. Patch stood as Erner came inside.

"Your coat," said Erner, handing it to Patch. "We'll be setting off shortly."

Patch put the coat on, immediately glad of its familiar feel. He looked at Erner, and noticed that the Apprentice Piper was uneasy. "Are you okay?" he asked.

Erner smiled nervously. "I should be asking *you* that. Patch, I want you to know that I—" He stopped and shook his head. "I'm sorry, about how things are."

Patch put his hand on Erner's shoulder. "I know," he said. "It's the way it must be, though. How's your boss?"

"Virtus Stone is unusually quiet," said Erner. "He's even moodier than normal."

"I could have guessed he was in a bad mood when he chose the Dispersal to deal with the rats," said Patch. "A bit over the top, don't you think?"

Erner shrugged. "The Virtus is the best Piper I've ever seen, by far. To him, the Dispersal is *easy,* and it was certain to do the job." He paused, before lowering his voice. "To be honest, it *was* overkill. I think he's cross from all this traipsing across frozen terrain, chasing you."

"I hope he cheers up on the journey back," said Patch. It seemed like a good opportunity to mention Wren. "Actually, there's something I need to talk to you about—"

"Silence!" came a voice. Rundel Stone swept through the doorway, and Patch took a step back from Erner. Even given the circumstances, Patch felt awed to be in the presence of a legend. "We leave in five minutes. The weather conditions are deteriorating. I've purchased another horse from the villagers for our *burden*." He looked with disdain at Patch when he said it; instinctively Patch opened his mouth to object, but the glare from the Virtus stopped him. "No speaking!" said Stone. "Understand? Not now, not while we travel. *Never.* You are a criminal. A *disgrace* to Piping. Oh, I know all about you, Patch Brightwater. I make it my business to know. A promising young student, you wanted to join the Custodian Elite, but instead you embarrassed yourself and vanished with your tail between your legs. Then you chose to *misuse* the skills you'd managed to learn, to lead me on a merry chase while my time would have been far better spent elsewhere, dealing with problems that – unlike you – *actually matter*."

Patch opened and closed his mouth in silence, like a dying fish.

"Five minutes!" said Stone. He turned to Erner. "Come, Apprentice," he said, and left. Erner gave Patch a regretful look and went with his master, locking the door behind him.

Wren poked her head out from her hiding place.

"So much for meeting your heroes," said Patch. "We'll get to speak to Erner on his own, sooner or later." He held his coat open. "Handmade by my grandfather, this coat. Deerskin. His gift to me when I first went to Tiviscan. A little big back then, but now it's perfect. Cool in summer, warm in winter, with endless pockets. Come on then, hop inside."

Wren wasn't too sure.

"I will *not* squash you," said Patch. "I promise."

When Stone and Erner came back a few minutes later, Wren was snuggled up in his pocket. Patch was led outside. The Elite Pipers' horses stood waiting, a smaller horse beside them. Next to the horses stood Greta, the only person there to bid him farewell; the other villagers of Patterfall had stayed indoors.

"Good luck, Patch," said Greta. She looked at Stone. "Don't be harsh on the lad. He meant well."

Rundel Stone said nothing in reply.

As Stone had instructed, Patch stayed silent as they rode. It made him miserable. He had too much time to think – about his past, and about his future. Neither was a place he was keen to visit. With Stone's expert Piping to clear the snow, it only took a day of travel for them to get out of the valley and reach lower altitudes. Heading south, winter's icy grip weakened quickly. Wren was a little pocket of extra warmth near his heart.

Each night, they camped in the cover of woods and forests, using three of the traditional Piper's shelters that had been part of Patch's training – tiny oilskin tents that, when folded up, took hardly any space in their horses' packs, but when assembled gave just enough room for a single curled-up sleeper. The tents kept out the cold, but even better was how the privacy let Patch help Wren learn her Merisax signs at night, until the light from the fire dwindled.

Each morning, Erner hunted for prey soon after dawn, when rabbit and fowl were more vulnerable to one of the various luring Songs. While he was gone, Stone got to work lighting a fire. Only on the third morning did they swap roles. When Stone went to hunt, Patch realized the chance had come to talk to Erner.

"Morning, Erner," said Patch, emerging from his little tent.

Erner had just struck his firesteel to light the fire. "Morning, Patch," he replied.

"Um, Erner?" said Patch.

Erner looked up, the fire doing well. "Yes?" he said, at which point Wren emerged from Patch's pocket, scurried to his shoulder, and waved.

"A rat!" said Erner, startled. Wren signed something, and Erner's surprise turned to astonishment. "That's Merisax hand speech!" he said. He watched the rat intently as she repeated what she'd signed. He stared in shock. "You want me to *what*?" he said, appalled.

"She didn't mean that," said Patch. "She's learning." He turned to Wren and signed: both hands opening and closing in fists. "*This* is 'Help me', Wren," he said. "What you just signed… Well, it's very much *not*, and I don't want to *ever* see you do that again."

Wren grumbled.

"No, I *won't* tell you what it means." Patch turned back to Erner. "Erner, this is Wren. She's human, she was cursed by a Sorcerer, and she needs help. She lived among the rats in the village, and I suspect she was the reason those rats were so successful at avoiding traps and poison." He glanced at Wren, who was trying to look as innocent as possible, but given how bright she'd shown herself to be, Patch had no doubt about it.

Erner's eyes widened in horror. "Wait…there were *people* among the rats?"

"None of the other rats were human," said Patch. "Luckily. Wren came to me when the Dispersal was about to happen, and I protected her from it, but with me in prison she'll need someone else to—"

"You *protected* her?" said Erner. "From *that* Dispersal? I felt how powerful it was."

Patch waved away the compliment. "Trust me, it wasn't easy. Look, we'd rather not involve the Virtus and he'll be back any minute."

"Why don't you want to involve the Virtus?" asked Erner.

Wren signed something incredibly rude again, and Patch thought that this time she knew *exactly* what she was saying. He turned to Erner. "She thinks that Rundel Stone is so stubborn he'd probably arrest her for being, I don't know, a talking rat without a *licence*. Or something."

Erner laughed wholeheartedly, then suddenly stopped. "Ah. I see your point."

Patch nodded. "Exactly," he said.

7

TRIAL OF A PIPER

Erner agreed to keep Wren's presence a secret, and to begin investigating a cure for her curse the moment they reached Tiviscan.

As they continued their journey, Wren's grasp of Merisax came on in leaps and bounds, and teaching her provided Patch with a welcome distraction from what awaited him when they reached their destination.

At last, ten days after setting off from Patterfall, the three horses trudged through rain on the rising road; ahead, they could see the sheer cliff on which Tiviscan Castle sat, overlooking forest. To the rear of the Castle was Tiviscan town, a ramshackle spread of buildings that flowed from the Castle's gates towards grassy plains and hills.

The Castle rose high and seemed larger than was

possible, since at its base it continued *into* the rock of the cliff. It was hard to tell where the Castle ended. Some parts of it were ancient beyond measure, older even than Piping. Originally, it was a village carved into the rock itself – networks of tunnels, tombs and homes that lay within the cliff. As the Castle grew, it grew down as well as up.

The oldest and deepest of those tunnels formed the dungeons where Patch would soon find himself. He thought of them, and shivered.

They reached the Castle gates, passing under the massive double archways and through the courtyard market, which was busy despite the rain. They dismounted at the vast central Keep, and Virtus Stone led them through the iron-clad Keep gate, into a dim stone entrance hall.

There were two sets of steps ahead. One set was plain stone, leading downwards. The other led up, and was far grander: the steps were marble, and the walls beside it were carved with images from the history of Piping.

The first carving showed the earliest days when Pipers knew only the simplest Songs. They were more like monks or knights back then, and travelled the world bringing help where they could, for no reward but food and shelter. A simple life, based on a proud code of honour – an ideal which was reborn much later, when the Custodian Elite were founded.

The next few carvings showed the discovery of new

Songs and new skills, as the Piper's Art was refined over centuries.

A great and glorious history, Patch thought, was carved into those walls.

And then he saw a carving that depicted a battle: army facing army, but only one side had Pipers in their ranks. It took Patch a moment to realize which battle was being represented, and when he did he sighed with sorrow.

The Pipers in that battle had been paid to fight. The opposing army was being slaughtered.

The history of Piping was not always great or glorious, thought Patch.

Stone stopped walking and looked at him, raising an eyebrow. He followed Patch's eyeline to the carving. "Ah," he said. "The Battle of Dornley Flats. I see you disapprove."

"Of course I do," said Patch. "Before then, Pipers could only fight for causes that were *just*, not for money."

"Pipers didn't invent war, boy," said Stone. "The many nations of these lands have always quarrelled with each other. Sometimes those quarrels grow. Sometimes they become wars. If Pipers have skills that are useful to an army, shouldn't they be able to profit from them?"

Patch didn't answer.

"Besides," said Stone, "no ruler – no king, queen, baron or overlord – wants the Pipers' Council as an enemy, for without the Council's approval they could hire no decent

Pipers to help in their battles. They'd be forced to use *outcast* Pipers, poorly skilled, poorly trained! Their forces would be at a severe disadvantage. That fact keeps the Pipers' Council safe, and all Pipers too, something you'd be wise to remember."

"Maybe," said Patch. It might have been the truth, but it left a sour taste in his mouth.

"Up past those carvings lies the Chamber of the Council," said Stone. "That's where you would have graduated if you'd proved your worth. Think how different your life could have been! As it is, your trial tomorrow could be the last time you ascend those stairs." He shook his head with a sigh and raised his arm, pointing ominously to the other steps. "We go *that* way."

Stone led them down the spiralling steps, followed by Patch, with Erner at the rear. It got darker as they descended, and a horrible stench rose from below.

They came to a locked gate. Stone knocked, and a burly man opened it.

"Prisoner for trial –" said Stone – "by the name of Patch Brightwater." He turned to Erner. "Accompany him to the holding cell," he said. "I'll inform the Council of our success."

"Come on through," said the burly man. He closed the

gate once Patch and Erner were inside. "My name's Furnel, lad," he said to Patch. "This way."

Furnel led them to a dank corridor lit by oil lamps. Patch saw a row of small cells, with one door open. Furnel pointed to the door, and Patch went inside. There was just enough space to lie down, and a sickly light came through the bars in the door. On the cold floor was some straw, and a rough blanket that at first touch felt like it might give him splinters. The door was shut behind him and he could hear Furnel and Erner walking away.

Wren came out of his pocket and ran up to his shoulder. *Horrible place*, she signed, anxious.

Patch nodded. Five years, he thought. Five years in a cell that would probably be even worse than this. And that was if he was lucky enough to have his sentence reduced.

A few minutes later, Erner opened the door and handed him a bundle of clothes. "The jailor insisted you change into these," he said. "Prison clothing must be worn by the accused at a trial."

Patch took them. Rough cloth trousers, rough cloth shirt.

"You can keep your boots," said Erner.

"What about my coat?" said Patch.

Erner shook his head. "I'll look after it until your release."

Patch set Wren on the floor and changed, then handed

Erner his clothes and coat. "There's one other thing I want you to look after," he said. He turned to Wren, whose eyes widened.

What are you talking about? she signed.

"I'll take good care of her," said Erner. "You have my word."

No chance! signed Wren. *I'm staying with Patch! Someone has to lift his spirits!*

"You can't stay with me, Wren," said Patch. "The dungeons are no place for you." She folded her arms and avoided eye contact. "Please, Wren. Erner will find the help you need. I'll make it through. In five years, I'll be out. And you can bring me that reward!" When he said it like that, it almost sounded *possible*.

Wren looked to Patch, then to Erner, and back again. Her shoulders sagged, and her head dropped. She nodded. *I'll miss you,* she signed.

Erner was carrying a satchel, and he kneeled down and opened the flap. "There's room in here," he said.

"Keep out of sight," said Patch. "People have a thing about rats. Safest to stay hidden!"

Wren hopped inside, with one last sad look at Patch. She waved, and Patch waved in return. "Look after yourself, Wren," he said. Erner closed the door, and Patch listened as his friend's footsteps faded.

He was alone.

After a long restless night, Patch was awoken with a bowl of hot stew.

"Is it morning?" he asked the jailer – Furnel, the same burly man who'd been on duty the night before. Given that no natural light seemed to reach his cell, he had no way to tell if it was daytime.

"It is," said Furnel. "Your trial begins in an hour."

Patch ate the food, his last meal before perhaps ten years of confinement, or five if he was lucky. When he finished, Furnel manacled himself and Patch together.

"I know you're not thinking of escape now, lad," said Furnel. "But things change when the sentence gets passed and the reality of it hits home. Trust me."

He led Patch up the central steps of the Keep until they reached the ornate door to the Council chamber. Furnel knocked, and the doors swung wide to a cacophony of voices.

The chamber was full.

Around the walls, rising rows of seats made it feel like a theatre.

Rundel Stone sat in a chair at one side, and Patch was led to a stool in the middle of the chamber. He sat and looked around the room quickly, trying to find Erner – and there he was, three rows up on the left, satchel in hand. Patch thought he could see a tiny nose peeking out from the bag.

He would be judged by members of the Piper's Council, usually two of them. A door in the far wall opened, and his judges started to come into the chamber. He watched, anxious to see who was going to rule over his fate.

He stared as all five members of the Council came in and sat at the judges' bench.

Lord Drevis entered first, followed by Lord Pewter, Lady Winkless, Lord Cobb and Lady Rumsey.

All of them would preside over his case. They wore ceremonial robes, fold after fold of garments stitched with gold, silver and brilliant indigo.

Patch turned to Furnel. "Isn't it supposed to be just *two* judges?"

"For something this infamous?" said Furnel.

Patch gave him a wary look. "Infamous?"

"Aye, lad. You were big news for a time, when the rumours started about a rogue Piper. People were scared! They thought the Hamelyn Piper himself might have escaped! I'm not surprised the whole of the Council is here. And look at the size of the crowd!"

The clap of a gavel sounded from the judges' bench, and the chatter of the audience began to settle. The gavel was in the hand of Lord Drevis, the head of the Piper's Council. Drevis, like Stone, was one of the legendary Eight. Indeed, he had *led* them in their successful capture of the Hamelyn Piper, and as a result was probably the most famous Piper

71

in the world. Another two claps of the gavel, and silence was finally achieved.

"The Court of the Council is gathered," said Drevis. "Accuser, state your case."

Rundel Stone stood from his seat. "This prisoner before you is Patch Brightwater."

"Prisoner shall stand!" called Drevis, and Patch stood, chain rattling.

"Thirteen years of age, Brightwater trained in this Castle," said Stone. "Last midsummer, his own failings led him to abscond after bringing shame on himself. He left the Castle, abandoning his training." The audience murmured darkly. "As the Council is aware, rumours began of a rogue Piper, playing the Dance throughout the land. A Piper able to change *form*!" The murmurs grew. "It transpires that Brightwater was at the root of the affair. However, the rumours of shape-changing were misplaced. He merely played the Dance in secret at various inns and taverns, to extract *moneys* and *favours*!" Stone addressed his next words to the audience, and spoke them with some relish. "His actions brought *disrepute* to the pure and glorious Art of Piping!"

The audience booed.

"The evidence?" said Lord Pewter.

Stone held up the two halves of Patch's broken Pipe. "The history of his crimes lies within the Pipe he used, one he had clearly crafted himself."

Lord Pewter gestured for Stone to bring the pieces to the bench. He took the broken Pipe and examined it carefully, then passed it to his colleagues. "A very traditional Pipe, but easy to get wrong," said Pewter. "I'm pleased to see how well you learned your carving, Patch Brightwater."

"Uh, thanks, Lord Pewter," said Patch. "It was cured over a hawthorn fire. Makes all the difference."

Stone glared at him. "The prisoner is to remain silent!"

"Come, come, Rundel," said Pewter. "I addressed him directly, his comment was allowed." He turned to Patch. "Think carefully, now, Patch Brightwater. Do you confess to your crime? Did you Pipe the Dance as the Virtus claims?"

There seemed little point denying anything. "I did," said Patch. A gasp came from the audience. "But it was not through greed, Lord. It wasn't riches I sought, only food and a bed to sleep in."

The Council turned to one another and entered muffled discussions. Finally, Drevis clapped the gavel and spoke. "Patch Brightwater, you have confessed your guilt. We must now consider the case for leniency. You have misused Piping, but I know your tutors thought well of you, and that previously you had shown yourself to be honest and of good nature – although not always of good judgement. Now, as you have done before, you have gone astray and chosen poorly." He looked to his colleagues. "We are all agreed?" They nodded. "This crime demands ten years in the dungeons of Tiviscan. The mercy of the Court allows us to reduce this to five years."

The audience murmured, nodding their heads. Erner gave him an encouraging glance. Patch looked to Erner's bag and could just about make out a thumbs up from a certain small paw.

Then a voice spoke: "Wait."

It was Rundel Stone.

"Yes, Virtus?" said Lord Drevis.

Stone got up from his chair and strode to the centre of the chamber. "I agree with your assessment of the prisoner. To my mind, he is indeed a *fool* more than a villain." Sniggers came from the audience. "However, there is one matter that I strongly disagree with."

"Go on," said Drevis, his eyes narrowing.

"This is a serious offence," said Stone. "When the Hamelyn Piper was imprisoned, the Dance was forbidden at once. In all these years, nobody has broken that law. Until now. Yet you wish to give the perpetrator a slap on the wrist?"

"Look at him, Rundel," said Lady Winkless. "There's no evil in the lad. Five years in the dungeons is already a severe punishment."

Stone shook his head, and when he spoke again there was a hint of anger in his voice. "You look at Brightwater, and see a boy who came here to study, a boy who then strayed from the path. I see *danger*. Here was a boy willing to play the Dance and ignore the law. Time has passed since Hamelyn, and people are starting to forget the horror of it. That cannot be allowed!" He looked around the chamber, the audience utterly silent. Yet, Patch noticed, Stone didn't look at *him*. "There has been *fear* since these rumours of a Dark Piper emerged, but before that, something curious had happened to the story of the Hamelyn Piper. On my search for Brightwater, for example, I saw an inn called The Piper and the Rats. The inn's sign showed a *jolly* scene, but it was the Hamelyn Piper that was depicted! Smiling! *Benevolent!*" His hand formed a fist as he spoke. "I spoke with some who even thought he might have been a hero. Who said the children had been taken to a wondrous place, to live happy lives. Who said that the people of Hamelyn must have done something to provoke him, or had treated their own children so *terribly* that the Hamelyn Piper needed to rescue them!" He paused, his anger seeming to overwhelm him for a moment. "How can that be? How can we have forgotten?" He looked around the chamber. Most would not meet his gaze. "The notion that the Hamelyn Piper was not evil cannot be allowed to stand," he said. "And so we cannot be lenient now. We cannot show pity. We must reassert the seriousness of what occurred in Hamelyn ten years ago. Brightwater's crimes must be treated with grim brutality. As such, I invoke the rule of multiple infractions!"

The Council all looked at Stone with stunned expressions, as the audience broke into uproar.

Patch bent down slightly to Furnel. "What does that mean?" he whispered.

"I think you'd best sit down, lad," said Furnel. "This ain't going to be pleasant."

Patch stayed standing.

"It's your right to insist, Virtus," said Lord Drevis, sounding almost dazed. He turned to the other Council members to discuss the matter, as the din from the audience continued.

At last, Lord Drevis clapped the gavel and the commotion in the chamber settled. "It is with sorrow that we must accept your request, Rundel," he said. "Patch Brightwater, your sentence will still be treated with leniency and reduced by half. However, the basic sentence is now ten years for each time you broke the law and performed the Dance." He looked to Rundel Stone. "In studying the broken Pipe, how many times did you assess?"

"One hundred and two," said Stone.

There was total silence in the chamber now. The faces of the Council paled, as the implications became clear to all.

"We will take it on ourselves to verify the figure, Rundel," said Drevis.

"Naturally," replied the Virtus.

"Patch Brightwater," said Drevis. "The sentence is ten years for each of the one hundred and two occurrences of your crime. You are hereby sentenced to one thousand and twenty years in the dungeons of Tiviscan, reduced to five hundred and ten by the clemency of the Council. Jailer, take him down." He clapped his gavel, looking somewhat ill.

The audience began its din once again. "God have mercy on you," shouted someone, "because Rundel Stone certainly won't!"

Patch fell back onto his stool, unable to take in what had just happened. He looked up to where Erner sat and could see him struggle with his bag as Wren tried to escape. "No!" Patch shouted at Wren. "Please! Don't!"

Someone from the audience laughed: "Beggin' won't help you!"

Patch kept his gaze on the bag. He saw Wren's paws, briefly. She signed something to him, then hid back inside.

Furnel dragged him out of the chamber and led him back down the steps, and through the dungeon gate once more, but instead of heading back to where he'd spent the night, Patch was taken to another spiralling staircase.

Down they went into the gloom below, passing level after level, and Patch thought, *How deep will I be put?*

Furnel took him down a long dank passage, one that

reeked of decay and was lined with cell doors. As they passed each door, shouts started up from behind: "Who d'ya have? Eh? Who've ya brought us?"

Furnel stopped at the last door in the corridor. There was a folded blanket on the floor, and Furnel picked it up and gave it to Patch. The burly jailer was subdued, and could hardly make eye contact. "It's not often I feel sorrow when I bring a prisoner down," he said, shaking his head. "This cell is the best I can do for ye, lad, given your sentence. Deep, sure enough, and at the very edge of the Dark. But it's by the outside wall of the Castle – so you have a window, such as it is." He unlocked the door and swung it open.

Patch stared. The door was several feet thick, as were the walls of his cell. He looked inside and saw that the cell was larger than he'd expected, perhaps five strides across. The "window" was an open hole barely the size of his hand, allowing a narrow band of light in from outside. The depth of the window showed that the outer wall was at least six feet thick, even thicker than the cell door. A bundle of rags was in one dark corner.

The stench in the cell was appalling.

"Your toilet is there," said Furnel, pointing to a hole in the floor. "You get food and water most days. There's your bowl and water jug." He pointed to a clay bowl and jug over by the rags. "Food and water tubes come in those holes by the door, see? Be sure you're ready to catch 'em." Patch noted small holes in the wall, and a mound of decayed food on the floor underneath. No wonder the smell was so bad.

Furnel unlocked the manacles on his and Patch's wrists. Patch rubbed at his chafed skin. "What happened to the last prisoner who was in here?" he asked.

"Oh, that reminds me," said Furnel. He walked across to the corner where the bundle of rags was, and lifted it up in his arms.

It wasn't a bundle of rags. It was a *corpse*.

Furnel carried it to the corridor and set it on the ground. Patch saw the dead man clearly now – ancient, and thin to the point of being just a collection of bones. "Innocent Jack, they called him," said Furnel.

"Why did they call him that?"

"On account of him being *innocent*," said Furnel. "Found guilty of murderin' a man through Piping, then the man showed up alive only last year." He shook his head. "Shame Jack died. His review was only a couple of months away. They'd probably have let him out!"

"How long had he been here?" said Patch, looking at the old face, its skin like parchment. *Must have been a long, long time,* he thought. *Perhaps it's possible to live long enough for the Council to come to their senses and let me go...*

"Jack was convicted when he was twenty," said Furnel. "So, let's see now –" his eyes went to the ceiling as he worked it out – "he'd been here almost fifteen years."

Patch stared at Furnel in shock.

"Time in here takes its toll," said Furnel. "Well, good luck, lad." He swung the huge cell door closed, and Patch heard the man's heavy steps vanish back along the corridor. Then he could *feel* the walls, unbearably heavy, crushing him...

He ran to the tiny window, stretching up on tiptoes to put his mouth to the slight draught that came in. Breathing deeply, he waited for the panic to subside.

He thought back to the message Wren had signed to him in the Council chamber: *Don't give up.*

But how could he not? Right now, there seemed to be only one thing that Patch Brightwater was certain of.

Like Innocent Jack, he would be in this place until he died.

8

THE HAMELYN PIPER

Patch's panic was just starting to lessen when he heard something that didn't help at all.

"Hey!" said a man's voice.

Patch pulled back from the window. "Who's there?" he said, looking around.

"Down here!" came the voice again, but it seemed to be coming from *everywhere*.

Aren't things bad enough, thought Patch, *without having to share my cell with the ghost of Innocent Jack?* "Who are you?" he said. "Please, just leave me alone!"

"Look, mate," said the voice. "We're going to be spending a *lot* of time together, so let's try and get along, eh? My name's Vague Henry."

"Are you…are you *dead*?"

Vague Henry sighed. "I'm your *neighbour*. Just look at the bottom of the wall. See the hole?"

Patch looked at the wall to his right. There was a dark area, smaller even than the five-inch window. It was level with the floor, and as he moved towards it he realized it actually *was* a hole. "I see it," he said.

"Stick your eye up to it and say hello!"

Patch put his eye to the hole. It was a long, dim channel cut through the thick stone wall, but at the other end – perhaps five feet away – was another eye, looking back at him. "Hello," he said.

"You've only got me as a neighbour, since you're at the end of the row," said Henry. "The holes are part of the plumbing, but it's a handy way to chat without having to shout and annoy everyone. So you're Patch Brightwater, eh?"

"How do you know who I am?"

"Word travels fast down here! Pleasure to meet you, Patch. We've not come up with a nickname for you yet, though. Not like Jack, your cell's previous resident."

"Innocent Jack," said Patch.

"Indeed! Used to be *Murderous* Jack, of course, before the whole innocence thing happened. Your nickname usually has something to do with why you're in the dungeons, see."

"So why do they call you Vague Henry?"

Henry paused. It was a long pause, and a strangely awkward one. "Dunno," he said.

Patch waited, but nothing more was forthcoming. "Uh... okay," said Patch at last, wondering if his question had been answered.

"What'll we call you?" said Henry. "Doomed Boy Patch? Bleak Young Patch? We'll get it. We've got plenty of time."

"Right," said Patch, the words "plenty of time" filling him with horror. He pulled away from the hole and lay on his back, staring up at the rough stone ceiling.

"Some advice for you," said Henry. "First up, when feeding time comes, the guard calls out 'tubes'."

"Furnel mentioned those," said Patch. "Why do they use tubes?"

"So they don't have to open the doors, lad," said Henry. "Be ready to catch it when it comes – especially the water! When it rains, you'll see the rainwater come in through holes like this one and run through grooves in the floor. See 'em? See where they lead?"

Patch looked to the floor and saw them. Grooves a couple of inches across ran towards the hole in the floor that Furnel had pointed out previously – the toilet. "I see them."

"Exactly. We get some of the, er, *waste water* from above us, and we're five levels down. So don't drink the rainwater, however thirsty you get, however clean it looks! And for your sake and ours, make sure your hole doesn't block up!"

"Will do," said Patch. "Henry, is it true that you can hear the Hamelyn Piper scream at night?"

"Oh, you'll hear him all right," said Henry.

"Doesn't it frighten you? Being so close to him?"

"The Hamelyn Piper? He's a wreck. His brain is nothing but mush by now. But no, I'm not frightened, not by him or any other Piper here. It doesn't matter how well a prisoner can lip-play to whistle up a Song. Hell, even if someone managed to get hold of a Pipe, it'd do 'em no good. They have precautions."

"Precautions?"

"Haven't you seen the depth of the doors and windows? If you look close, you'll see that every way out of your cell is lined with little furrows."

Patch looked into the hole that led to Henry's cell. Dark as it was, he could make out a slight twist here and there on the stone, a pattern carved into the rock. "Sound baffles?" said Patch. He'd heard of them in training – they confused any Songs you played, and took the edge off the magic enough to render them useless. They only worked for conduits that were long and thin, so they were no good as a general defence; they were more a curiosity of Piping theory. In here, though: perfect.

"Precisely," said Henry. "The workers down here are almost immune to Piping, lip-Piping at any rate, but the baffles make sure. It's why the walls and the doors are so thick, and why they feed us with the tubes. Inside your cell, you can't affect anyone else. So don't let the Hamelyn Piper frighten you. He's harmless now. Especially with what they did to him!"

"The Iron Mask," said Patch, nodding to himself.

When Patch was younger, his grandmother had often told him the story of the Hamelyn Piper, but only when he pestered her. She preferred to tell him about the adventures of the Eight as they hunted him down and caught him, rather than the horrors that had led to their quest in the first place.

She would say, "I don't want to frighten you, Patch."

And he would insist, "It doesn't scare me, Nan."

Eventually she would give in, and Patch would thrill at the tale. But he had lied to her about it not scaring him. He knew that once she was done – the instant his candle was blown out and the door shut – his courage would fail and he would lie in his bed and tremble, wondering when the long bony fingers of the Hamelyn Piper would wrap around the door handle.

She always began with the same words, words which, even when he thought of them now, brought back a strange combination of adventure and terror: *Have you heard of the town of Hamelyn, Patch? It was once overrun with rats...*

★   ★
★

Have you heard of the town of Hamelyn, Patch? It was once overrun with rats.

Of course, *every* town has its rats, but one summer there were so many that the Mayor of Hamelyn brought in rat-catchers from all around, and they did their work. In the past, this had always done the trick.

But not this year.

At first the rat-catchers were happy. The more rats they caught, it seemed, the more rats they *saw*, and as they were paid for each rat they killed, there was real money to be made!

Then they began to grow nervous.

"It's not natural," they said to one another. "We catch a thousand a day, yet their numbers just keep rising!" They began to think the town was cursed, and one by one the rat-catchers left.

The townsfolk were angry with the Mayor for letting them leave, but what else could the Mayor do?

A Piper!

Much more expensive than rat-catchers, yes, but a Piper was the answer.

One thousand gold coins were raised and locked in the Town Treasury. By early evening the Mayor was sitting in the Town Hall surrounded by the most powerful people in Hamelyn, writing a letter to summon a Piper: *one thousand gold coins*, it said, *to the Piper who rids us of our rats*.

As he was placing his seal on the envelope, the door to

the hall opened wide. There stood a Piper so tall and so thin that he seemed to be built entirely of edges.

"I heard you had a problem," said the Piper.

"You did?" said the Mayor, wary. He looked at the letter in his hand. "And *how* did you hear?"

"From the twenty rat-catchers I met along the road," said the Piper. "But now I've arrived, and the rats will soon be gone! For five hundred gold coins."

The Mayor nodded, and tried to stop himself from grinning. *Five hundred!* he thought. *Only five hundred!*

He carefully placed the letter in his pocket before standing, and walked over to the Piper. "A hefty price," he said, looking up at the considerably taller man.

"Well, if you'd rather find another Piper—" began the stranger.

"We accept!" said the Mayor. He offered out his hand and the Piper shook it.

The Piper smiled. Those in the hall smiled back, even though they all thought that the Piper's teeth seemed a little sharp, and the smile a little cruel.

The Piper cleared his throat. From his coat he produced a long thin Pipe, and began to play. As he played, he took slow strides out of the hall, then along the street outside.

The first rats appeared from the shadows, watching him, but soon they followed in the same slow rhythm: step – step – step!

More and more rats poured out from every house, every street, and by the time the Piper reached the edge of the town there was a vast shifting carpet of rats coming after him. The Mayor and all the people watched this huge procession leave, cheering that the town would soon be free of its rat plague.

The River Weser lay ahead, beyond the walls of the town. At the river's edge, the Piper stopped walking. He raised his arms out to his sides, and the rats reached him.

The townsfolk shuddered, seeing from a distance how the wide column of rats engulfed the Piper, crawling up his coat then down the other side into the water to drown. It was almost an hour before they had all completed their final journey and the Piper was revealed again.

He lowered his arms and returned to the town. The townsfolk cheered and applauded. The Piper took an extravagant bow and smiled. The Mayor stood outside the Town Hall, waving to the crowd to make sure he would always be remembered for such a great success.

As the Piper reached him, the crowd fell silent.

"My job is done," said the Piper. "I will take my payment."

The Mayor summoned the Town Treasurer, who brought a bag that was so heavy it needed its own cart. "You have counted the coins?" asked the Mayor, and the Treasurer said he had. "Here is your payment," said the Mayor to the Piper. "Five hundred gold coins!"

The Piper opened the fastening at the neck of the bag and thrust in his hand. When he pulled it out, it was only *sand* that ran through his fingers.

A shocked gasp spread through the crowd. The Mayor stared at the Treasurer. The Treasurer stared at the bag; he darted forward and tipped the contents of the bag out. Nothing but sand!

"You try to trick me?" said the Piper.

"No!" said the Mayor, terrified by the malice he saw in the Piper's gaze. The Mayor looked to the Captain of the Town Guard, and pointed to the Treasurer. "Arrest this man!" he cried. "And bring five hundred gold coins from the treasury vault!"

The Treasurer protested as he was taken away. Soon, the Captain returned and shook his head. "There is only sand in the vault, sir," he said.

The Mayor was speechless. He looked at the Piper, who scowled.

"I see you have a thief in your midst," said the Piper. "I will return tomorrow to collect my payment."

The Piper turned and walked out of the town.

The Mayor looked to the Captain. "Find the money!" he said. Then he turned to his most trusted advisor. "You are now the Treasurer! Raise more, in case we can't find the missing coins!"

The next morning, the River Weser burst its banks downstream as the rat corpses blocked the flow of water. Fields of wheat and barley were destroyed. The townsfolk set about clearing the corpses and built pyres to burn them on. By afternoon the air was thick with the smoke of the pyres, and the stench of burning rat flesh.

The stolen money was not found; the previous Treasurer had refused to admit taking it, whatever unpleasantness was done to him. In the end, the Captain of the Town Guard stopped torturing him and concluded that he was innocent.

The new Treasurer, wary of the fate of his predecessor, managed to raise enough for the Piper's pay, but it was difficult. When the money was gathered, it was all witnessed by trusted men of the Town Guard, who then stood watch over the vault.

As dusk approached the Piper was seen coming along the road to town. This time the crowd was silent as he came. There was a fearfulness that was shared by all.

The Piper was brought to the treasury, where the vault stood closed. It had not been left unattended, not even for a moment.

"Greetings, Piper," said the Mayor.

"Greetings, Mayor," said the Piper. His smile seemed dangerous. "My payment?"

The Mayor nodded to the new Treasurer, who opened

the door of the vault and handed the Piper the first of the bags that were inside. The Piper untied it and tipped it out.

Sand.

"No!" cried the Mayor.

"No!" cried the Treasurer.

The Piper shook his head, tut-tutting. "Such a *terrible* crime problem you have here," he said. "What *are* we to do?"

The Piper's eyes were aimed directly at the Mayor, that sinister gaze drilling deep. The Mayor could see a darkness there, unlimited and uncaring. He cleared his throat. "We have no more money," he said. Suspicion and fear almost overwhelmed him. He thought of how the rat-catchers had been so wary of the rats, some of them believing the infestation was unnatural; he thought of the money disappearing repeatedly, with no apparent culprit.

He could see suspicion in the eyes of others around him, too, all looking at the Piper. But what could they do? People looked from the Piper to the Mayor, waiting for someone to speak.

"Don't worry," the Piper said at last, but in a voice that was far from soothing. "Tonight I will take my pay. I will take things that are often unwelcome. Things that *everyone*, at some point, wishes were gone. Could I be fairer than that?"

The Piper turned and left. Silence filled the entire town until he was far in the distance.

The Mayor looked to the Captain. "Ready your men," he said. "Guard the gates. Let *nobody* in tonight."

Night came.

In the distance, the pyres still burned.

The guards were ready. The townsfolk locked their doors.

It was midnight when the sound of Piping began. The music grew louder. The people of Hamelyn could hear their own children stir from their beds, laughing. The children came out, unlocked the doors and danced into the streets. The adults all found that they could not move, could not even *speak*.

They could only watch.

And the Piper, his eyes burning like the distant pyres, danced by each house and smiled a wide, sharp smile, and the children of the town followed him towards the town gates, dancing with unbounded joy. The gates were flung open by an invisible force, and the Piper led the children out of Hamelyn.

It was not until morning that the townsfolk could move again. They fell to the ground, wailing in horror at what had happened. Then they ran, seeking their children, following the road, seeing where the grass at the edges had been trampled by the dancing.

On and on they went, until the trampled grass veered onto a smaller pathway that went up Koppen Hill. Near the top of the hill, the trail ended by a sheer face of rock.

The children were not there.

The townsfolk heard the sound of sobbing, and found one small boy, who had been lame since birth.

"I couldn't keep up," he cried, again and again, despairing.

"Where are the others?" asked the adults. "Where are all the other children?"

"He promised us a Land of Play, with all the toys and sweets we could want," said the boy. "When the Piper reached this point, a doorway opened in the rock and they all danced inside. But I couldn't keep up! I was too late!" He burst into angry, desolate tears. "The door shut before I got to it!"

They found no sign of a doorway. In all, one hundred and thirty children had been taken by the Hamelyn Piper.

It took over a year to catch him.

The Pipers' Council assembled a group to track down this evil creature who had brought shame on their kind – a group who became known as the Eight, their exploits now legendary.

When the Piper was finally caught, he refused to reveal what had become of the children. Many wanted to see him die for what he had done, convinced he would never reveal the children's fate, but the Council kept him alive, and gave him the cruellest punishment they could devise. The Iron Mask: fastened around the head of the Hamelyn Piper, it prevented him ever using his abilities again, as no magic could escape it, Song or otherwise.

But it had one more function. Once put in place, whatever the Hamelyn Piper said next would be the only thing he could ever say again, unless he was to tell where the children had gone. When the Mask was fitted to the Piper's head, the Council addressed him.

"Piper of Hamelyn!" they said. "Do you still refuse to tell what you did with the children?"

"Aye!" the Hamelyn Piper cried, his eyes at first defiant; but then his eyes became defeated, and lost, as he finally knew that his reign of evil was ended, and the world would be forever safe from him.

They locked him in the deepest darkest place within the dungeons of Tiviscan, and "Aye!" is still the only word he speaks.

For he has never revealed where the children went.

"Sleep well," said a voice, bringing Patch crashing back to the present. He realized the voice belonged to Vague Henry, but those were the words his grandmother had always said to him as she left him in his bed.

He was a long way from there now, in this cold cell in the dungeons of Tiviscan. The dungeons that would be his home for the rest of his days.

"Goodnight, Henry," said Patch. He stood and looked around to see where best to sleep. The corner where the corpse of Innocent Jack had lain was, for the moment, ruled out, so Patch chose the opposite corner.

He lay down and closed his eyes, trying his best to cover himself in the meagre blanket he'd been given. Rather than consider what the future held, he thought back to the past again.

There was so much more to the Hamelyn Piper's story, of course; the quest of the Eight to catch him was, in itself, an epic tale of courage. But of all the things he'd learned during his training, the most shocking was the Hamelyn Piper's *next* crime, and how close it had come to triggering another war between dragons and humans.

It was shocking, because Patch's grandmother had never told him about it.

One week to the day after the children of Hamelyn were taken, there had been another atrocity: in the Dragon Territories, young dragons had vanished from an isolated school. One hundred dragon children, gone. The ten adult dragons who were their teachers and guardians were poisoned, and only one of them survived, managing to reach another settlement and reveal what had happened.

"A human came," the dragon had said. "A *Piper,* riding a griffin! He played his Pipe and the children followed him, flying over the horizon, laughing as they went."

The Hamelyn Piper had struck again.

When the evil Piper was finally captured, the dragons wanted him executed for his crimes. The refusal of the Pipers' Council was absolute, however, and tensions between Pipers and dragons, high at the best of times, increased. The dragons threatened war against the Pipers. One by one the many nations of the world made their choice: they would stand with the Pipers, whatever happened.

The last war between humans and dragons had been hundreds of years ago, and the loss of life had been horrifying; but suddenly, a new war seemed inevitable.

Yet war was averted. Just.

Among humans, meanwhile, the notion that the Hamelyn Piper had taken the dragon children was treated with suspicion, as if it was only a rumour invented by the dragons to stir up resentment. It was rarely spoken of, and this was probably why Patch's grandmother hadn't included it in her tales.

Humans had always feared dragons, and *fear* could easily turn to *hate*.

For many people, the hatred they had for dragons was so great that they could never have sympathy with them, whatever the situation. Even if their children had vanished.

For some, having fewer dragons would always be a good thing.

✦ ✦ ★

It took a while before he stopped feeling so cold, but Patch finally started to doze on the floor of his cell. Then, as sleep was beckoning, he heard it: from elsewhere in the dungeons came a terrible sound.

"There he goes," sighed Henry. "He'll keep at it until he's hoarse."

"Aye!" screamed the Hamelyn Piper, again and again, deep in the Dark. "*Aye!*"

Patch trembled, hands over his ears, but nothing he did blocked out the noise. It was two hours before the screaming stopped.

9
NO PLACE
LIKE HOME

"Tubes!"

T Patch's eyes snapped open. All he could remember was the nightmare he'd been having, the Hamelyn Piper's long fingers creeping along the floor towards him.

"*Tubes*, Patch!" yelled Henry. "Come on, get up! Tubes!"

Everything came back to him. He hurried to fetch his bowl and jug, turning to the door just as the metal tubes came in through the holes two-thirds of the way up the wall. Sludge oozed from the wider of the tubes, and water came from the other. He reached them in time to collect half of his meal, the rest having joined the rancid pile on the floor.

He looked cautiously at the contents of his bowl, pushing the food around with his fingers. It was a thick gloopy mush, with gristly bits dotted through it. Wary, he raised his fingers to his mouth and tasted it, ready for the most horrible flavours he'd ever encountered, but it was mercifully bland. Even after eating all of it, he was still hungry. He looked at the food that had fallen before he'd reached it, glistening on top of the rank heap that had been there yesterday – the remains of all the food Innocent Jack had presumably failed to collect before they'd noticed he was dead.

Surely he could salvage the rest of today's meal? Just scrape it off carefully, not taking any of the mouldy food below, or the *maggots* that were squirming in amongst it?

"No," he said to himself. But how long might it be before he took that next step, and ate the maggots and mouldy remnants without a thought?

What would he become in a year? In ten years?

He set down his empty bowl and walked to the tiny window, his only view of the outside world. The sun was bright, and on his tiptoes he could see the forest on the distant hills. He would never walk in a forest again, he realized; never feel the sun on his face.

He fell to his knees, sobbing hard, and there he stayed, lost to his misery. When he heard footsteps approaching up the corridor he was unaware of how much time had passed.

The footsteps halted and the lock in Patch's door clunked. He got up and went to the middle of his cell as the door swung open, and the first thing he saw was the purple and black of a Custodian Piper's robes.

It was Erner, carrying his satchel and a parcel. Behind him stood a guard even larger than Furnel.

Erner stepped into the cell and the door slammed closed, the noise reverberating for a few moments. He looked around and spotted the hole in the wall that led to Henry's cell. He walked over and fetched Patch's blanket, then went to the hole and blocked it up.

"Do you mind!" Vague Henry shouted, his voice muffled. "I'm trying to hear what's going on in there!"

Erner walked back to Patch. "Better if we can talk in private," he said. "I didn't come alone."

Wren's head peeked out of Erner's satchel. Patch held out his arm and she hopped onto it, then along to his neck, which she hugged.

Patch grinned, tears falling. "It's so good to see you," he said. "*Both* of you."

Erner nodded, smiling. "I've been enjoying Wren's company very much," he said. "Her Merisax is very good, considering how short a time she's been learning."

"She's a bright girl," said Patch. He glanced at Wren, who gave a proud nod.

"She is," said Erner. "Virtus Stone and I have been assigned duties elsewhere, and I fear Wren would be in too much danger if she came with me. I suggested leaving her with a trusted colleague, but she insists that I tell nobody else about her yet. Besides, she's desperate to keep you company. She should be safe enough with you, now that you're in your cell. I'll be back in two or three weeks."

"What about curing her of her curse?" said Patch.

"By the time I'm back, I hope to have a reply to *this*!" he said, and with a flourish he produced an envelope, complete with an official Custodian Elite wax seal.

Patch read the address. "Brother Tobias, Marwheel Abbey," he said.

"Indeed," said Erner. "I asked Virtus Stone if he knew of anyone capable of curing a Sorcerer's curse, given how… well, you know how it is with Pipers and Sorcerers."

Patch knew very well how it was. While the obvious course of action might be to ask a *Sorcerer* for help, the notion of a Piper doing so was almost unthinkable.

Sorcerers were few and far between, secretive and wealthy. They used a different, older form of magic that they thought was far superior to Songs, and so they looked down their noses at Pipers. In return, Pipers didn't have much liking for Sorcerers; they also didn't *trust* them. Sorcerers often had questionable morals and little regard for laws, although if it ever came to a clash between them and the Custodian Elite, the Custodians had the advantage of greater numbers – Sorcerers always worked alone.

"Didn't Virtus Stone want to know why you were

asking about curses?" said Patch.

"An apprentice is expected to extend their knowledge as much as possible," said Erner. "I ask him so many strange questions, he didn't bat an eyelid at that one. He just told me to contact Brother Tobias at Marwheel Abbey. I've kept my letter vague, and explained that a victim of a shape-changing curse needs help."

"Well, let's hope that Brother Tobias has the answers," said Patch, looking at Wren.

He'd better, she signed. *I want to be human again soon!*

Patch smiled at her, overwhelmed with gratitude that she would choose to stay with him. "In the meantime we can work on improving your Merisax," he said.

There was a heavy knock on the cell door. "Time!" came a shout.

Erner sighed. "Visiting prisoners is frowned on," he said. "And even when it can be arranged, they keep it brief. So, here –" he handed Patch the string-tied parcel he was carrying – "the wrapping is a new blanket – a warmer one – and there are a few other items inside. They're strict about what can be given to prisoners, so if I were you..." He leaned closer and whispered. "Unwrap it in secret!"

The door started to open again. Wren gave a tiny squeak of panic and ran down Patch's back, her claws digging through his thin clothing and into his skin. She clung there, out of sight, and Patch grimaced.

"Come on," said the guard to Erner.

Erner looked at Patch. "I'm sorry," he said. "I still can't believe what happened at the trial. I'll do what I can for you, but…" He shook his head.

"Thank you, Erner," said Patch.

Erner nodded, silent, then stepped out of the cell. The door closed with another thunderous slam.

Patch sighed with relief as Wren's claws stopped digging into his skin and she climbed back up to his shoulder. "Right then," he said quietly, raising the parcel. "Let's see what we've got here!"

Quietly in the corner of the cell, with Wren on the floor beside him, Patch untied the string. Inside was one of the tiny oilskin tents they'd used on the journey to the Castle, which folded up smaller than a fist. Patch found himself staring at it. No more cold nights, he realised, as long he was careful not to let the guards see it. There was also an apple, a curious little wooden box, and a small bag of wheat grains that had Wren's name written on it, in a scratchy style that Patch guessed was Wren's own writing. "Yours?" he said. She nodded, with narrowed eyes.

Touch it and you're dead! she signed, then pointed at the apple. *That's for you.*

Patch smiled and set the bag down beside her. He looked at the strange wooden box. "What's this?" he asked.

Fox and Owls, signed Wren. *Ever play it?*

"My grandfather tried to teach me once," he said. "I couldn't get the hang of it." He fiddled with the box until the top popped open. The inside of the box lid was a game board, and a dozen little pegs were the playing pieces.

Well, now I can teach you, signed Wren.

"We have plenty of time," said Patch, and the phrase didn't fill him with horror the way it had when Henry had said it. As he ate his apple and tried to remember how to set the board up for a game, Wren wandered off into the cell. After a while, Patch heard a crunching sound. Wren was on the top of the rancid food pile, merrily picking up the maggots and eating them.

Wide-eyed, he watched her as she polished off another of the wriggling grubs.

Wren noticed him watching. *You don't mind if I...* she started.

"No," said Patch. "You go ahead. Is it just the maggots, or are you going to eat the rest of the pile?"

Wren screwed up her little face in revulsion. *What, this mouldy old stuff?* she signed. *Don't be disgusting!*

They settled down for some Merisax practice, and after taking Wren through the signing of numbers Patch could tell she was distracted by something. "Are you okay?" he asked. "Do you want a break?"

Wren shook her head. *I've just been dying to ask a question*, she signed. *But it might be upsetting for you.*

"Go on," said Patch. "Ask away."

Why did you leave Tiviscan and abandon your training? she signed. *At the trial, they mentioned bringing shame on yourself.*

Patch took a deep sigh. "Ah," he said. "That."

You don't have to tell me if you don't want to, signed Wren.

"You may as well know," he said. "It happened at the Trials Ceremony, just before summer."

The trials?

"Each year, all the trainee Pipers engage in trials to show how well their studies have gone, and demonstrate their abilities. When a trainee reaches thirteen, though, it's a special time. That's when they can be chosen to begin training for the Elite."

Like with Erner? she asked.

"Yes. He was chosen, and did two years of training before passing his final trials to become an Apprentice. But it's not just the Custodian Elite. There are other specialities, you see. Those who excel in Arable Piping, for example, might be accepted into the Arable Elite. If a nation faces famine, say, or disease wipes out entire crops, the Arable Elite will help prevent disaster. I was like Erner. I wanted to join the Custodian Elite. They enforce the laws of Piping, but that's only part of what they do. They also act like the

Pipers of ancient days. They help those most in need, and bring justice to places that justice has forgotten. For that, a trainee has to be among the very best."

And you are, aren't you?

He shrugged. "I hoped so. Even when I first found I had a talent for Piping, I knew what I wanted to do. Pipers are mainly used by the wealthy. The bigger towns and cities can maybe afford them regularly, and the richest farmers, but for most people they're too expensive. The Custodians were always different. They're not paid by anyone. I mean, every Piper is expected to do their duty, do what's right, but Custodians apply basic laws of justice, even in countries that don't *have* those laws. In every civilized nation, the Custodian Elite have the power to make a difference, and defend the defenceless! If only there were more Custodians, the world would be a much better place to live."

And that was your dream? signed Wren. *To become one? Make the world a better place?*

Patch nodded. "When I first came to Tiviscan, the Tutors were very excited. I showed great skill in the Piping of *people*. Unprecedented, I was told! It's why I'm so good at the Dance. I could even affect *myself* with what I played, which I'd thought was normal, but for most Pipers it's nearly impossible. It's like trying to tickle yourself – it just doesn't work. They told me I could be anything I wanted to be, so I studied as hard as I could, and I tried my very best, because I knew that the *only* thing I wanted was to join the Custodian Elite. And then last summer, the Trials Ceremony came. With all the trials over, the ceremony began, and I knew I'd done really well. Every trainee, every Tutor, and the Pipers' Council themselves, were all gathered together, and at the very end of the ceremony the list of trainees selected for Elite training was read out."

Oh no! signed Wren, looking anxious. *They didn't call out your name!*

Patch shook his head in sorrow. "They called my name, all right. Just not as a Custodian. I couldn't believe what I'd heard, and I stood up, and I shouted. 'The Custodian Elite!' I cried. 'It has to be the *Custodian* Elite. No other will do!' But my trial results weren't quite good enough, and that was that. It felt like my world had ended." He paused, then looked at Wren. "Have you ever wanted something so badly that anything less just wouldn't do?"

Absolutely, she signed. *What happened next?*

"Being chosen for *any* Elite training is such an honour, you don't turn it down. Nobody had *ever* turned it down."

You turned it down? signed Wren, and Patch nodded. *That's all you did? It doesn't seem so bad.*

Patch winced. "I turned it down very, *very* rudely. To the faces of the Pipers' Council; in front of everyone. My disappointment had turned to anger, you see, anger that just bubbled out of me before I even knew what was happening.

I called Lord Pewter a stupid old drunkard who stank of rotting cheese; I yelled at Lady Winkless that she couldn't Pipe her way out of a sack. And I didn't stop there."

Oh dear, signed Wren. *That doesn't sound good.*

"The Council watched me in disbelief, with their mouths hanging open, as I insulted them one by one. When I finished there wasn't a sound. Everyone – the Council, the Tutors, the students, *everyone* – was staring at me. I couldn't believe what had happened! I did the only thing I could think of. I turned and ran. Away from Tiviscan. Away from Piping."

Wren put a paw on his hand. *You must have wanted to be a Custodian very much.*

"It was everything to me. A few days later I thought of returning, but I couldn't face it."

Wren nodded. *What branch of the Elite had they offered you?* she signed. *Arable?*

Patch shook his head. "It doesn't matter now." He felt a little distant for a moment, before snapping out of it. "My turn to have a question answered," he said. "How did you manage to get a Sorcerer angry enough to curse you like this?"

I was kidnapped, she signed. *The Sorcerer wanted a maidservant. This was last summer, too. As your life was changing, so was mine. When I almost managed to escape, he caught me, and that was that.*

"He turned you into a rat."

Exactly. I fled into the forest, terrified of the dangers around me from hawks and the like. I was even fearful of other rats at first, but they proved to be generous creatures. Stupid, but generous. I found a little rat community near some local wheat fields and stayed with them for a few weeks. Ten rats, terrified of the farmer's dog, half starved. They knew there was something unusual about me, and started to follow my lead. The dog was easy to outsmart, and soon everyone was well fed, but it came time for all of us to move on. As we travelled, we'd come across other rats, and they'd tag along. We snuck onto a barge transporting barley, and spent a week on it. I'd hoped we would make it to a warmer place before winter, but we were discovered and had to flee the barge. Turned out we were in the middle of the Breydram Valley, and winter came faster than I'd expected.

"Patterfall was your only refuge," said Patch.

Yes. We tried to push further downstream, but gave up in the end and stayed put. At first I thought we had plenty of food to last us through winter, but a population explosion put paid to that idea. Rats will be rats, and they just wouldn't be told.

"The villagers were terrified that you'd eat them. So was I, come to that."

They're much more mild-mannered than people believe. The villagers needn't have feared, but the rats didn't get the chance to prove it... She looked at Patch. *Would they have suffered?*

He shook his head. "I know the Dispersal is horrifying, but as far as I know the effect is instant. They wouldn't have suffered at all."

She nodded, tears in her eyes. *I didn't make a very good leader in the end,* she signed.

He picked her up and put her on his shoulder. She snuggled down, and they sat together in silence for a time, until they both felt ready to get back to the Merisax number system.

In the afternoon, shortly after the food and water arrived, Vague Henry shouted loud enough and long enough that he couldn't be ignored, and Patch removed the old blanket from the hole between their cells.

"Thank the stars!" said Henry. "Set something in front of it if you want to stop me peeking in, but please don't block it up like that. God help me if it rained!"

"Sorry," said Patch. "I forgot it was there." He gathered up the blanket and left it a little way in front of the hole, perched over the narrow channel in the floor so Henry couldn't see into Patch's cell. "That okay?" he said.

"That's fine," said Henry. "No harm done." He didn't waste time moving on to a subject he was clearly more interested in: "So, um, your visitor? A Custodian Piper, then? I saw that much."

"A friend," said Patch. "He came to commiserate with me on how things turned out."

"Oh," said Henry. "I just wondered if you were holding up okay? I mean, I thought he'd given you more bad news or something, since—"

"Since?"

"Since you've started to talk to yourself. And don't say you haven't!"

It occurred to Patch that if Henry thought he was crazy, he could chat with Wren as much as he liked without worrying about how loud he was talking. "Let me deal with things my own way, Henry," he said, smiling. "I'll be fine."

After a little more Merisax practice, Wren was eager to get started on Fox and Owls. She took the game board and rearranged Patch's failed attempt at placing the pieces.

Which do you want to be? she signed. *Fox or Owls?*

Patch shrugged. "Remind me of the difference."

Okay, signed Wren. *I'll start with the basics. There's only one fox piece, and two owls. Say you be the fox, then you move, and I move one of the rabbits, then I move both owls, then you move a rabbit and it starts again. Easy!*

Patch smiled, bewildered by the game but curiously happy. The cell around him had suddenly stopped being so oppressive.

He looked at the pile of rotting food and vowed to get it cleaned up soon. He faintly wished for a chair, or a mirror.

It feels more like a home than a prison, he thought. *Just because I'm here with a friend.*

10

UNWELCOME ARRIVALS

Overnight it started to rain heavily. When they woke, the importance of Henry's warning about not blocking the hole in the wall became clear – the channel in the floor had turned into a murky stream, flowing towards the toilet hole.

Patch saw the opportunity to clean things up. He gritted his teeth and scooped up handfuls of the rotting pile of food, carrying it to the toilet hole and letting the filthy rainwater wash it away. Once finished, Patch used a little of the water from mealtime to clean his hands.

Outside, the weather kept getting worse, and with it the murky stream threatened to overflow its channel, but as the hours passed the flowing water became a little less filthy, and the stench in his cell began to fade.

Henry, meanwhile, kept trying to get Patch to converse. He seemed sure that Patch was falling apart, talking to himself and – God help him! – actually *laughing* occasionally.

"I'll be okay," Patch told him.

"I'm just worried," said Henry. "I asked some of the others if they could help, and all I managed to do was land you with your nickname."

"Which is?"

"The Mad Piper, I'm afraid."

Patch laughed out loud, which presumably didn't settle Henry's nerves one bit.

The heavy rain continued unbroken for the next two days.

Patch, meanwhile, was improving at Fox and Owls. At the start, Wren had always won within a dozen moves, but now it was taking perhaps twice as long for her to be victorious. In one game, his owls had taken *four* rabbits, and he'd clapped with excitement.

Then, after a particularly vicious thunderstorm that continued until dawn, the rain faded at last. The dungeon seemed oddly quiet with the rain gone. The drainage channel in the cell had little more than a trickle running through it.

When chatter started to grow from the prisoners along the corridor, it was hard to miss in the relative silence. With

Wren on his shoulder, Patch went over to the hole in the wall. "Henry?" he said. "What's the fuss about?"

"All this rain has caused serious flooding lower in the dungeons," said Henry. "They're having to move some prisoners from the deepest levels until it's sorted out."

There were footsteps in the corridor. For a moment Patch wondered if it was Erner again, but this time the sounds stopped short of Patch's door.

It was Henry's turn for a visitor. "Henry Trew!" called a voice.

"Yes?" said Henry.

"Ready your things, you're to be moved up a level." Other prisoners called out to ask if they would be moved too. "Shut up!" yelled the guard. "None of you lot are going anywhere."

The whole corridor complained.

"We'll be bringing a prisoner up shortly from a flooded cell," said the guard. "Keep the noise down or you'll not get a meal today! Now, hurry up, Trew!"

"I'll just fetch my things," said Henry. He came back over to the hole. "Patch! Did you hear? I'm getting an upgrade! Moving up a floor, until it's sorted out. Maybe they'll let me stay up there!"

"I'll miss you, Henry," said Patch. "Good luck upstairs!"

"God bless you, Patch. And I'm sure whoever they put here in my place will, um—" Henry paused, and Patch knew why – *any* prisoner from the deeper levels would likely be unpleasant company.

"It'll be fine, Henry," Patch said. He looked at Wren, who seemed fretful. "Don't worry," he told her. "I mean, how bad could it be?"

It wasn't long before they found out.

An hour later Patch heard the sound of rattling chains in the corridor, soon followed by the shouts of the other inmates: "Who's your prisoner, eh? We don't want no scum here!"

The clanking stopped at Vague Henry's cell. Patch and Wren heard the door open, and they both went to the hole and looked through. A narrow shaft of light from the window fell on the prisoner, who was shuffling into the centre of the cell.

You want me to go in there and take a look? signed Wren.

"No!" whispered Patch. "Stay here, where it's safe."

The prisoner stood in the light, but all Patch had sight of was the legs, chained together, thick manacles at the feet. The prisoner was facing the window, and Patch presumed the light was so unfamiliar that they were mesmerized. They might not have seen any sunlight in years.

The cell door slammed shut, catching Patch by surprise. He'd expected the guard to remove the chains before leaving, but apparently not. The prisoner's arms came into view, wrists also manacled with a long chain between them. That was when the sobbing began, deep and agonizing, as the prisoner fell to their knees and out of the shaft of light.

After a while, the prisoner's hands came back into the light, twisting around, almost playing with it. *Yes*, thought Patch, *this is someone who hasn't seen daylight in a while.*

Wren sneezed. Suddenly the shape in the gloom snapped up into a sitting position, chains clanking.

Patch and Wren pulled back from the hole.

Sorry! signed Wren.

Let's wait a bit before we have another look, Patch signed back.

The chains in the other cell rattled as the prisoner moved around within. Eventually the rattling stopped, and after a few minutes of silence Wren and Patch glanced at each other and nodded.

They looked through the hole.

An eye was looking back at them, full of desperation.

And there was something around the eye, Patch saw. Some kind of metal.

Iron.

Patch pulled back, and so did Wren.

"Oh," said Patch. "Oh no."

"Aye?" came a quiet voice through the hole. It sounded like pleading. "Aye?" More sobs followed, and then the prisoner spoke again, louder and louder, becoming more and more angry, the same word every time. "Aye! *Aye!*"

The other inmates knew immediately what this meant.

"Guard!" came the shouts. "Take him away! You can't do this! Anyone but him! *Anyone but him!*"

"*Aye!*"

"Guard! You can't leave him here!"

"*AYE!*"

"*Show us some mercy!*"

Patch grabbed the old blanket and stuffed it into the hole, pulling his hand out quickly – fighting the childish terror that the fingers of the Hamelyn Piper would close around his wrist. He lifted Wren from the floor and ran to the little tent at the far side of the cell. They stayed there all night, awake and shivering with fear as the Hamelyn Piper screamed.

Soon after dawn, Patch took the sleeping Wren from his lap and set her on the soft blanket Erner had brought. He went to the hole and pulled out the old blanket, then looked inside the other cell.

The Hamelyn Piper was asleep near the hole, and Patch could see the Iron Mask clearly. It seemed to be made from many smaller sections, forming a mesh that wrapped around the back of his head and obscured most of his face, save for his eyes and mouth. It looked grubby and tarnished, unsurprising after almost a decade of imprisonment. The Hamelyn Piper's beard – if that was a word that could be used for such a jumble of hair – had grown through the mask, and seemed to have been haphazardly cut quite recently. The guards had probably taken advantage of the move to do this most basic of maintenance.

As the other prisoners awoke, the complaints about the new arrival started up again, growing in volume all morning. The response from the guards came later – when the tubes arrived, it was only water that came, and no food. That night the Hamelyn Piper screamed again, and the prisoners complained again, and the only difference was the hunger that gnawed at Patch. Wren nibbled at her grain, offering Patch some, but he refused to take it from her.

"They'll feed us tomorrow," he said. "They'll have to."

But the next day, the food was still withheld. Complaints about hunger were now almost as loud as the complaints about the Hamelyn Piper.

The day after, the prisoners had learned their lesson. Any grumblings were quickly silenced by a scolding from the others, and the food came at last.

Once Patch's bowl and jug were full, Wren asked to sit in the tiny window as she sometimes did. Patch was quietly jealous, as Wren could scurry to the far end of the six-foot-long hole and see much more than Patch, who was limited to a tiny piece of sky and distant hill.

As he finished his food he heard Wren squeak urgently. He came to the window.

You need to see this, she signed, looking worried. She hopped onto his shoulder and he went up on his toes, straining to look out of the window. It took a moment for his eyes to adjust to the bright sky, but eventually he saw dark spots against the blue: birds flying.

"Starlings?" he said. Wren shook her head, agitated. He looked out again at the dark spots in the sky. It had to be starlings, he thought, with so many of them – a vast flock, coming over the distant hill.

Wait. The *distant* hill?

The trees on that hill were so far away they seemed tiny, yet he could see the individual birds, see them *flap*… How was that possible? He froze, staring at the dark cloud. He looked at Wren, and she nodded.

You understand now? she signed.

"Yes," said Patch, watching the dark cloud come ever closer. It wasn't a flock of birds.

It was *dragons*.

Thousands of them.

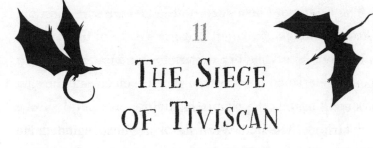

11
THE SIEGE
OF TIVISCAN

Warning bells rang out on the Castle battlements, something Patch had heard in the occasional drills during his training.

"It's been centuries since anyone dared attack Tiviscan," he told Wren. "They'll be readying the Castle defences now, with the garrisoned Pipers preparing the Battle Horns." Those huge horns were mounted permanently on the roof of the Keep, able to create barriers of turbulent air strong enough to protect against flaming catapult attacks, say – or to knock dragons out of the sky. He shook his head, stunned. "*Why*, though? Nobody wants war. What could they hope to achieve? Sending such a huge army?"

The dragons were obscuring more and more of the sky as they came ever nearer, the flock filling their little window now.

No, thought Patch. It wasn't a *flock*. That wasn't the right word.

The right word depended on the creatures in question: a *flock* of birds, a *swarm* of bees, or a *pack* of dogs. There was a word especially for dragons, too, and until now Patch hadn't understood why that word had been chosen, instead of something more appropriate for fire-breathers. Surely, he'd always thought, a *burning* of dragons would make more sense? Or a *firestorm*?

But seeing the dark cloud approach, blocking out more and more light, he understood at last why the right word was *darkness*.

A darkness of dragons was coming. And it wouldn't be long before they reached the Castle.

Wren scurried up to the far end of the window for a better view. After a moment, she came back. *Some of the dragons are carrying something,* she signed.

Patch looked past her, trying to make it out. Yes, there it was – small groups at the front were linked in some way, a shape hanging down below them.

"Are those…?" said Patch, squinting. "Are those *rocks*?"

Wren nodded. She hopped onto Patch's shoulder. Closer and closer the dragons came.

"What would they need huge rocks for?" He looked at Wren. "Not to—"

Wren nodded again.

Patch stepped back from the window and kept going until he reached the cell door.

The other prisoners were yelling to be released – "So we can help defend the Castle!" cried one, although Patch very much doubted their sincerity – and the general air of panic and doom was overwhelming. He sat at the base of the door, Wren on his shoulder, and waited.

The sounds of shouted commands, fearful cries, and angry prisoners were soon joined by another sound.

The beating of giant wings.

"Here they come," said Patch. He cupped his hands around Wren as a roar of fire came. Flame lit the window and the cell, then a black shadow flew past, heading up. After a moment there were screams and explosions. The dragons they'd been watching couldn't have reached them so quickly. He realized that some must have come in low, unseen, then shot up at the last instant to surprise the garrison. Certainly, he couldn't hear any sign of a barrier Song being played on the Battle Horns.

"I wonder if—" he started, but then the wall exploded and everything went black.

Patch felt something hitting his nose repeatedly, but all he could hear was a high-pitched continuous tone. He opened his eyes. The air was thick with dust. Wren was on his chest, slapping his nose with her paw.

Sit up, she signed.

"What happened?" Patch said – or *tried* to say, as his voice didn't seem to work. He clapped his hands but couldn't hear it. He was temporarily deafened; time to switch to hand-speech. *What happened?*

The dragons used their rocks, Wren signed, pointing at the wall.

Patch coughed as he looked. At least now he couldn't complain about having a small window. A large chunk of the wall had gone, taking the window with it.

His hearing was starting to recover. Wind howled past the damage in the wall, and there were groans and shouts from the prisoners and beyond, but it seemed that there was a definite lull in the attack. He set Wren on the floor and went to the hole, climbing up into it. The view was dizzying. The forest and hills were now home to the many dragons, bursts of flame coming here and there as shows of bravado. He looked up at the outside wall above him. "My God," he said.

The damage was considerable. Huge slabs of stone had fallen away, but the attack had been tightly targeted. He climbed back down to the cell floor and realized he was shaking. "This is madness," he said. "What could they possibly want—?"

He stopped talking and slowly turned his eyes to the wall of the cell next to them.

"They've come for *him*," said Patch. "They've come for the Hamelyn Piper. All these years they've waited, and finally they've come. Somehow they heard he'd been moved, and they must have known exactly where he was moved to!"

What will they do next? signed Wren.

Patch laid out his blanket and started to put his belongings on top, preparing to turn it into a parcel again. "I'm not waiting to find out," he said. "We're lucky that attack didn't kill us. If they do it again we're dead!"

Wren jumped onto the Fox and Owls board as he reached for it, his hand trembling. *What are you doing?* she signed.

"We're leaving."

How?

Patch pointed at the newly created hole in the wall. "That way." He nudged her off the game board and packed it up.

Wren looked at the hole. She stared at Patch. *We're climbing down?* she signed. *You're not serious!*

Patch nodded, trying to sound confident rather than terrified. "They'll assume I died in the attack, Wren! This is my chance of freedom."

You're crazy, she signed, and he thought she was probably right.

"I can lip-play a bit of courage into both of us," he said.

125

"And there's a climbing Song I know that'll help." He wrapped the blanket-parcel to leave plenty of string spare, and tied it around his waist.

But at that moment, the warning bells rang out again.

Outside, a lone figure was flying towards the Castle from the assembled dragons. Patch wondered how much damage the previous flaming assault had done to the huge Battle Horns. Not enough to put them out of use, it seemed – as the solitary dragon approached, the low pulsing hum of the Horns began, building a defensive Song. They'd been caught by surprise once before, and this time they were taking no chances.

The dragon representative carried a white flag in one front claw, and something else in the other.

A scroll! signed Wren.

"Their demands, I assume," said Patch. He climbed up into the hole again to keep sight of the dragon. This time, Wren scampered up with him. She seemed confident enough, he saw, climbing on the shattered wall, even in the blustering wind. A rat, he knew, could fall from such an enormous height and walk away after landing. For him, the result would be very different. *Messier*, for a start.

Patch watched the dragon as it came closer to the Castle. It wore a battle harness – a hardened leather chest plate on the front, and packs and straps on the sides which held equipment and supplies. The animal certainly looked fearsome enough. Patch could see what he thought were battle scars, discoloured areas on the creature's underbelly and flank. There had clearly been some trauma affecting its muzzle. And wings.

And tail, come to that.

It was male, Patch could tell, lacking as it did the giveaway spines on its back. It – or rather, *he* – came within a hundred feet of the battlements and stayed there, wings beating steadily as he tucked the white flag into the top of the battle harness.

The dragon unrolled the scroll he carried and began to read in an impressively booming voice. "By the authority of the Triumvirate of the Great Circle of the Red Sand, I demand that you hand over the prisoner known as the Hamelyn Piper. Failure to do so will be met with the displeasure of the dragons here gathered. You have thirty minutes to respond." He rolled up the scroll and turned to fly back to the other dragons.

"We have to go right now," said Patch. "If we're here when they attack again, we'll be killed."

Wren jumped onto his shoulder and gave him a thumbs up; Patch found the water jug on the floor, on its side but still with some water in it. He rinsed the dust from his mouth and licked his lips, ready to whistle up some courage.

But before he could begin, a deep rhythmic melody filled the cell. It was coming from the Battle Horns.

"That's an attacking Song they're building," said Patch, looking out to where the dragon with the scroll was still flying away from the Castle, barely a fifth of the distance back to the rest of the dragons. "Don't tell me they're going to—" The melody suddenly picked up pace, the underlying low hum from the Battle Horns pulsing now, rapid and deep. "They *are*!" he said, shocked. "They're sending their answer already! They're going to bring that dragon down!"

The dragon messenger looked over his shoulder and started to flap his wings harder. Too late, though – the sound from the Battle Horns grew so loud and so strong that it made the air shimmer and twist, and the space in front of the Castle took on a multicoloured sheen. The colours shot out towards the lone dragon like a rainbow turned into a torrent of flame, making a sound that was half-thunder, half-scream. The dragon was engulfed by the blast, and he tumbled hundreds of feet down through the air, vanishing into the dense pines in the forest far below. The crunch of impact made Patch wince.

Cheering began from the Castle walls, but in the dungeons a shocked silence fell. One prisoner shouted out: "We're dead! The fools have killed us all!"

The Battle Horns maintained their deep pulsing rhythm. Out of range in the distant trees, dragons were taking off and circling, gathering their numbers. "There are just too many of them," said Patch. "The Battle Horns won't be able to stop them all. They'll get through and the Horns will be abandoned. We'll be defenceless."

And then he heard a voice that had been silent all this time.

"Aye?" said the Hamelyn Piper, his voice almost mournful.

Patch looked out of the gaping hole and saw the rock-wielding dragons closing in. Behind them he saw *other* groups of rock-wielders, who were rising sharply at high speed, releasing their rocks well out of range of the Battle Horns. The air shimmered as the Horns did their work, but the rocks were flying up, arcing, coming down again, this time within the Castle walls.

There were crashes and screams, and the Song of the Battle Horns was silenced.

The dragons had already taken out the most important defence.

Cannons thundered from the battlements high above, but it was the rock-wielders heading right for the dungeon walls that Patch was watching now, almost hypnotized by the sight.

Wren's piercing squeal snapped him out of it. She scampered to the outer wall in the corner farthest from the Hamelyn Piper's cell, and he dived towards her as the rocks hit their target.

Impact after impact came. The cell shook violently. Stones shattered and flew. He tried to shield Wren with his body as he covered his ears with his hands. He yelled in terror, certain that he was moments away from a painful death.

The attack stopped.

Patch stood, shaking. On the floor under him Wren was holding her paws around her head. She peeked out and looked around.

There was no dust this time. It had cleared quickly in the strong breeze, because there was almost no wall now. The only remaining part was the small piece beside them that had miraculously remained intact. Patch looked up at the ceiling and saw a worryingly deep crack in it. He looked across to the Hamelyn Piper's cell. Much of the wall between the two cells had collapsed, and the external wall in that other cell was entirely gone. The Hamelyn Piper was on the floor, half-covered in rubble. A single word came from him, frail and almost lost to the wind. "Aye…"

Patch found himself staring at the most dreaded of Pipers, yet somehow he felt no fear of the masked man and started to walk towards him. He was aware of movement out in the distance. He turned and saw dragons holding their position in the air higher up, making sure of no further defensive assaults from the Castle, while a line of dragons formed some kind of honour guard, maintaining

130

their height. Past the end of that line a group was coming closer, at the centre of which were three who wore incredibly ornate battle harnesses, flanked by black-armoured dragons.

The Triumvirate and their guards, Patch guessed. The rulers of the Dragon Territories, here in person to claim their quarry. They would reach their target soon, but Patch still walked towards the edge of the Hamelyn Piper's cell, drawn there by an irresistible need to *see*.

The attack had wounded the man badly. A large slab of stone had crushed his legs. The Iron Mask was visibly damaged at the front. Patch watched with horror and fascination as the Hamelyn Piper's hands came up and tore at the Mask, until the front opened outwards and it clattered to the cell floor.

Patch stared at the thin face, the Hamelyn Piper's eyes now locked with his own.

"Aye..." said the man, with a cough of pain that brought up blood. But the Mask's protective charms, the charms that had forced him to repeat the same word over and over, had no more hold over him now. "Aye...am..." he said.

Patch marvelled at how he felt no terror, even though he was in the company of the most evil Piper ever to have lived. And he realized what the man had actually said.

What he had *always* been trying to say.

It wasn't "Aye". It wasn't the single word of defiance

that the story claimed. Instead, it was only the first word in a sentence that he had never been able to finish.

Until now.

"I...am..." said the man, relief in his voice. He swallowed and took a breath, still looking directly at Patch. "I am not the Piper of Hamelyn."

The sound of wings announced the arrival of the black-armoured dragons. Patch stepped away quickly, knowing he was at their mercy, but they ignored him. Instead, they lifted the slab the man was trapped under and yanked their quarry from the rubble.

There was no fear written on the man's face, Patch thought, only a sense of *release*.

A short way from the Castle the Triumvirate waited. They gave their guards a nod. The dragon carrying the prisoner let out a deafening screech and flew high into the air, higher than the Castle battlements. The other dragon guards, together with the Triumvirate themselves, formed a circle. When ready, the prisoner was released, falling towards the circle in silence.

The circle of dragons aimed upwards and breathed their fire, creating a blast of flame that caught the man right in the centre and tracked the path of his fall.

All that emerged from underneath the circle were the blackened chains that had held him. Of the man, there was nothing left but ash, drifting in the wind.

Patch looked back to where the Iron Mask had fallen. He climbed over what was left of the dividing wall, then took the Mask and returned to his own cell.

Wren was angry with him, squeaking loudly to get him to come back. Fragments of stone fell on his head as he ran to Wren, and the moment he reached her a loud cracking came from the stone around them. Wren climbed up to his shoulder, scowling.

You scared me! she signed. *Promise me you won't do anything that stupid again!*

But before he could make any promise at all, the floor shuddered under them and shifted outwards in a sudden jerk. Patch found himself dropping down, a scream leaving his lips as he fell.

12
NOT QUITE DEAD

Patch came to an abrupt halt, sprawled on his knees on the small section of cell floor that had broken away. It had landed on a wide rocky ledge jutting out from the sheer cliff the dungeons had been built into; beside them, in the jagged rock of the cliff face, was a crevice about ten feet high and two across.

He shared a look of bewilderment with Wren. She suddenly squealed with terror and pointed up: above them another huge chunk of wall was falling. Patch grabbed Wren and scrambled off the ruined floor, into the crevice. He winced as the falling chunk crashed into the space he'd just stepped out of, then stood with his eyes shut, not daring to look as debris rained down behind him.

There were other screams. He opened his eyes and

turned, staring as masonry and prisoners alike tumbled down past them. The piece of floor they had been on had already vanished, and the ledge that had stopped their fall had been sliced away from the cliff face.

They'd fallen fifty feet or so. Above them at least eight cells were open to the elements now – eight cells whose walls had gone, several having lost most of their floor. Shouts for help echoed around the devastation.

He put Wren on his shoulder and was suddenly aware of something in his other hand – he was still clutching the Iron Mask. He tied it to the parcel at his waist.

Very slowly, Patch bent his knees, keeping his back pressed hard against the rock. He worked his way as far into the crevice as he could, and found he could actually sit. Wren was staring ahead blankly, just as stunned as he was.

"I'll, um, wait until I stop shaking before I climb anywhere," he said.

It took a while.

As they waited, the shouts and calls echoing around the Castle above them grew less and less urgent. Apart from the occasional piece of stonework tumbling past them, the structure of the dungeons held together.

Soon they could hear gruff voices hollering to each

other, describing the damage and assessing what could be done to shore up the Castle until repairs could be attempted.

Patch wasn't shaking any more, but with all the activity that was going on he decided to wait until nightfall before risking the climb. As things stood, the Pipers would assume he'd died – certainly, he didn't imagine they'd be hurrying to hunt through the rubble for bodies. If people saw him climbing, that would all change.

In the distance, the dragon army was preparing to leave, apparently unhurried. There certainly didn't appear to be any sign of reprisal from the Castle – the dragons had come here to kill the Hamelyn Piper, and now that it was done the fight seemed to be over.

Far below, the forest at the base of the cliff showed the scars where the largest chunks of masonry had crashed to the ground. There was another scar that Patch could see – a smaller area further out, where the broken tops of trees were visible. He pointed it out to Wren. "Is that where the dragons' messenger fell, do you think?"

Wren looked for a moment then signed her reply: *Could he have survived?*

Patch thought back to the dragon dropping out of the sky, and the crunch of the impact. "I doubt it." The dragons had presumably collected their colleague's body during the attack. Patch felt a wave of empathy for the messenger, accompanied by a strong feeling of shame at how the Pipers had attacked him from the rear while he carried a white flag.

The dragon army rose and began the long journey back to their homelands. The darkness of dragons receded, until at last it looked like a flock of birds in the distance, just as it had when Wren had first seen it approach.

Once the dragons had gone, the sound of hammer on stone and the bawdy conversation of workmen drifted down to them.

Patch set Wren down beside him in the crevice, and a moment later she lurched to one side and grabbed a juicy beetle that had blundered too close. She tucked in, ripping the insect's head off with her first bite. As she crunched into the abdomen she noticed Patch's grim expression. She polished off the rest in two mouthfuls. *They're actually pretty good*, she signed. *A bit like caramel.*

"I'll take your word for it," said Patch.

As night fell the work on the Castle ceased. Patch and Wren risked a quick glance up and saw the roped-timber reinforcements that had been put in place, all rather impressive considering how speedily it had been assembled.

In the sky the moon shone through wispy cloud.

"I think it's safe to go," he said. He checked the parcel at his waist and took a moment to better secure the Hamelyn Piper's Mask. He lifted Wren back onto his shoulder. "If I fall, jump away from me. You'll survive the landing as long as I don't come down on top of you." Wren just gave him a hard stare. "Okay, okay. I won't fall. Right. Time to whistle up some courage. Quite a bit of it, I think."

Patch built the Song of Courage as best he could without a Pipe. As a very young boy, he'd stumbled onto some rhythms and melodies that made him feel a little braver; anyone who had ever felt emboldened by joining in a normal song of hope or patriotism could understand the kind of feelings he'd been able to create when he was young. The power of music was clear even to those who knew little of the Piping Arts. But as he'd learned the ways of the Pipe at Tiviscan, his eyes and ears had been opened to the *real* power that music could conjure.

He felt strength flowing through his blood.

Confidence. Certainty. Courage.

I can do this, he thought.

He stepped to the edge of the crevice they had taken refuge in, and looked down.

I can't do this, he thought.

He stepped back from the edge. It was a *long* way down. Long, and craggy, and *sharp*.

Are you okay? signed Wren.

Patch took a breath and nodded. "I've a little courage now," he said. "Next, I need help with the *climbing* part." He began the Song of the Climb, slowly building it up, the rhythm steady. In his mind, he could already feel the satisfaction of his hands moving over rock, finding purchase, knowing how much weight a handhold could support.

As he whistled, he put out of his mind the knowledge of where many Songs came from, where many had originated and been refined.

War.

Pipers had accompanied armies for centuries, and had also ventured on smaller missions: infiltration, sabotage. The Song of the Climb, for example, would have helped a group of fighters tackle terrain that an enemy thought impossible.

And while not all Songs had such origins, most of those that affected *people* came from the battlefields of history.

He whistled, eyes closed, until he felt a kinship with the rock itself. It would show him where to place his feet. It would guide his fingertips to where they would cling. He was ready to start the descent. He kneeled and lowered his legs over the base of the crevice.

The moonlight was unnecessary; instinct alone was leading him down the face of the cliff. Only the rock seemed real. Everything else faded away, coming back into focus from time to time and prompting him to change what he whistled. Whenever terror crept into his bones, he whistled for courage; when his sure reach for handholds faltered, he went back to the Song of the Climb.

When at last they were safely down, he stopped whistling and stared back up, unable even to *see* the crevice where the climb had begun. How long had it taken? Somewhere between hours and centuries, it seemed.

He looked at Wren, her expression one of awe. She hugged his neck.

Patch took her from his shoulder and gently set her down.

"We made it," he said, falling to his knees. Then he spent ten minutes retching, his last prison meal forced out of him in a thin stream of bile.

Where to now? signed Wren, when he'd stopped being sick.

Patch wiped the spittle from the side of his mouth. "Erner's letter, remember?" he said. "We go to Marwheel Abbey, to find a way to cure you! Unless you've decided to remain a rodent?"

No chance of that, she signed.

Now that the climb was over, Patch noticed how cold he was feeling. Tiviscan always enjoyed a mild winter, but his meagre prison clothing wouldn't do much to keep him warm. "I wish I had my coat," he said, rubbing his hands together. "Are you cold too?"

I'm all right, signed Wren. *Being furry comes in handy.*

"Well as long as we keep moving, I should be okay on the journey to the Abbey." He pointed to the trees ahead.

"We go that way through the forest. We have to get far from Tiviscan without being discovered. I'm an escaped prisoner now, Wren. I have to be cunning and resourceful! A day's walk will take us to the Penance River, which we can follow north."

And after I'm cured, what about you? She pointed to his waist, where the Mask was tied. *You're the last person to see the Hamelyn Piper alive. Perhaps you'll be famous!*

Patch shook his head, untying the Mask to take a proper look at it. "Obscurity is all that I want, Wren. If Rundel Stone found out I was alive, he'd make sure I went back to the dungeons." He held the Mask closer, peering at it. The parts that seemed damaged simply popped back into shape after some prodding, although the lock itself was beyond repair.

Every inch of the Mask's inner surface was covered in symbols that reminded him of the ancient magical textbooks in the Tiviscan library. He wiped it to see the runes more clearly, and was astonished at how much cleaner the metal was where he'd wiped. What he'd taken for tarnish seemed to be merely dirt. "The Mask came off the Hamelyn Piper's head just before the dragons took him," he said. "I don't even know why I picked it up. I should just drop this here and be done with it." Studying the metal, he could see that it wasn't welded together. It was made from overlapping pieces connected with *joints*, similar to the ones that

141

allowed it to hinge shut over the wearer's face. He tried to move some of the pieces against one another, at first without success, but then parts of the Mask seemed to fold up. He tried again with another section, and this time the entire Mask flattened down into a rectangle the size of his hand.

He looked at Wren. "Interesting," he said. "Should I keep it, do you think?"

She nodded. *A souvenir*, she signed. *Of when you saw the most evil man in history finally get his reward!*

"I'm not sure that watching a man die is something I want a souvenir of, Wren," Patch said, but then it occurred to him – Wren hadn't heard what the man had said. *I'm the only one to know the Hamelyn Piper's last words,* he thought. *If I should even think of him by that name any more!* Suddenly the knowledge was a terrible burden: the prisoner had suffered a great injustice, if those last words had really been true, and worse – it would mean that the *real* Hamelyn Piper must still be free.

And if that was the case, surely it was Patch's duty to tell the Council? *They'd lock me up again*, he thought. *Whether they believed me or not, I'd spend the rest of my days rotting in a cell.*

He tied the folded Mask to his waist. He would need money soon enough, he reckoned, and strange magical objects always had value.

He put Wren on his shoulder and made his way through the light vegetation at the forest's edge, then through thicker bushes until they were in amongst the vast pines. By the time the first hint of predawn twilight was visible in the sky, they were far enough from the base of the cliff – and from Tiviscan – for Patch to breathe easier.

A little further on, the undergrowth became more challenging. The sky was brightening rapidly, letting Patch look further ahead to spot the clearest path. He could see a much brighter area beyond a thicket. "Is that a clearing?" he said. Wren shrugged, but as they got closer they could see splintered treetops high up, and a dark shape on the ground ahead.

The messenger? signed Wren.

Patch paused. Surely the dragons wouldn't just have left their fallen comrade? Yet as they got closer, they saw that it *was* the messenger, broken and still. The dragons had abandoned their sole casualty of the battle. "I don't understand," said Patch. "Why didn't they retrieve the body?"

That's really sad, signed Wren.

"This poor soul was attacked from the rear," said Patch. "Seeing that happen made me ashamed to be a Piper. But now this lack of respect from his own kind!" He scowled, surprised by how angry he felt. "It's not like dragons at *all*. During training I learned quite a bit about their culture.

When a dragon dies, the body is taken by members of the Order of the Skull – the most ancient and secretive part of their religion. The body is buried deep, in total secrecy, the location never revealed."

Wren frowned. *So a dragon's family don't even have a grave to visit?*

Patch nodded. "It's been that way for thousands of years. Mind you, humans have always thought various parts of a dragon have magical properties. There are plenty of idiots who'd buy any old potion if you pretended it had powdered dragon tooth in it. Can you imagine the trouble that'd be caused if there were dragon graves to rob?"

When Patch had first seen the messenger he'd noticed an odd discoloration on the scales, which suggested terrible old wounds; now, he could see the same thing around its closed eyes and mouth. The snout seemed misshapen, and was presumably broken. The wings were limply spread out, and one had a long bleeding tear near its base.

"A proud creature, reduced to this," he said. "Meeting its fate after showing true bravery, yet ending up mourned only by us, Wren. An escaped prisoner and a cursed rat."

He stepped closer. It wasn't very large for a dragon, he realized, its head perhaps four feet long and two across. Something nagged at him about the markings, especially those on the wings.

Couldn't we do something? signed Wren.

"Well, we couldn't exactly *bury* him," said Patch. "Unless we had a week or two to spare."

You could say a few words, she replied.

Patch nodded. He thought back to what he'd learned of their culture, then cleared his throat. "Today, we ask the Gods of Fire and Scale to look to the ground, and see this fallen warrior, that they may bring him to the Mighty Flame and—"

At that moment, Wren tapped his cheek. He glanced at her, irritated that she would interrupt such a solemn occasion, but she was pointing furiously towards the dragon. He turned his gaze to see what was bothering her.

The dragon's eyes were open, and looking right at him.

"Could you *stop* all the mumbo jumbo, please?" the dragon said in a deep voice. "I've already had a terrible day, and the last thing I need is *religion*."

13

THE MESSENGER

It took a few seconds for Patch to get his mouth to work. The sudden reality of standing next to a living dragon, especially an injured and obviously *irritable* one, had quickly pushed him close to panic. He racked his brains to remember the most respectful form of address, and came up with *seken* – roughly the equivalent of *sir*. "I'm glad to see you're alive, Seken!" he said.

The dragon eyed him carefully and grunted. "Don't call me that."

Patch's eyes widened. "I'm sorry, I thought it was the correct term—"

"Oh, yes, it's the correct *term*," said the dragon, sitting up. "For a dragon. But I'm *not* a dragon, and after today I suspect I'll have nothing more to do with the pig-headed *idiots*."

"*Not* a—" began Patch, then his voice trailed off. He looked again at the creature, and those nagging feelings he'd had before resurfaced. Aside from the obvious tear, the wings were discoloured in places; the snout was misshapen, but he'd thought it had been badly injured in the fall and not looked at it too closely. Now that he *did* look closely, he saw a snout that ended in a hooked shape more reminiscent of a *beak*; he saw wings that were covered in the stubs of cut feathers, as well as areas of the thick leathery skin that dragons had. There were stubs of feathers around the snout too, but those were charred.

Now that the creature was sitting up, Patch could see that the legs each had densely packed brown feathers running down them. And while the front claws were very like those of a dragon, the rear were more like the feet of some enormous falcon, or…

Well, thought Patch. *Of course!* A smile crept onto his face as the truth dawned on him. The creature in front of him seemed to grow even more irritated because of the smile, but Patch couldn't help it.

Some features of a dragon, and some of a *griffin*. "You're a dracogriff!" he said. He glanced at Wren and saw the confusion on her face. "Half-dragon, half-griffin!" he told her. "I'm sorry, it's just I've never met a dracogriff before. Actually I've never met a *dragon* before, not really, or a griffin come to that, but when it comes down to it they're two a penny! A *dracogriff*, though! Now that *is* an honour."

Why is it an honour? signed Wren.

The dracogriff sat up suddenly, looking at Wren with astonishment. "Your rat can talk!" he said, wide-eyed. "I know Merisax hand speech when I see it! I've spent the last seven years as a bodyguard-for-hire in the Islands of the Eastern Seas. Merisax came with the territory. Is *talking* the nature of its curse?"

"Curse?" said Patch.

"Yes. As you approached, you referred to yourself as an escaped prisoner and a cursed rat."

Patch blinked. He looked at Wren.

Oh great, she signed. *We've only been fugitives for a few hours, and we've already given ourselves away.*

"Please," said the dracogriff. "You have no need to fear that I'd hand you over. I'm certainly no friend to Pipers. Even if you *are* one." Patch stared at him, open-mouthed. "I *also* heard you say that what they did to me made you ashamed to be a Piper."

"I did?" said Patch. "I did. Damn. I need to be more careful what I say in future. Being an escaped convict is harder than I thought."

"As I said, you've nothing to worry about from me," said the dracogriff. He held out his front claw. His *hand*, Patch corrected himself – that was what dragons and griffins called them, and it seemed impolite not to think of them as such. Patch offered his relatively tiny hand out in return, and they shook. "I'm Barver. Barver Knopferkerkle."

"Barver Nop-fur-ker-kill," said Patch, trying to get his mouth around it.

"That's it," said Barver. "Dragon surname, griffin forename. Your turn!"

"Patch Brightwater," said Patch. "Imprisoned a week ago, now free and hopefully presumed dead. This is my friend Wren Cobble, a girl cursed by a Sorcerer into the form of a rat. I taught her some hand speech when we met so that we could talk. She's a quick learner."

Barver looked closely at Wren. "Your markings *are* pretty," he said. "I especially like the red rings on your tail."

Thanks very much, signed Wren with a smile.

"A Sorcerer's curse, eh?" said Barver. "It always saddens me that Sorcerers are such *awful* people. Think of all the good they could do if they were nicer!"

Tell me about it, she signed.

Barver turned his attention to Patch. "Aren't you a little *young* to have been imprisoned?"

Patch felt himself bristle. "I'm thirteen," he said, as imposingly as he could manage. Wren suppressed a laugh, and he glared at her.

"I meant no offence," said Barver. "It just seems harsh, to experience such adversity so young." He looked up through the trees. Patch and Wren followed his gaze, and could clearly see the damage to the Castle through the branches. "I saw the flames burn brightly as the Hamelyn Piper was executed," said Barver. "I heard the screams as other prisoners fell to their deaths. Yet you lived. It seems fate has plans for you!"

"I hope not," said Patch. "I'd rather just find somewhere I can earn a living and get some peace and quiet. I reckon I've earned it."

"How did you survive the fall?" said Barver. "Humans must be hardier than I thought."

"I climbed down the cliff," said Patch. "How did *you* survive the fall? I heard the crunch when you hit the ground!"

"It was a bad one, I admit," said Barver. He slowly folded his wings up along his back and stretched his legs, wincing.

"Are you sure you should be moving anywhere for a while?" said Patch.

"I'll certainly not be flying for a few weeks," said Barver. "But apart from that it's just bruises."

"Incredible," said Patch. He and Wren shared an amazed look, and both raised their heads to the sky, through the broken treetops, thinking about how far Barver had plummeted.

"How much do you know about dracogriffs?" said Barver.

"That they're rare," said Patch. "Beyond that, not much."

Barver nodded. "There are two broad kinds. One is called a *higher*. The other is called a *lower*. Highers have a blend of the prettier aspects of dragons and griffins, but they're a bit delicate. Lowers have a blend of the more *durable* qualities. We're ugly, but very hard to kill. Naturally, dragons and griffins prefer the pretty ones, but I know which I'd rather be!" He grinned, and as he did his strange blend of features suddenly seemed to make *sense*. Wren and Patch both found themselves grinning too.

I like him, signed Wren.

"Me too," said Patch.

"So, my new friends!" said Barver. "Where are you headed?"

"The Penance River flows through the forest," said Patch. "Following it will take us to the Collosson Highway, and then to Marwheel Abbey. We've heard that someone there can help lift Wren's curse."

Barver grinned. "Then we should set off at once!"

"We?" said Patch.

"You don't mind if I tag along? I seem to have been abandoned, and I'll not be able to fly for quite a while. The company would be appreciated."

Patch looked to Wren.

Why not? she signed.

"Why not indeed," said Patch. "Although I have to say, Barver, you don't seem all that cross about the dragon army leaving you behind. I think if I was you, I'd be *seething*!"

Barver waved his hand like he was swatting a fly.

"I won't waste my anger on that lot," he said. "They weren't very keen on me accompanying the army when we left the Dragon Territories, but it seems they were even *less* keen on me going back with them." He shrugged. "As I said, dragons prefer the pretty kind of dracogriff. They tend to look at me as some kind of unfortunate *mistake*."

Wren was outraged and signed some things that made quite clear what she thought of the dragons.

"You should mind your language," said Patch, wincing. He noticed that the scroll of demands Barver had read out was still tucked into his harness. "When I saw you approach the Castle, I'd assumed sending you to deliver the demands must have been some kind of honour."

"I volunteered when nobody else came forward," said Barver. He frowned. "Makes me wonder if they all knew something I didn't." He shook his wings a little and stretched again. "Anyway, enough of all that! Which way is the river?"

Patch pointed towards an overgrown area of bushes that looked worryingly thorny. "That's the most direct way, so if we head over *there* –" he pointed towards a more accessible route – "it should be easier going."

Barver nodded and trotted off towards the wall of thorny bushes, flattening a path as if it was nothing more than tall grass.

Patch smiled at Wren, shrugged, and followed.

They could hear the soft murmur of flowing water as they approached the river. Barver paused and turned. "Can either of you smell something?" he said. "Bears, maybe? Or wolves?"

"Bears?" said Patch. He looked at Wren and she gave him a frightened glance, but following in Barver's trail made Patch feel about as safe as he'd ever felt in his life. "Oh, I don't think we've much to worry about on that score, Wren," he said.

"Actually, not a bear," said Barver. "Something *dead*." He lifted his snout high and sniffed deep and long, turning his head this way and that. "Over there," he said. "*Human*," he added, then led the way to a small rise covered in ivy-choked trees. He stopped and pulled at the ivy.

The corpse underneath was revealed. The skull grinned out at them, ragged remains of flesh clinging to it. It wore a long coat, which was torn in several places – gashes from sharp claws. Within the coat, little but bone remained.

Patch stared at the skull, and couldn't help imagining his own skull there instead. "Have I mentioned how glad I am that you're here, Barver?" Wren, who was also staring, nodded in agreement.

"It's at least a few months old," said Barver. "Probably a bear attack. A gruesome enough death, but quick." He pulled at more of the ivy, and discovered a hardy shoulder-slung leather bag, similar to Erner's satchel. "What do we have here?"

Patch picked up the bag and untied the fastening strap. Inside was a simple cotton tunic, a sheathed knife, a firesteel, a small waterskin, and the mouldy remains of an old hunk of bread – which he took out and discarded. "He just carried the basics of survival," said Patch. "Perhaps the poor soul travelled along the river, in search of a new life." He shook out the tunic. It was a little musty, but basically clean, so he set Wren on the ground before taking off his coarse prison shirt and putting the tunic on. It was a vast improvement. He gave the torn coat a sorrowful look. "Shame about that," he said. "It seems well made."

Barver shrugged. "It's not beyond saving. And a good wash in the river will shift much of the smell." He gave Patch a look. "Speaking of which…"

"What?" said Patch.

"Go to the river, Patch Brightwater, and scrape the dungeon stench from your skin. It makes my eyes sting even more than the odour of this corpse." He turned to the gnawed jumble of bones on the ground and looked at it, thoughtful. "In the meantime I'll see what can be done with that coat."

14

A Clean Start

Cold, was it? signed Wren.

Patch tried to nod in response, but it was hard because he was shivering so much. He'd stripped off and jumped into the river, but the water had turned out to be rather more chilly than he'd expected. Half-screaming, half-whimpering, he'd cleaned himself as quickly as he could before leaping out and returning to Wren.

He'd already untied his blanket parcel, leaving its contents on the fallen tree trunk next to Wren, so that he would have his blanket ready to wrap round himself. He dried off as best he could, then he dressed and put his meagre belongings back into the damp blanket. Wren hopped onto his still-trembling shoulder, and they returned to where they'd left Barver.

To Patch's amazement, Barver was holding the dead man's torn coat, stitching up the rips. Patch had never imagined that the clawed hands of dragons and griffins were capable of much dexterity, but Barver wielded a needle and thread with the skill of an expert.

Barver reached into his harness and produced another reel of thread. He smiled when he saw them nearing. "A few large slashes and a couple of minor tears, that's about it," he said. "I'll be finished shortly." He looked closely at Patch, his expression suddenly concerned. "Should your lips be *quite* that shade of blue?"

"The w-water was a b-bit c-c-cold," Patch said. "I'm not k-k-k-keen on being c-c-cold."

"My apologies, I should have thought!" said Barver. He set down his sewing and took a few steps forward, then with a broad swipe of his tail cleared an area of the ground down to the soil. He made a small mound of earth at the centre. "Stand back," he said, lowering his head to the mound. He opened his mouth wide and a gurgling noise came from his throat. He coughed and thumped his chest a few times. "Hang on, I'll get there," he said, and opened his mouth again.

This time, an intense flame poured from his throat, flowing over the mound of earth. It sounded, Patch thought, like a blacksmith's forge with the bellows being pumped. The heat reaching him was already significant, and very welcome.

Barver kept the fire coming until the earth started to glow, stones within it audibly cracking. "There you go," he said. "Get yourself warmed up!"

Around Barver's half-griffin muzzle there were blackened stubs, one of which was currently on fire. Patch licked his finger and thumb and reached out, pinching the stub to extinguish the flame.

"Thank you," said Barver. "My dragon and griffin features don't always work together. Griffin feathers on a fire-breathing face, for example. They don't last long, trust me."

Patch sat and let the heat fill him. On his shoulder, Wren stretched her paws out to the warmth. Barver held the coat up, examining his work. "I'll wash it when I'm done," he said. "Shouldn't take long to dry on a heated boulder." He returned to his stitching.

Patch and Wren watched him with an obvious bemusement. It wasn't long before the dracogriff caught their expressions. "Anything wrong?" he said.

"Sorry," said Patch. "But it's just...well, the sewing?"

"My mother taught me," said Barver. "For my wings." He unfurled his left wing a little. Patch and Wren looked, and saw that the tear they'd seen when they'd first found Barver was now neatly stitched. Barver traced his fingers along the line of the injury. "I treat my wings *terribly*," he said with a gentle melancholy. "Always have. They're about as hardy as those of a typical dragon, but I'm used to the *rest* of me being so much more resilient." To underline his point, he picked up a thick fallen branch from the ground and smashed it over his own head. "See? I was a clumsy youth and my wings often got torn. They heal better when stitched, and my mother got tired of having to keep doing it, so she made sure I learned. And I've had plenty of practice, believe me."

For a few quiet minutes, Barver stitched the coat while Patch and Wren warmed up near the glowing mound of earth. Patch opened out the blanket he'd used to dry himself, setting his belongings to one side and holding the damp blanket up to the heat.

Oh, show him the Hamelyn Piper's Mask! signed Wren, pointing at it.

"I don't want any fuss," mumbled Patch.

Barver had seen what Wren had signed, though. "The Hamelyn Piper's Mask?" he said.

Patch shrugged. "I was in the cell next to him. Like you, I saw him die, although I was *much* closer. His Mask fell off him before he was pulled from his cell. I picked it up."

"The actual Iron Mask of the Hamelyn Piper?" said Barver, fascinated.

Patch picked up the Mask and demonstrated how it unfolded. He tossed it to Barver.

"Astonishing," said Barver, turning the Mask over in

his hands. He reversed what Patch had done and the Mask folded up again. "We've seen history made today. A dark and evil thing, finally brought to an end." He shook his head slowly and gave the Mask back to Patch. "Well, the sooner I get this coat washed and dried, the sooner we can set off again." He picked up the coat and made his way to the river.

Patch put his belongings into the traveller's leather bag, and looked at the small pile of bones that was all that now remained of him. "This traveller was heading for a new life," he said. "Hopes and dreams, all brought to a terrible end." He shook his head. "Looking at those bones makes me think," he said, wistful. "However bad things have been, we're alive; we're luckier than that poor soul."

It makes me think, too, signed Wren.

"What?" said Patch.

Wren grinned. *Stay away from bears*, she signed.

They made good pace alongside the river, and Patch was glad of his new coat. Barver had managed to clean it well, and although a slightly odd smell still clung to it, the warmth it provided was more than enough to compensate. Spring wasn't far away now, but the air still had a deep chill to it.

As evening approached, Barver found a secluded clearing for their camp. Exhausted, Patch put up his little tent and lay down for what he thought would be a short rest before eating.

When Wren woke him with a loud squeak in his ear, night had fallen.

Patch came out of the tent. Barver was sitting by a small fire, holding a spit over the flames – rabbit, Patch saw. His mouth watered.

"Awake at last!" said Barver. "Wren was telling me all about your exploits, yours and hers both. She told me the story of Patterfall and of her own curse, and I gave her some tales of my adventures in the Eastern Seas." He took the spit away from the fire and sniffed the rabbit, then handed the spit to Patch, who tore off a piece of meat and ate it. It tasted sublime.

"That's *amazing*," Patch said around his mouthful.

"A few common herbs to bring out the flavour," said Barver. "Now, Wren… Shall we finish our game?"

Wren nodded and scampered over to where – Patch now saw – the Fox and Owls board was laid out. *I taught him*, signed Wren to Patch. *He picked it up pretty quickly.*

Patch ate his rabbit and watched the game, which was hard-fought by Barver. Wren's victory came in the end, but it was much closer than Patch had ever managed against her.

In the warmth from the fire, with his belly full, he realized with a degree of shock that he had a *future* to look forward to. Barver's mention of the Eastern Seas had made him think. The Islands of the Eastern Seas were mostly outside the influence of Tiviscan and, as such, uncertified Pipers could still work there if they were careful.

He could work there.

Of course, the Islands were also overrun with pirates and criminals, but it was something for him to consider: a future as a Piper, even if it wasn't the one he'd always dreamed of. But there was one thing he would need to do before even *that* future was possible.

He would need to make himself a new *Pipe*.

He'd already noticed plenty of mature boxwood bushes in the forest, so it wouldn't be hard to find some suitable branches that he could use.

A new Pipe, for a new life.

That night, he slept well.

15

THE THREE OUTCASTS

The next evening, as dusk approached, they reached the Collosson Highway – a rather grand name for what amounted to a slightly-wider-than-normal muddy road. They were confronted with another smell in the air, but one that was rather more pleasant than a dead traveller: the smell of food cooking.

"Beef stew," said Barver, his eyes half-closed. His stomach gave a rumble so loud it echoed.

"Fresh bread," said Patch, his mouth starting to drool.

There must be an inn nearby, signed Wren.

"It's a shame the dead traveller wasn't carrying any money," said Patch, mournful. There was a curious tinkling sound to his left, and he turned to see a glorious sight. Barver was grinning, and in his hand was a small purse.

"Let this be my treat," said Barver. "Since I returned from the Eastern Seas I've not known many I'd care to spend time with, and now I meet a condemned criminal and a cursed rat and find them to be honest, decent and agreeable company. What do you say? We'll have a feast, and I insist on getting you a proper bed for the night. Then we'll reach Marwheel Abbey fed and rested."

A bed, thought Patch.

A proper *bed*. He almost wept.

The inn lay round the next bend in the road, and it looked as perfect as it smelled.

The innkeeper was petrified the moment he saw Barver, but soon enough Barver's friendly manner – and his money – smoothed things over. "A feast, if you please," said Barver, offering up a shiny golden coin. "And beds for the night."

"Will the smaller of our stables do you for sleeping, my large friend?" asked the innkeeper. "It's clean and warm, and you'll have it to yourself."

"Sounds perfect," said Barver.

The innkeeper spotted the rat on Patch's shoulder and frowned. Wren gave him a wave and bowed.

"Trained rat, eh?" said the innkeeper. "Clever."

"You don't know the half of it," said Patch.

The innkeeper showed them to a table at the back of

the inn. Patch had a tankard of small ale brought to him; Barver had a bucket of the same, and insisted on a thimble for Wren, the innkeeper delighted by the level of training this "pet" rat displayed.

Patch looked at Barver's bucket. "I would've thought you'd drink something stronger," he said. Small ale was a very weak brew of barley and oats, tasty and thirst quenching with hardly any alcohol.

Barver shook his head. "Anything strong irritates my fire ducts," he said. "This is just about right for me."

Patch nodded. "A toast," he said, raising his tankard. "To you, Barver, and to you, Wren! Only days ago, I was alone and in despair. Today, I'm happy and with friends!"

"Thank you," said Barver. "But I'd rather we raise a toast to my mother. She was the reason I recently returned from the Islands of the Eastern Seas, and it is her gift to me that is paying for our meal. To my mother!" He raised his bucket. "May she rest in peace."

Wren's face fell, and so did Patch's.

Oh, Barver! signed Wren, distressed.

"It's good for me to talk about it," said Barver. "In the dragon tradition, she left me what's called a Vanishing Gift – the money now in my purse. In her honour, I must spend it all within one month." He shook his head, his eyes moistening. "But I'd not spoken to her in years. We'd fallen out, which was why I left for the Eastern Seas in the first

164

place. If my father had still been alive things might have been different, but me and my mother never spoke again. By the time word reached me that she was dying, it was too late. Her funeral ceremony had happened, and the Order of the Skull had taken her body to its final secret home."

They fell into silence for a moment.

"Then we *must* raise a toast to your mother," said Patch. They raised their ales and took a drink. "I'm so sorry, Barver."

Barver nodded, grateful. "She left a letter for me. I'd hoped there might be some kind of apology for the way she'd acted, but instead it was instructions for a last wish. I feel overwhelmed by it all. Things have been so rushed, you see. The day after I got back to the Dragon Territories, they began raising the army to claim the Hamelyn Piper. My mother had always been fascinated with him – an *obsession*, really. It seemed fitting that I should volunteer, and see with my own eyes what happened. I think she would have been appalled at how it turned out. Revenge is such an unpleasant thing."

Why was she obsessed with the Hamelyn Piper? asked Wren.

"She was an advisor to the Dragon Triumvirate. *Highly* respected. Even her relationship with my father hadn't tarnished her reputation, and dragons are very touchy about one of their kind falling in love with a griffin, believe me.

165

She'd first taken an interest in the Hamelyn Piper when the *human* children vanished, but when the dragon children were stolen her obsession was complete. And while the other dragons wanted war with the whole of humanity – as if it was their fault! – *she* was a voice of reason. Without her guidance, I think another war might have been unavoidable."

"Then we have much to thank her for," said Patch.

"True," said Barver. "But it was that same obsession which drove such a wedge between us. She became ever more distant, and was often cold to me. One question burned within her, the most important question of them all! *Why* had the Hamelyn Piper taken the children?"

Because he was insane, signed Wren. *Me and Patch saw him, remember? We saw his eyes! Crazy!*

Patch felt his cheeks redden, and wished above all else that he could just *forget* what the prisoner had said. He wanted to tell his friends the truth, but he also knew that doing so would lead to trouble. It was easier to pretend that the Hamelyn Piper *had* been mad, and so anything he'd said at the end was meaningless. "Did your mother ever suggest an answer to that question?" he said.

"Some claim the children were taken to a mysterious and beautiful place," said Barver. "To show that humans and dragons could live in harmony, and prevent wars from ever happening again. Fairy-tale nonsense! It's a miracle it didn't *start* a war at once, instead of preventing them in future. No, my mother didn't think any of the popular theories made much sense. If she had her own ideas about it, she never shared them with me." He took a drink of ale and sighed. "Then again, she stopped sharing *anything* with me. That was why we grew apart."

The food was soon brought out, and it was impressive. A pair of roasted boars at its centre, the table soon strained under the weight of cheese and bread and cake, nuts and fruit and bowls of spiced porridge, soups and stews and biscuits and salted fish.

Barver's table manners were almost a shock to Patch. He'd expected the dracogriff to consume the feast one vast mouthful after another, but instead he took his time and ate with delicate care. He didn't hold back on praise for the wide variety of dishes that had been cooked for them.

"Living out in the Islands of the Eastern Sea, you get used to decent food," said Barver to the delighted innkeeper. "This is all superb!"

They continued with the meal, Patch and Wren eating until they were almost in pain. Patch looked at his own plate, tempted by the various bits and pieces that were left on it. The idea of not eating everything he'd taken was unthinkable to him, but it would be a few minutes yet (and probably a belch or two) before he could fit anything else in.

He delved inside his bag and pulled out several pieces of boxwood that he'd cut from bushes as they'd walked. He studied the wood and chose the best pieces, straight and free of awkward knots. Before long, he'd planned out the new Pipe in his mind. The knife the dead traveller had carried in his bag was a good one, and Patch set about stripping the bark.

What are you working on? signed Wren.

Patch smiled. "A Pipe," he said. "I don't quite feel whole without one."

You've done this often? signed Wren.

"Twice before," he said. "Not everyone makes their own, but making it yourself lets you get to know it right from the start." He blew away some shavings. "I'll need some fine woodcarving knives, though, before I can really get to work."

I can't wait to hear you play it! she signed. She sat back and patted her stomach. *You know, after this meal I'll probably sleep for a month.*

Barver nodded. "It's a very welcome feast." He let rip with a thunderous burp that seemed to last for ever. Done, he gave a satisfied smile, while Patch and Wren laughed.

Barver started loading his platter up with food again, two-thirds of the feast now gone.

Patch mopped up soup with some bread. "What will you do, Barver?" he asked. "When we go our separate ways?"

"I'll fulfil the last wish of my mother," said Barver. "Her letter gave me instructions – there is a place I must go, and a second letter to open when I'm there. After it's done, I'll return to the Eastern Seas. There's nothing for me in the Dragon Territories. I've always been a bit of an outcast, but I think I prefer it that way." He smiled, and nodded to Wren. "And you, an outcast from your human form, but not for much longer! What will you do when the spell is reversed?"

I'll go home, she signed. *I miss my parents terribly, but I refuse to go back to them until I'm cured.*

"And you, Patch?" said Barver.

"Once Wren's free of the curse, I'll see her safely back to her home. Then—" He set down the stripped boxwood he was holding. "I'm making this Pipe because I feel incomplete without one, but I'll never be a true certified Piper. I'm an outcast, too. I can make a living, but it must be far from Tiviscan. Far from its *dungeons*."

"Well," said Barver, "if you happen to find yourselves in the Eastern Seas, just ask for me at any inn on the Islands. They'll be able to point you in the right direction." He raised his bucket of ale. "To the three of us! Outcasts all!" They each took a drink. Barver wiped the froth from his mouth. "There's an old griffin tale called The Three Outcasts," he said. "Have you heard it?"

"No," said Patch; Wren shook her head.

Barver looked wistful for a moment, then drew in a breath and frowned. "Probably better you haven't," he said. "It doesn't end well."

16

MARWHEEL ABBEY

The next morning, they saw the Abbey long before they reached it. The road took them up over a high ridge, and on the descent they could see a wide expanse of farmed land with cottages dotted throughout. At the centre was a vast, ornate grey-stone building. A large central rectangular section was impressively high, and topped with densely packed spires. Around it, smaller annexes had their own profusions of smaller towers and pinnacles. The overall impression was that the architect must have had a considerable fondness for hedgehogs.

"Marwheel Abbey," said Patch. "Down there, Wren, lies the answer to your predicament."

Wren peeked out from Patch's pocket, where she was sheltering from the morning chill. She looked and nodded, returning to the pocket without a word. Patch could understand – she was nervous. There was a lot riding on this visit.

They reached the Abbey entrance – huge wooden doors, the frame intricately carved with flowers and animals. The doors were closed, and a bell-chain hung down next to the frame. When Patch pulled it a delicate tinkling came from the other side, followed by the echoing approach of footsteps.

A small inset hatch opened in the door directly in front of Patch, revealing the face of a young monk. "Yes?" said the monk.

"Would it be possible to see Brother Tobias?" said Patch.

"If you give me a moment I'll find out," said the monk. He caught sight of Barver and let out a curious noise, as if someone had trodden on a vole. He looked petrified. "Oh. I...um. Back in a minute." The hatch shut. Hurried footsteps charted his rapid retreat.

After a while, the hatch opened again revealing a different monk. He was much older, with blue, penetrating eyes on a lean and weathered face, the left side of which had a deep scar running from jawbone to forehead. With the man's gaze on him, Patch felt like a rabbit being sized up by a wolf. "I'm Brother Tobias," said the man. "Who exactly are *you*, lad?"

Patch opened his mouth, and suddenly realized that

giving his real name might not be the best idea. "Um...
Henry," he said. "Henry...Smith." He felt a little wriggle in
his pocket from Wren, and could almost *see* her exasperation;
the way it had come out, calling himself "Archibald
Fakename" would have sounded just as convincing. "And
this is my friend Barver Knopferkerkle, a dracogriff."

Tobias nodded briefly to Barver, apparently unconcerned,
then turned back to Patch. "I understand you wish to see
me about something?"

"I'm a friend of Erner Whitlock, an Apprentice
Custodian. He wrote to you about a problem regarding the
victim of a curse?"

The man's eyes widened and he looked at Barver again.
"Lord, really? That's one *heck* of a curse."

Patch glanced at Barver, who seemed bemused rather
than offended. "No," said Patch quickly, "Barver actually *is*
a dracogriff." He held open his coat; Wren poked her head
out of the pocket and waved. "This is Wren. She's the one
who needs your help."

"A rat, then!" said Tobias. "That's more what I was
expecting. You'd better come inside."

Tobias opened the large main doors, and led them along
a tall, arched corridor, which was spacious enough to give
Barver no trouble moving around. Patch noticed a few

fearful glances from the monks as they passed, but only a few ran off in terror.

"We've had some griffins here in our time," said Tobias. "But never a *dracogriff*. You're very welcome. Although, given recent events, you might find things a bit awkward for a while, being part dragon."

"Recent events?" said Patch.

"Yes," said Tobias. "Did you come to us from the south?" He nodded to Barver. "Did you fly?"

"A fall has left me too wounded to fly," said Barver. "For a week or two, at least."

"We came from the north," said Patch. "By road."

"Shame," said Tobias. "I'd hoped you could add to the news we've been getting from travellers on the West Road about an attack on Tiviscan Castle!"

Patch forced out a vaguely convincing gasp. "Goodness no," he said. "Was anybody hurt?"

"A dragon army assaulted the Castle, it seems," said Tobias. "The only fatalities were a few of the prisoners in the dungeons, one of whom was particularly noteworthy. The Hamelyn Piper!"

Patch gasped again. "Gosh," he said.

"The dragons finally got their wish," said Tobias. "And the Hamelyn Piper's secrets have now died with him. There's understandable anger that the Castle was attacked, but frankly the Hamelyn Piper's death is being widely

174

celebrated. I suppose if he was ever going to reveal the truth about the children, he'd have done so by now…" They reached another set of double doors. "Ah! We're here. Come through."

The doors led outside to a walled garden. A solitary monk tended some of the plants, and looked anxiously at Barver.

"It's okay, Brother Jessop," said Tobias. "There's no reason to be scared."

"Morning," said Barver. The monk nodded without a word and turned back to the plants, trembling visibly.

"The infirmary garden," said Tobias, gesturing to their surroundings. "I'm a Healer, or at least I try to be. I've been running the Abbey infirmary for some years now, and we grow as many of the key herbs here as we can. Sit, sit."

There were stone benches in the middle of the garden. Patch and Tobias sat on them, while Barver hunkered down on the ground. Wren emerged from Patch's pocket and came out onto the bench. She stretched. *Come on then*, she signed. *Get down to business.*

Patch nodded. "So, Apprentice Whitlock wrote to you and explained?"

"That he had met someone who had been shape-shifted by a Sorcerer's curse," said Tobias. "That's the essence of it, yes?"

"It is," said Patch. "Rundel Stone himself suggested your name as Wren's best chance of finding a cure."

"Yes," said Brother Tobias, sounding annoyed. "Whitlock mentioned he was Rundel's Apprentice. I'm afraid, Wren, that you have come here with false expectations. I sent a reply to Apprentice Whitlock telling him as much, but not soon enough to save you a journey."

Wren sagged, and Patch didn't know what to say.

"What?" said Barver. "You can't just snatch away the girl's hope like that!"

Brother Tobias shook his head in sorrow. "I'm sorry. Rundel had someone else in mind, I suspect. Someone we both used to know."

"It sounds like you and Rundel Stone are old friends," said Barver.

"Old friends?" said Tobias. "Rundel doesn't really *do* friends. We were colleagues. But it was this *other* person I spoke of that is the true expert in matters of sorcery. I think Rundel sent you to me in the belief that I could take you to them, but I cannot. I made a solemn vow, a long time ago." Wren was staring ahead of herself, tears falling. Brother Tobias looked at her, a pained expression on his face. "I really am sorry, Wren."

"Please," said Patch. "Tell us where this expert is, we'll go and ask directly."

Brother Tobias looked at Wren and seemed torn for a moment, but he shook his head. "That's not going to work," he said. "Even if I broke my vow and told you, it would do you no good. The danger is too great. It's complicated, but there you have it. For your own safety, I'm not going to say any more. There are others who I think can help, however. Let me gather what information I can, and give you a list of names."

Patch put his hands out to Wren; she hopped onto them and went to his coat pocket to curl up.

Barver let out a deep sigh. "Well then, we must seek a cure elsewhere. Brother Tobias, we would appreciate those names as soon as possible."

"I think they are all a considerable distance away, I'm afraid," said Tobias.

"Not a problem," said Barver. "If I'm flight-ready soon, I'll take her wherever she needs to go."

Wren peeked out of the pocket and wiped away a tear. She shook her head. *You have your mother's last wish to deal with*, she signed. *I'm not going to make you delay that.*

"Nonsense," said Barver. He looked at Tobias. "Any hot springs around here? That tends to sort me out quick-smart."

"No hot springs," said Tobias. "But I'm sure we can do better than that." He called to the monk who was still tending the plants. "Brother Jessop? Could you find Brother Duffle and ask him to come out here?" Brother Jessop seemed only too happy to go. "Brother Duffle has experience with non-human healing. I insist you stay and let him help you, Barver. The Abbey can extend all of you hospitality for a few days."

Barver nodded. "I'd be very grateful," he said. He reached for his money purse and pulled out a coin. "I'll make a donation, naturally. Also, if there's any stitching or darning to be done I'll be only too happy to help."

Tobias gave him an odd look. "Uh…okay. The money is very much appreciated. The infirmary has been dealing with an outbreak of firefoot recently, various supplies are depleted. This will help considerably."

At that, a plump monk bearing an overwhelmingly excited expression entered the garden, heading straight for Barver.

"It's true!" cried the monk. He took Barver's hand and shook it repeatedly. "A dracogriff! Welcome! Welcome!"

"Brother Duffle," said Tobias. "This is Barver, our visiting dracogriff, and his friends, Henry and Wren – she is human, the victim of a Sorcerer's curse. A recent fall has left Barver unable to fly, and I thought you might take a look?"

"Absolutely!" said the monk. "Tell me, Barver, can you spread your wings a moment?" Barver did as asked, and Brother Duffle spent a few minutes looking over his new patient. As he did, he mumbled to himself. "I see, I see," he said at last.

"And your prognosis?" said Barver.

Duffle shook his head and tutted. "You've not been taking very good care of yourself! Your shoulder is in terrible shape, your wing skin is peppered with wounds that have never healed fully, and I suspect you've torn every muscle in your body at least once in your life."

Barver nodded, impressed. "You seem to know your stuff, Brother," he said. "But can you get me flying again soon?"

"Indeed!" said Duffle. "A poultice of my own creation will make short work of the old wounds, and a combination of hot rocks and massage will do *wonders* for your shoulder." He cleared his throat. "Um, could you just lie down for a moment, first?" Barver did, bemused. Brother Duffle stood beside Barver's head and took hold of his wing above the shoulder. "Just hold still," said Duffle. "This might... tickle." With unexpected force, he wrenched the wing back then pushed it forward.

There was a deeply unpleasant crunching sound, and Barver howled. He stood at once and backed away, glaring angrily at the monk. Brother Duffle toppled over, but the smile on his face was as broad as ever, and it soon widened even further – Barver started to move his shoulder, and suddenly grinned. "Good gods," said Barver. "What on earth did you just do?"

Duffle looked immensely chuffed. "Your *secundum humeri* had a dislocated *alae vallo*," he said. "Could have been like that for ages. I'm surprised you hadn't noticed."

"I have no idea what you just said," said Barver, stretching out his wings. "But you, Brother Duffle, are a genius!"

At the request of Brother Tobias, Brother Duffle led them out of the gardens and round to the side of the Abbey, which was dotted with a ramshackle collection of smaller stone buildings. He walked up to one and opened the door, revealing a large interior with a crudely built fireplace in one wall. Half the room was taken up by assorted piles of wooden boxes.

"The pigsties!" said Brother Duffle, smiling. "Oh, don't worry, we've not kept pigs at the Abbey for at least forty years. A fireplace was added so it could be habitable when necessary, although now it's mainly used for storage. Hence the boxes."

Barver peered into the nearest box and pulled out a piece of cloth, on which was embroidered "Grettings frum Marwel Abey". He looked in another box and pulled out a small misshapen lump of wood that, eventually, he identified as a model of the Abbey itself. A very *bad* model. "What is all this?" he asked.

"Souvenirs," said Duffle. "Handkerchiefs, little Abbey models, and other stuff. Some of our Brothers spend their days making them, and we sell them to visitors as a way to increase the Abbey's funds. Anything that's not quite up to scratch, we put in here. We might try and fix them, or, well...find another use." He gestured to the fireplace. "The Abbot often says that a wasteful heart is the first step to evil! Although please don't burn anything saleable."

"Understood," said Patch.

"I'll arrange a sleeping mat and bedding for later, and some candles," said Duffle. "For now, settle in and rest your weary feet. Barver, I'll return with my poultice shortly, and we can begin the rest of your treatment. The muscles in your shoulder will need a few days to settle before you can risk flight, but you'll soon be on the road to recovery." He bade farewell and left.

Barver chuckled to himself, moving his shoulder in circles and muttering, "Amazing!" every now and again.

Patch tapped gently on his coat, just where his chest pocket was. "Come on out of there," he said, gently. "Have an explore. I'm sure there'll be a nice beetle or two you can find."

Wren stuck out her head. Her eyes were still wet with tears, and her little nose was running. Patch went to the boxes and found one of the souvenir handkerchiefs. He tore a small square from one corner and gave it to her. "Here," he said. "More your size."

Wren took it and blew her nose. *I think I just want to sleep*, she signed.

"Don't be like that," said Patch. "It's not so bad. Once

Barver can fly and Tobias gives us his list, it won't take long to get you cured."

She shook her head, despairing. *But what if none of those people can help me either?*

"Nonsense," said Patch. He was trying to sound as positive as possible, even though he was thinking the same thing. What if she *was* beyond help?

A distraction was needed, so he took off his bag and rummaged for the Fox and Owls board. "You and Barver should play." Beside the board were the boxwood pieces he'd stripped ready for his new Pipe. A thought struck him, and he looked over to the models of the Abbey. Bad as they were, surely it meant the Abbey had some woodcarving knives? "Actually, I think I might pop out for a bit and see if I can borrow some tools. I can spend the time getting my Pipe made."

Will your Pipe take long? signed Wren. *I imagine it needs weeks of work.*

"Goodness no!" said Patch. "Carving it only takes a few hours. Then I can cure it and decide on a glaze." The thought of his new Pipe was giving him some much-needed optimism.

Wren blew her nose again, and set the mini-handkerchief down beside her. Suddenly, her stomach gave a little rumble. She looked up at Patch with a fragile smile on her face.

You're probably right about those beetles, she signed, and scampered off to hunt.

17

THE NEW PIPE

Patch returned to the pigsties a few hours later. He'd managed to borrow tools from the small group of woodcarvers in the Abbey, on condition that he stayed in the workshop as he used them. His Pipe was a joy to carve, the boxwood having a particularly good texture that made it almost soap-like to work with. The central airways didn't take long to finish with the tools at hand, and the headpiece likewise was completed very quickly. This gave him plenty of time to cut the fingerholes – first the primary set, then the more intricate ones. Without feeling rushed, he took great care in their placement, although he was careful to keep his work out of sight to avoid awkward questions. As soon as he saw any of the other woodcarvers coming near, he swapped his Pipe for another piece of boxwood which he whittled into a crude bird.

Before returning to Barver and Wren he gathered a few more things he needed, including some hawthorn sticks and flat stones from the Abbey grounds. When he entered the old pigsties, an overwhelming smell assaulted his nose – a mixture of flowers, garlic, vinegar and sulphur. Barver was sprawled on the floor with his eyes closed, as Brother Duffle worked the muscles of his weakened shoulder. Some of the boxes of junk had been moved to give Barver space to spread out his wings, which were smeared in places with a greenish gloop that, presumably, was the source of the stench.

Wren, meanwhile, was dozing in front of a fire built up mainly from rejected souvenir Abbeys. They burned rather well.

Duffle nodded a greeting and stopped his massage. "That'll do for today," he said. "I'm going to make a start on an ointment for tomorrow, Barver. I have a few ideas I want to try." Barver opened his eyes, rose onto all fours and folded up his wings. He stretched, and an alarming crack came from his spine. "No, no!" said Duffle. "You should stay flat for a while longer. Your back is much more delicate than you think!" He lifted his near-empty poultice jar and went to the door. "See you tomorrow," he said, and left.

"See you, Brother Duffle," Barver called as the door closed. "Successful day, Patch? Or should I say, *Henry Smith*?" He winked.

"It went extremely well," said Patch. He set down his bag and produced his newly-carved Pipe, then played a simple scale and nodded, very happy with the sound. "I'm going to start the curing process now. How's your treatment coming along?"

Barver brought one wing up to his face and licked at the green gloop. "It's certainly *delicious*," he said, then grinned. "Brother Duffle gets *so* cross when I eat his poultice. It's doing my wings the world of good, I must say. Duffle told me it's laundry day tomorrow, so I'm going to sit in the laundry house and soak up some steam. It's the nearest thing to hot springs he can manage. A few more days, and he says I can try a small flight." He stretched his wings out as wide as the room allowed. "My shoulders and wings feel better than they have in years." He took another lick of the green poultice. "I know I shouldn't, but I just can't resist. It's too tasty."

Wren sat up and gave a big yawn. *I'll take your word for it*, she signed with a grimace.

"This from the one who loves maggots and beetles," said Patch, moving to the fireplace, where the model Abbeys burned brightly. He took the poker and tongs from beside the hearth and spread the Abbeys out. Once the fire was less fierce, he added his hawthorn and made a little chamber using the flat stones.

Is this for curing your Pipe? signed Wren.

185

"It is," said Patch. He produced a pot of sandy earth and poured half into the chamber, then laid his Pipe inside and covered it with the other half. He added a few more Abbeys around the sides, and sat back, pleased with his work. "An hour in there, and the Pipe will almost be done." From outside came the tolling of the Abbey's bells. "That's dinner time!" he said. "I'm off to the refectory. You want me to bring a bucket of anything back, Barver?"

"Yesterday's feast will last me a week," said Barver, licking more poultice. "I really shouldn't snack."

Bring some for me, signed Wren. *I've already eaten all the beetles I could find.*

When Patch returned from the meal an hour later, Barver was sleeping in front of the fire, with Wren curled up beside him. She greeted Patch with a wave, and ran over to see what he'd brought her – a little wooden bowl of stew, with a small hunk of bread. She tucked in as Patch checked on his curing Pipe. He prodded the stones and the sandy earth spilled out. With his hand wrapped in the bottom edge of his tunic he removed the Pipe and let it cool for a few minutes before examining it carefully.

"A good result," he said, testing various combinations of fingering. The notes from the Pipe were steady. "I've borrowed a pot of varnish, so I can get the glaze done once

I've sorted out the other ingredients." He reached for his bag and took out the varnish. As he did, the folded Mask of the Hamelyn Piper clattered to the floor.

Barver opened his eyes and sat up. "Can I take another look at that?" he asked. Patch handed it to him. Barver twisted the rectangle, opening it out into the Mask and studying it. "To think, this was created by Casimir himself! My mother read me the stories of the Eight, and I think he was my favourite!"

"I didn't think dragons were interested in the Eight," said Patch.

"Not usually," said Barver. "But my mother certainly was." He had a dreamy look in his eye as he spoke. "At first, news of the Eight was only rumour – a special team assembled to find the Hamelyn Piper and bring him to justice! It was an exciting idea for a young dracogriff, all that adventure and intrigue... But it was only once they'd succeeded that the tales of their adventures started to come out. Every week, it seemed, a new part of their exploits would be told! With her position as an advisor to the Triumvirate, my mother got copies of the pamphlets as they appeared, and I still remember them all. First was *The Call*, when the Pipers' Council brought in a dozen of the greatest heroes they could find, and tested them. Lord Drevis – a Virtus in the Custodian Elite at the time, not a member of the Council – was chosen to lead them, and one by one the heroes proved their worth or were shown lacking, leaving the Eight we all know. Next was *The Terror of Imminus Rock*, where the Eight hoped to find a great Sorcerer to help them, but discovered instead an island full of monsters! And then came *The Caves of Casimir*, where—"

"Okay, okay," said Patch, laughing. "I was only three when it was happening and too young to understand, but by the time I was seven I knew every chapter back to front. My nan must have been tired of reading them to me."

I loved those stories, signed Wren. *Our village had a copy of the collected pamphlets.*

"*Palafox, Corrigan, Kellenfas, Stone*," said Barver, reciting the names of the Eight. "*Casimir, Hinkelman, Drevis and Throne*. Casimir was so mysterious! A Piper who spent decades trying to understand sorcery, and called himself the Sorcerer Engineer."

Wren nodded with enthusiasm, but Patch decided not to comment. While Casimir had created the Mask and various other useful magical devices, Patch reckoned that the sheer courage and Piping skills of Stone, Palafox and Corrigan had been more important.

Barver went to the boxes at the back of the room and took a handkerchief, using it to rub at the Mask. "There are fine symbols engraved on the inner side," he said. "I don't recognize them. Do you?" He passed it back to Patch, who looked closely at the parts Barver had cleaned up.

"They're an old runic language," said Patch. "No idea what it says, but... Oh, that's interesting." In the places Barver had cleaned, the darkness in the engraved lines was glinting. "I'd thought it was just dirt in the engraving," he said. "It's not." He passed the Mask back to Barver.

"What, then?" said Barver, examining it.

"I think the letters are inlaid with obsidiac," said Patch.

At once Barver let go of the Mask, dropping it as if it was red hot. "*Black diamond*," he said, sounding angry.

Wren looked confused. *Black diamond?* she signed.

"It's the dragon name for obsidiac," said Barver. "The first humans to chance upon it in the Dragon Territories thought it was ordinary obsidian, just simple volcanic glass. But soon they realized it had magical properties, and because it was only ever found in the lands of dragons they called it 'drac-obsidian', a name which eventually became 'obsidiac'." He shook his head slowly. "Dragons, though, have long known that it is a dark, evil substance. Corrupting. Black diamond is a much more suitable name. Just as diamond is a rare form of beauty, black diamond is a rare form of darkness."

Patch picked the Mask up again, and fetched the knife from his bag. He used the tip of the blade to scratch at the dark glints in the runes. "Not leaving a mark," he said. "Pretty sure it's obsidiac."

Barver scowled.

Why do you hate it so much? signed Wren.

Barver sat down in front of the fire again, and added some more model Abbeys. For a moment he watched the flames in silence, then he looked at Patch and Wren with sorrow-filled eyes. "For dragons, black diamond is so dangerous it's something only the *gods* can use. Digging it up is a kind of blasphemy."

"I thought you weren't religious," said Patch.

"I'm not," said Barver. "But most dragons *are*. There is an uneasy peace between humans and dragons, but there are those who dream of more, of cooperation and coexistence, working together. Truly sharing this world. Black diamond makes this impossible."

What do you mean? signed Wren.

"Humans come to the Dragon Territories to steal black diamond, and dragons hate them for the blasphemous theft. Dragons *burn* the humans caught stealing it, and humans hate them for the killing. Black diamond creates a circle of hatred. The world would be a better place without it."

He fell silent again, watching the fire.

Wren turned to Patch. *When I was the Sorcerer's captive,* she signed, *I read some of the books in his castle. One mentioned an old legend that obsidiac could give unnaturally long life. Is it truly that powerful?*

Patch shook his head. "Don't believe everything you

read. Sorcerers are *famous* for wasting their lives looking for immortality. It is very powerful, though. An obsidiac-glazed Pipe is supposed to be as good as they come. The obsidiac is powdered and flaked, then bound in a resin varnish and used as a Pipe glaze." Absently, Patch started looking closely at the Mask again.

"Don't even think about it," growled Barver.

"Oh, I doubt I could remove it from the grooves," said Patch, still looking at the Mask. "It's known for being extremely tough, so unless I—" He trailed off, the tone of Barver's warning finally sinking in. "No," he said. "Of course not."

There was a cold silence.

After a few moments, Wren broke the tension. *What else can you use as a glaze?* she asked.

"Some flowers are good," said Patch, flustered. "But they have to be fresh. This time of year, the ash of feathers might be the best bet."

Feathers? asked Wren.

"Yes," said Patch. "Eagles are particularly effective." He frowned, wondering where he would get any.

"Eagle, hmm?" said Barver, his voice softer now. "How about *griffin* feather?"

"That's good too," said Patch. "Falcons as well, and buzzards. Has to be carnivores, you see, and—" He stopped, the penny dropping. "Ah," he said.

Barver was holding up three of his own feathers. "How many do you need?" he asked.

The following morning, Barver was awake the moment the dawn bells sounded.

"What's got into you?" said Patch, yawning. "Don't fancy a lie-in?"

"I'm off to the laundry," said Barver. "They get the fires lit early, so the water's hot by now. The laundry room fills with steam, Brother Duffle told me. I'll get half an hour before they need me out to get the laundry started. It'll do me the world of good."

"Well, I'll see you later," said Patch. With Barver gone, Patch went to where he'd hung his Pipe after glazing it the night before. The glaze, with its dracogriff-feather ash, had given the Pipe a rich dark colour, a deep reddish brown that Patch hadn't seen on a Pipe before. He touched it to test the varnish. "Dry!" he said, excited. He gave it a look over, then put it to his lips and played a few scales. "Good tone," he said. "Let's see if dracogriff feathers are up to the job!" He thought for a moment about which Song he should try. "A Lift, perhaps?" he said. "Yes. A Lift!"

And what's that? asked Wren, emerging from the folds of the blanket she'd spent the night in.

"Battle Pipers do it a lot," said Patch. "Lifts the mood.

Raises morale." He paused, thinking back. "When I told you about the ceremony at Tiviscan, and the moment I learned I wasn't to join the Custodian Elite, you asked me what branch of the Elite they'd offered me. I didn't give you an answer."

I noticed, signed Wren. *I figured you'd tell me when you were ready.*

Patch nodded, feeling sombre. "It was the Battle Elite. That was the branch that wanted me."

Not something you would consider? asked Wren.

"With Battle Piping, there are Songs with the power of cannon fire; Songs to set distant tents ablaze. But it's the Songs that increase hatred and bloodlust that are most valued. And I was so good at playing Songs that affect people, you see. That's why they wanted me. I'd dreamed of making a difference in the world, Wren. Making people better at *killing* each other wasn't what I'd had in mind."

Wren thought for a moment, then smiled. *I'm proud of you*, she signed.

"Thank you," said Patch. "Although I wish I'd just told them as much, rather than insulting them all and running away." He shook his head, then looked pointedly at Wren. "So...do I have a volunteer for the Lift?"

What, me? signed Wren. *No chance. That's an untested Pipe!*

"Oh come on, you're perfectly safe. The chances of a new Pipe actually going *wrong* are tiny."

Find another idiot to try it on, she replied. She scurried over to the door, pointing through a knothole. *One of them*, she signed. *They always look like they could do with a bit of cheering up.*

Patch joined her and crouched low to peer out. There was the usual solemn flow of monks, mostly individuals, sometimes pairs, quietly making their steady way around the Abbey in the time left to them before morning service. "I don't know," said Patch, although it appealed to a mischievous part of his mind. "A new Pipe is usually pretty weak. It might be hard to tell if it worked." He felt something tickle his hand, and looked down to see an ant crawling over it. "Aha!" he said. "Perfect."

Wren was sceptical. *How do you tell if an ant's morale improves?* she signed.

"Trust me," said Patch. "Ants are always good for practice. Plus I can keep my playing nice and quiet."

Fine, signed Wren. *Just make sure I'm not part of your experiment.*

"Don't worry," said Patch. "Stay beside me, we won't be affected. With things like the Lift it's a simple matter of moderating the direction, range and nature of your subject, to guarantee that the Song doesn't spill out beyond the desired target. Easy peasy."

Easy? signed Wren. *Isn't that what happened to make the villagers dance in Patterfall?*

Patch winced at the thought. "That was a lapse of concentration," he said. "Could happen to anyone." After carefully placing the ant in the middle of the room, he put his Pipe to his lips, furrowed his brow, then started to play.

The Lift was a very simple Song at its core, and Patch had always been good at it. No wonder, really – it shared many of its patterns with the Dance, although it didn't *direct* the subject in any way and was much less potent. All it did was perk them up, and the resulting effect varied considerably from subject to subject.

Patch built up the heart of the Song. It took him back to the days when he'd sat in the woods by his grandparents' home, whistling and seeing the effect it had on the wildlife as they drew near, intrigued and playful.

The little ant, which had started to march back towards the doorway, stopped. Its tiny head tilted up slowly, then moved down again; then up, then down. It started walking once more, but there was a definite *swing* to the motion, left and right, and it sped up and slowed down to the Song's rhythm. It began to take an extra little step to each side as it went, and from time to time it turned in a circle on the spot. It continued in the same way until it reached the door.

Wren looked at it, delighted. *That's one happy ant*, she signed. The ant tapped out the music for a moment, then made its way under the door and outside. Wren watched its progress through the knothole. Suddenly she turned back to Patch. *Hold on,* she signed. *I think your Song has spilled out a little!*

Patch stopped playing, and the Song faded gently. "Oooh, listen to that," he said, distracted by the Pipe. "The sustain is impressive! It usually takes a few more—"

Wren interrupted him with a cough, and pointed at the knothole. Patch crouched down to look out again.

The monks were still making their way around the Abbey, but now their pace had picked up, oh-so-slightly; from time to time, some had a bit of a skip in their step. The clearest change, though, was that most were smiling. There were even, shockingly, a few laughs to be heard.

Did you have another lapse in concentration? signed Wren.

"Not this time," said Patch. The Pipe was silent at last, and he looked at it with genuine satisfaction. "This packs a punch, let me tell you. Dracogriff feathers are now *officially* my favourite."

How long will the Lift affect them? asked Wren.

"That depends on the monk," said Patch. "Some, I imagine, will decide that they're *far* too serious for all that smiling. Others, well…it might stay with them for a few hours." In the distance, through the meandering monks, he caught sight of someone who definitely did *not* have a smile on his face. "Look who it is," said Patch. "Brother Duffle."

Duffle had a stern expression, but there was a hint of puzzlement there, too. He paused, looking at the smiling faces of the strolling monks. He shook his head and continued, making a beeline for the pigsties.

Wren frowned. *What's troubling him?* she signed. *I hope Barver's okay!*

"What is it, Brother?" asked Patch when Duffle reached them.

"There's a dire situation," said Duffle. "Brother Tobias needs you in the infirmary, right away!"

18

DESPERATE TIMES

With Wren in his pocket, Patch followed Brother Duffle to a small room within the infirmary. On one wall were shelves of old books, bottles and containers. Brother Tobias was standing by a table on which sat various sizes of pestle and mortar, and bunches of herbs and plants in the process of preparation.

"You can leave us, Brother Duffle," said Tobias. "Thank you."

"I'll return to Barver," said Duffle. "Some light massage as he takes in the steam, I think."

Once Duffle had gone, Tobias gave Patch a cold look. "*Henry Smith*," he said. "An interesting choice of name. As an escaped convict, you could have spelled trouble for the Abbey, Patch Brightwater!"

Patch felt his ears redden, but before he could ask how Brother Tobias had learned the truth, the monk turned and left the room through a second doorway. As he went, Patch could see he was holding something in his hand. He almost gasped to see it – a Pipe. What was a monk doing with a Pipe?

A moment later he *did* gasp, because through the doorway Tobias had left by, someone else entered.

Erner Whitlock.

"Patch!" cried Erner, hurrying over to him. Wren emerged from Patch's pocket and climbed up to his shoulder. "It's really you! And Wren! I thought you were both *dead*!" Erner flung his arms around Patch and gave him a hug, a look of immense relief on the Apprentice Custodian's face.

When Erner let go and stood back, Patch stared at him. "Oh no," said Patch. "Oh no, oh no, oh no…"

Erner looked at him, confused. "Why do you look at me with such horror? I can't tell you how thankful I am to see you alive! Virtus Stone and I were travelling to Yarmingly when news came through of the attack on Tiviscan. We heard that the Hamelyn Piper was dead, and that some prisoners had died too. Including the young lad who'd only just been locked away, they said! The Piper of Patterfall!" He shook his head, clearly distressed. "An awful thing to hear, Patch. *Awful*. When we arrived at the Abbey just an hour ago, Brother Tobias told me that Wren was here, accompanied by a dracogriff and a young lad calling himself Henry Smith—" Erner shook his head, smiling now. "I didn't dare hope, but here you are. Both of you!" When Patch and Wren still said nothing, Erner's confusion returned. "But still you look at me so strangely—"

Patch's mouth felt horribly dry. He kept glancing at the door, expecting Rundel Stone to enter at any moment. "Don't you understand? You've found me alive, and it's your duty to see me delivered back to the dungeons! Where is your master, anyway? I would have thought Rundel Stone would be *incredibly* pleased to be able to slap some manacles on me!"

Erner's smile dropped away. "My duty…yes. Perhaps it is. In all the relief of seeing you, it hadn't occurred to me. But Patch, please…I'll not tell a soul, not even the Virtus. Stay as Henry Smith, and you'll be safe. Nobody will know!"

Wren tutted. *Brother Tobias already knows*, she signed.

"Oh, ah, yes," said Erner, wincing. "Brother Tobias. I'm sorry. I blurted it all out when he told me you were here, Wren. I'll tell nobody else!"

"I know you mean well," said Patch, still glancing nervously at the doorway. "But Virtus Stone would never allow such a thing. Where is he, anyway?"

And what was the dire situation we were told about? signed Wren. *Was that just a trick, to get Patch to come here?*

200

Erner shook his head, looking grim. "No trick," he said. "You see, things have become rather complicated." He walked to the doorway. "Follow me, and I'll explain."

Erner led them through to the main part of the infirmary. Twenty simple beds were in a long hall, and each bed was full – there were men and women, old and young, being tended by three monks.

At the far end of the hall was a curtained area, and from there Patch could hear the sound of a Pipe. Once they reached the curtain, Erner pulled it aside. By the wall was a bed, and sitting on its edge was Brother Tobias, playing the Pipe he'd carried out with him.

Patch listened, impressed by the complexity of the Song Tobias played – a healing Song, and far more intricate than any he'd ever managed to learn. "Wow," he said.

Erner nodded. "Impressive, isn't it?" he said, his voice barely above a whisper. "Brother Tobias was a Piper before he took holy orders. He could make a fine living, yet he's chosen a life in the Abbey and to give his skills for free."

For the first time, Patch turned his eyes to the patient lying in the bed, and he almost jumped. There lay Rundel Stone, his eyes closed and his skin horribly pale. "What happened to him?" said Patch.

"We were called to the village of Yarmingly," said Erner.

"There had been a death, and the dead man was a close friend of the Virtus. The cause of death was obvious, and gruesome – several blows to the back of the head. We'd been there only a few minutes when Virtus Stone cried out and collapsed to the ground. Half-conscious, he ordered me to bring him here. I had to stop often and play a healing Song, just to keep him alive. Brother Tobias and his monks have treated him since, but he has not woken, and the cause of his condition is a mystery."

Brother Tobias stopped playing and beckoned them. "Quickly, Erner! He's coming round!"

Erner rushed to the bedside; Patch moved to follow, but Wren squeaked at him from his shoulder.

You should keep your distance, she signed. *Better Stone doesn't see you!*

Stone gave a spluttering cough, and opened his eyes.

"Virtus!" said Erner. "It's me, Apprentice Whitlock! Can you tell me what caused your collapse?"

Stone gripped Erner's arm. "An *enigma enicatus*!" he said, struggling for breath. "A death puzzle. A *box*, Erner. A small metal box. I found it under a book on the floor, near to where Ural lay dead. I felt its sting as I grasped it and realized my mistake too late!"

Ural…thought Patch. The name of Stone's dead friend was somehow familiar, but he couldn't quite place it.

Brother Tobias checked Stone's hand. "There! A small

mark, some kind of needle." He looked at Erner. "Did you see the box he speaks of?"

"Well, I did find this on the floor near the Virtus," said Erner. He reached into his pocket and pulled out a small metal cube, about an inch across.

"Don't touch it!" cried Stone. He knocked the box from Erner's hand. The effort was too much for him – he slumped back, and his eyes closed.

Erner looked at Tobias, shaking his head. "I already *did* touch it, Tobias, yet it did nothing to me."

"Death puzzles have specific targets," said Tobias. "You touched it without incident, but Rundel was stung. That means *he* was a target." He rushed to his room and returned with wooden tongs and a jar. He picked the metal cube from the floor and dropped it inside the jar, then held it up for a clear view.

Stone opened his eyes again, straining to speak. "Identify its targets, and you find the killer!"

"Forget finding the killer," said Brother Tobias. "Your *life* is the priority now, Rundel. Healing Songs can keep you alive for a time, but I fear I can't treat this, not fully. There's sorcery at work here." He paused. "You suspected as much, Rundel. You didn't come here to get help from me – you came to get help from *her*. Didn't you!"

Wren frowned at Patch. *Her?* she signed. *Who does he mean?*

"Yes," said Stone. "I sensed it was no simple poison. A Sorcerer's poison, needing a Sorcerer for the cure. You know where you must take me!"

Tobias looked away. "You're asking too much!"

"Please, Tobias!" cried Stone. "*Please!*" He tensed and cried out in agony, then went limp.

Tobias examined him. "Unconscious," he said. "And refusing to die. Stubborn as ever." He shook his head and hit the nearby wall in frustration. "That settles it, we have no choice." He looked directly at Patch. "I only pray that the expert we both seek has the answers we require."

"The expert we *both* seek?" said Patch. "Both?"

Tobias nodded. "You'll be coming as well. Wren's best hope is also Rundel's. I told you there was too much danger, and I meant it, but now Rundel's life is on the brink. Where we're headed, your dracogriff friend will keep us safe, to a point. We must leave at once. It's a full day's journey by horse, Erner, and while we're gone you must stay here and play that healing Song, to the best of your ability, for one hour out of every four. It'll be gruelling work, but it's the only thing that will keep Rundel alive. Can you manage it?"

"I can," said Erner.

"And, um, where exactly are *we* going?" said Patch.

"You've heard of the Gemspar Range?" said Tobias.

Patch frowned. His training had involved studying notoriously treacherous locations throughout the world, and the Gemspar Range was high on that list. "Home of vicious criminals, and unbounded danger," he said. "It has quite a reputation. There's also the mythical Witch who, legend says, makes the central peak of the range her home – Gemspar Mountain itself! A foreboding craggy deathtrap, by all accounts."

"Afraid of old myths, are you?" said Tobias.

"Oh please," said Patch. "I know there's no actual *Witch*, but the Gemspar Range is a hostile place, home to the worst smugglers and wrongdoers in the land. The Witch was just a story to frighten people away from the area. But those are all pretty *scary* old myths, Brother Tobias. Even *you* have to admit it."

"I'll grant they're unpleasant tales," said Tobias.

"Unpleasant?" scoffed Patch. "Horrible murders, horrible monsters, a horrible warty old hag of a Witch! Kept me up at night, some of those tales. She was said to have extra joints in her arms that she could make grow a hundred feet long. Her enemies would be strangled in their beds with their doors locked, the only clue being a sprinkling of soot from the fireplace. Her eyes were supposed to shine bright in the dark, so you could see her blink in the depths of the forest." He shivered. "Besides brigands, I'm surprised *anyone* wants to make their home somewhere so creepy! Your *expert* must really like privacy."

"That is certainly true," said Tobias. "She *absolutely* does."

"So, um, who exactly are we going to see?" said Patch, an awful feeling stirring in his guts.

Brother Tobias widened his eyes. "We're off to see the Witch of Gemspar Mountain!" he said.

Patch whimpered.

19
GEMSPAR

The Abbey possessed only five horses, and the group took three of them. Patch was given the smallest, a friendly black and white mare. He tied his bag to his saddle, and Wren opted to sit on his shoulder rather than be cooped up for the journey in his pocket. As well as Tobias, they were joined by a burly monk called Brother Madder, who was armed with a decidedly un-monkly broadsword.

Barver was reluctantly dragged from the warmth of his steam treatment, and looked rather grumpy when Brother Duffle led him to the front of the Abbey to join the others.

"Be careful!" Duffle told him. "Absolutely no flying, and if you *must* kill any brigands, don't strain your shoulder in the process."

"Okay, okay, I promise," said Barver, and Duffle waved

him farewell. Barver looked at Patch and Wren. "Bit of a rude awakening to have to leave that lovely heat and come out here," he said. "Duffle was vague about where we're going. Can you fill me in on the details?"

Wren told him everything. When she got to the part about the Witch, Barver went strangely quiet.

The presence of Barver unsettled the horses a little, so he kept himself to the back of their column, with Patch next, then Tobias, and Madder leading. They kept up a rapid pace, riding mostly in silence.

They stopped to rest only once, letting the horses drink from a stream and graze its banks. Patch took his Pipe from his pocket to take a look at some of the lowest finger holes – while playing the Lift earlier, he'd felt some rough edges on the mouthpiece that he needed to fix, but he'd not had a chance to deal with it until now. He used the tip of his knife to gently smooth the wood.

Brother Tobias approached him. "Ah!" he said. "Erner Whitlock told me you were a trainee Piper before you were put in the dungeons. I suggest you put your Pipe away, though. I have my Pipe with me, too, but I'll only use it if the worst comes to the worst. Be in no doubt: *Barver* is our protection in Gemspar. The brigands there have evaded capture from the Custodian Elite for a very long time. Anyone they see with a Pipe is likely to have a dozen arrows in them before a single note can be played. A dracogriff will give them reason to stay well clear of us."

Patch nodded. Before they set off, he made sure to put his Pipe in his bag.

By afternoon they could see the peaks of the Gemspar Range, and by evening they had reached the forest on the slopes of the first of the mountains. The path was rough, growing narrower with each passing mile, as the forest grew thicker.

Brother Madder held up his hand for the party to stop. "From here on," he told them, "there must be absolute silence. If anyone sees anything suspicious, they should draw my attention by clapping their hands together twice."

"And, um, what are we looking for?" asked Patch.

"Brigands. Bandits. Thieves," said Madder. "Given Barver's presence, anyone who attacks us will have to be especially crazed. That would make them especially *dangerous*."

Barver raised a hand. "I want to clarify the rules of engagement," he said. "Is fire breathing okay?"

"Feel free," said Madder.

"And am I allowed to *eat* anyone who attacks us?"

"Absolutely," said Madder, with a sly grin.

Patch and Wren stared at Barver. The dracogriff shrugged. "I'm kidding!" he said, although they weren't sure if he was.

From then on, Patch scanned the gloomy forest constantly. He saw nothing with his eyes, but his mind spotted dozens of non-existent, cut-throat villains hiding behind every trunk, every bush, every pine cone, every leaf. He broke out in a sweat as his anxiety grew.

The peaks of the Gemspar Range towered above, but it was another hour before the razor-jag tip of Gemspar Mountain itself became visible: bare black rock that seemed to cut and slice at the sky.

Behind him Patch could hear Barver's stomach gurgle continuously, the only sound coming from his otherwise stealthy friend. Patch slowed, dropping back a little from the others, and turned to Barver. Heeding Brother Madder's earlier warning of silence, he used hand speech.

Are you okay? he asked.

I think it's Brother Duffle's poultice, answered Barver. He rubbed his belly, looking queasy. *I don't think it agreed with me.*

Do you need to rest?

Barver shook his head. *It'll pass*, he signed, and sure enough it did seem to settle down.

The forest path began to weave as they ventured through a valley deep in the Range. Steep climbs became precarious drops, and the path led them through twisting high-walled gullies that Barver was only just able to fit through.

The narrow path, with high trees all round and little sky to see, gave Patch an increasing sense of claustrophobia. Then, as they rounded a series of tight bends, a clearing lay ahead. Patch smiled with relief and turned round to look at Barver.

Barver wasn't there.

Terrified, Patch clapped his hands twice. At the head of the group, Brother Madder turned and stared, seeing at once that their main protection had vanished. He guided his horse to Patch.

"Where is he?" whispered Madder.

"I don't know," said Patch. "He was behind me a minute ago."

Madder eyed the trees warily and went back around the bends they'd just passed. After a few moments he returned. "No sign of him," said Madder, his intense gaze darting around the trees. "We may be in trouble."

"You think somebody—" said Patch, disbelieving.

Wren was horrified. *Somebody nobbled Barver?* she signed. *How?*

"To the clearing, quickly!" said Madder, taking his horse to the front and picking up speed.

It was too late.

The vegetation around them erupted into life. Fifty well-armed bandits burst from behind every tree and bush, with a huge cry of "*Yaaaaarrgh!*"

They were caked in grime, and a smell like month-old pigswill filled the air. The bandits shook their various weapons at the travellers, growling menacingly as the leader stepped forward and addressed their victims. He was especially grubby, his hair long and matted, his blackening teeth on display as he grinned. Patch very slowly started to reach back to his bag; despite the warning Tobias had given, if they'd hurt Barver he was going to try and take out some of them before he was disarmed.

"Welcome to our forest, wanderers!" said the leader. His fellow robbers jeered and waggled their blades some more. "A dangerous forest, too! It's lucky that we chanced on you this day!" Another jeer came, with some coughing from the less-healthy members of the group. "Me and my friends wish to offer you protection against the evils here. A basilisk walks the woods!" A mock-scared "Wooooo!" came from the bandits. "An evil Witch haunts the mountain!" An "Ahhhhhh!" from the thieves. "Worst of all, the most feared band of murderous villains also prowls these parts!"

He paused for dramatic effect.

"And that's *us*!" he said, flourishing his sword as the brigands cheered long and loud. "Who better to offer you protection from our blood-keen knives, friends, than we ourselves? So if you would, a simple fee!" He paused again, and the grinning outlaws looked at him with anticipation, waiting for the punchline. "*All you have!*" cried the gloating leader, as every blade – long sword, short sword, knife and dagger – moved in to point steadily at the travellers, each blade-tip no more than a foot from flesh.

Patch's hand froze halfway to his bag. He looked at the brigand whose sword-tip was nearest his throat, and slowly brought his hand back to his horse's reins. Playing a Pipe would be *much* harder without fingers.

Madder, his broadsword half-drawn, gave an angry growl and shook his head. "Without Barver we have no chance," he muttered. He put the sword back in its scabbard and reached into his cassock, producing a small pouch. He threw it to the bandit leader. "Take it, and let us be on our way!"

The leader caught the pouch and looked at the contents. He raised an eyebrow. "This is all you have?" he said. "I think not!" He stroked his chin for a moment then suddenly looked at Madder's horse, pretending to be surprised. "Goodness!" he said. "A horse! And another! And a third! These should cover your fee, I think." The malice in his voice was matched by that in his eyes.

Madder gritted his teeth. "So if we give you our horses too, we can go on our way?"

"*If* you give us your horses? When we *take* your horses, then we'll see! Right, lads?" A sinister cheer came from his fellows.

"Might I ask what you did with our companion?" said Madder. "Is he alive?"

"Companion?" said the leader. "What companion?" He dismissed Madder's question with a shake of his head, and at that moment spotted Wren on Patch's shoulder. She was standing defiantly with her arms folded, glaring. The leader was fascinated. "What on *earth* is that?" he asked, then smiled. "What curious markings!"

From behind him another bandit – face wide with fear – cried out: "Dragon!"

The leader turned to him with a look of complete scorn. "Don't be stupid, man!" he said. "It's obviously a rat!"

But by then all of his men were staring past him with widening eyes, their bravado gone. Patch and Wren turned to see, and grinned: Barver was striding around the bend in the path. His expression was one of outrage – although, Patch saw, there was also a hint of glee at the reaction he was getting.

The dracogriff stopped, eyeing up the terrified brigands who, for now, seemed rooted to the spot. "If you've hurt any of my friends," cried Barver, "I will have to eat you. *Alive.*" There was a moment of silence, broken only by one or two sobs of dread. Barver let rip with a huge burst of flame and a thunderous roar, then charged forward. The thieves scattered at once, squealing like piglets as they fled.

Barver had set his sights on the leader. He seized the man by his feet and dangled him upside down. "I wonder how *you'll* taste," he said, leering.

"They're all fine!" cried the leader. "Your pals! All fine! Just our little…joke! Yes! A joke!"

But they weren't *quite* all fine. The horses had been seriously scared by Barver's fiery entrance, and were in a panic – particularly Patch's, which was hurtling around the perimeter of the clearing, whinnying in terror.

Patch was barely able to hang on to the reins; Wren was off his shoulder and clinging on for dear life to the saddle. The horse wasn't slowing – indeed, each time it caught a glance of Barver, the animal managed to go even faster. Patch reached back to his bag, trying to grip the horse with his legs so he wouldn't fall. At last, his fingers wrapped round his Pipe.

"Yes!" he cried, almost losing his balance. "Don't worry, Wren! I've got this!"

There was a Battle Song he knew, one that could be used against cavalry. It slowed a horse down, whatever the plans of the rider or the horse. Patch quickly looped the reins round his left arm and gripped even harder with his legs, leaving his hands free to Pipe. "Hold on tight!" he said to Wren. Her little face grimaced with effort as she clung to the saddle.

This was no time to be subtle, he knew; he went for it, and built the Song up as fast as possible. Finally, he played the key melody that would slow the horse down.

It stopped dead.

Patch kept going.

Over the horse's head he went, and the ground came up

fast to greet him with a hard, stony welcome. When his head stopped spinning, he sat up and looked behind him. There was his horse, slightly confused; and on the saddle sat Wren, giving him a thumbs up.

Patch stood, trying to ignore the pain in his shoulder and the smarting of his scraped knees. He went to the horse and took the reins, leading it back to Barver and the others.

All the brigands had abandoned their leader, who was now lying on the ground with his wrists and ankles tied, a gag in his mouth, and Madder's sword against his throat.

"So what happened to you?" Patch called to Barver.

"I had to go," said Barver, sheepish.

"What?"

"I had to *go*. Brother Duffle's poultice—" He rubbed his belly. "Sorry about that."

Wren jumped from the horse to Patch's shoulder and scowled at Barver. *We thought something had happened to you!* she signed.

"We're all okay," said Patch. "That's what matters." He looked at the brigand leader. "What do we do with him?"

Madder grinned, leering close to their captive's face. "What indeed!" he said. "All your friends have gone. And they won't be back."

The leader tried to speak through his gag. "Mmmpph!" he said. "Mmmph mmmpph!"

"A few years back I would've cut your throat on principle," said Brother Madder. "But I'm a man of God these days."

Tobias kneeled down beside him. "Maybe he can be useful," he said, pulling the gag down. "We're here to seek help from the Witch."

The leader laughed. "The Witch doesn't help people," he said. "Unless they want help to *die horribly*."

"You've met her?" said Tobias.

"None meet her and live!" said the leader. "We stay clear; she leaves us alone. You'd be wise to do the same. I've heard things screaming in the trees when I've got too close to her territory. You're idiots if you seek her out!"

Brother Madder pressed the blade of his sword a little harder against the man's throat. "Less of the backchat, scum. Is she easy to reach from here?"

"Follow the path until it splits, and you'll know which way to take. Trust me, you'll know…"

Madder took his sword away from the leader's neck and forced him to his feet. "You'd best run along now," said Madder. "Before I decide to kill you anyway. I'm sure God would grant me forgiveness if I asked nicely."

"Untie me, eh?" said the leader, his bound ankles making him wobble as he stood. "Please? Dangerous place this forest. Lots of undesirables, you know?"

Barver strode up to him and brought his head down until he was face to face with the trembling prisoner. For long seconds he studied the man. "You know what they say about the *eyes*," said Barver with a grin.

"They're the windows to the soul?" said the leader.

Barver shook his head and put the gag back over the man's mouth. "Tastiest part of the face," he said. The leader let out a muffled squeal and started hopping towards the trees, falling over every few hops. Barver watched him go, with a look of pure satisfaction.

Brother Madder swapped horses with Patch. "She knows me," said Madder, letting the animal nuzzle him. "And if I take her up to the front of the line, she'll not panic again."

Patch took Madder's horse, and went to put his Pipe in his pocket.

Tobias nodded to him. "Let me see it then, lad," he said. Patch handed the Pipe over, and Tobias examined it. "Your Song was a little stronger than needed, but given the situation it was impressive. Whitlock told me you were talented, and he was right."

"I have my moments," said Patch.

Barver tutted. "Listen to him! He's being modest. They offered him a role in the Battle Elite, but he turned it down, not wanting death and destruction to be his life."

Patch raised an eyebrow and gave Wren a pointed glance. "Do you share everything I tell you with Barver?" he said.

Friends don't have secrets, signed Wren.

"I too was in the Battle Elite," said Tobias, and Patch noticed the man's expression change suddenly, looking almost haunted. "You made the right decision, lad. The scars cut deep, and they stay with you for the rest of your days. And I don't just mean *this*." He gestured to the terrible scar that ran down the side of his face.

After another hour of travel they came to the split in the path that the leader of the brigands had told them about. On the path to the right, the forest continued without change, and songbirds perched among the leaves and tweeted happily. To the left, the trees were stunted, diseased things, the bushes spiky, and blackened by fungus. The only wildlife Patch could see were crows, sulking in large groups on leafless branches.

"Well," said Madder, with a wary smile. "He said we'd know the way to the Witch when we saw it."

They took the leftward path.

The peak of Gemspar Mountain loomed high above them. Patch felt uneasy when he looked at it, as if the sharpness of the rocks was pricking at his eyes.

As dusk approached, Brother Tobias held up his hand and called for a halt. "We're almost there I think," he said, sounding anxious.

"How should we approach her domain?" asked Brother Madder.

"The two of us will leave our horses and proceed on foot," said Tobias. He turned to the others. "The rest of you wait here. We're taking a great risk, and I can't say for certain how the Witch will react. We'll be back by dark."

With the horses tethered, Patch and his friends were happy enough to watch Tobias and Madder walk off to meet the Witch, but their nerves grew frayed as the light started to fail with no sign of the monks returning. Moonlight was all they had, lending yet another sinister edge to the forest.

What if they've been killed already? signed Wren, on Patch's shoulder. *Or eaten? Or turned inside out and rubbed with salt and then eaten? While still alive!*

"They'll be back soon," said Patch. "There's no need to worry. Barver will protect us."

From behind that tree? signed Wren.

Patch turned to look. Sure enough Barver was hiding behind a large oak, peering around it fearfully. "Oh, come out here, you big wuss," said Patch.

"I don't like it," said Barver, edging out from hiding. "All this creepy stuff. I just don't."

A low moan came from the forest ahead of them. Nobody said anything, but Patch stood up slowly and started to walk in the direction of the sound.

Wren squeaked at him. *You're going* towards *the sound?*

she signed. *Count me out.* She scurried down his leg and ran to Barver.

"It might be Tobias and Madder," whispered Patch. "Maybe they need our help." He felt for his Pipe, whatever use it might be, then remembered it was in his bag. "Barver?" he said. "Come on!"

Barver shook his head. "Uh uh," he said. "Absolutely no way."

There was another low moan, longer this time, followed by what could only be described as a *cackle*.

"Okay," said Patch. "So it's not Tobias and Madder."

Two bright circles appeared in the gloom, fifty feet from where they stood. Patch's legs wobbled. The light from the circles (Patch didn't want to think of them as *eyes*, not yet) made it easier to see the shape *around* the circles, and the two long dark lines on either side of it.

The shape was that of a bent figure. The two *very* long lines were about the width of arms, held out as if to embrace. Or to *grab*.

Patch backed away. The circles of light went off and came on again.

"It blinked!" said Barver.

The next moan was louder, longer, and far more ghastly. The cackle that followed was unmistakable. The dark figure shifted slightly, moving towards them one slow step at a time.

Patch kept backing off until he bumped into Barver, who was rigid with fear and staring at the wailing *thing* that was approaching.

Wren climbed over to Patch's shoulder again. They huddled together, the three of them, trembling and whimpering.

And the Witch of Gemspar Mountain drew ever closer.

THE WITCH

The Witch was wearing a black cowl. Its arms, ten feet long, ended in deathly white claws that twitched with each step it took. The disc-like eyes glowed in the midst of a face as craggy as the mountain itself, and under the eyes an oversized mouth gaped open, revealing discoloured teeth like ancient tombstones.

Patch could feel his sanity draining away, such was the terror he felt, and from the sound of her whimpers Wren was the same. The scariest noise of all, thought Patch, had to be Barver's hitched breaths: the dracogriff was paralysed with dread.

Then the Witch let out a hideous screech and Patch decided that no, actually, *that* was the scariest noise of all. As one, the group answered with their own long, drawn-out scream, which only faded when another voice cut through the air.

"Alia, stop it! They're with me!"

The Witch instantly halted. Without moving her mouth she answered in a voice that didn't sound anything like the cackling wails she'd been making so far: "Who said that?"

From the trees to the far left of the cowering group, Brother Tobias emerged, Brother Madder beside him.

"It's me! It's Tobias!" he said. "We need—" He paused and shook his head. "*I* need your help, Alia. Please. For old times' sake."

The Witch's long arms slowly lowered until the claws were on the ground. The light in the eyes faded. From behind the Witch, a second figure emerged in a grey hooded robe. It walked in front of the Witch's still form, then over to Tobias and Madder. Its hands – on the end of ordinary-sized arms – reached up and pulled back its hood.

Patch gaped. The figure was a woman, and a beautiful one at that. She was looking at Tobias with a defiantly raised eyebrow.

"Brother Tobias," she said. "I always knew some day you'd come walking back through my door." She frowned and glanced around at the trees. "Metaphorically speaking."

As Tobias and the woman spoke, Patch looked again towards the Witch, squinting to try and see better in the moonlight. He had a moment of realization, and all his fear vanished suddenly. With one eye on the newcomer in the grey robe, he walked towards the Witch.

Wren was on his shoulder, and she wasn't happy. *What are you doing?* she signed. *Stop!*

"It's okay," said Patch. "Take another look, Wren."

As they got closer, it became obvious. The frightening face was just paper, glue and paint; the terrible claws were jointed wood.

It's a puppet! signed Wren. *A big, horrible puppet!* She hopped off Patch's shoulder onto the "Witch" and vanished under the black cloth that covered it.

Barver arrived by Patch's side. "Never tell anyone about this," he said. "Not in the Islands of the Eastern Seas, anyway. I wouldn't live it down."

Wren reappeared on top of the Witch's head. *The eyes are lamps,* she signed, clearly impressed. *There are all sorts of levers back here!*

Barver reached out to one of the long arms and waggled it up and down. It broke off in his hand.

"Hey, leave that alone!" called the woman. She walked over, Tobias and Madder behind her.

"Um, sorry," said Barver. He half-heartedly tried to poke the arm back into position, and when he let it go it fell to the ground. "I didn't mean to break it."

The woman lifted the end of the arm and slotted it back

into place. "It's far more delicate that it looks," she said, tetchy. She stared at Barver. "And *what* are you?"

"The name's Barver," he said. "I'm a dracogriff."

She turned to Patch. "And you?"

"Patch Brightwater," he said. "Uh, human."

The woman shook her head, unimpressed, but then she saw Wren sitting on top of the Witch-puppet. "Ah! Now you…you're a different prospect entirely. Cursed, eh?"

Wren nodded. *I'm here so you can cure me*, she signed, but the woman waved a dismissive hand at her.

"No, no, stop all that," she said. "I don't understand a word."

Tobias stepped in. "Alia, this is Wren. She's part of the reason we're here. Everyone, this is Alia, the Witch of Gemspar Mountain."

"Obviously not the *original* Witch," said Alia. "So, the rat curse is *part* of why you came. What's the rest of it?"

"I need help with a patient who is close to death," said Tobias. "A poison runs through his veins, one that is dripping with sorcery."

Alia shrugged. "And why should I care?"

"The patient is Rundel Stone," said Tobias.

She scowled at him. "I say again, why should I care?" Tobias said nothing and just looked at her. After a few moments Alia sighed and shook her head, clearly irritated. "Oh all *right*. Give me a minute to pack up." She reached under the black cloth that covered the main bulk of the Witch-puppet, and pulled. The arms grew shorter and folded themselves under the cloth. She nodded at Wren. "Do you mind?" she said politely, and Wren hopped from the puppet to Patch's shoulder. Alia pushed down on the head, which retracted, and then shoved hard against what remained of the puppet. It pivoted down, and Alia gathered up the cloth and shut a lid. The entire puppet was now contained in a wheeled box, like a small handcart.

Wren couldn't resist giving a little round of applause.

"Everyone get your things and follow me," said Alia. She nodded to Barver and pointed to the cart. "Make yourself useful and push that. Just try not to damage it!"

She led them through the trees to a forbidding path between high volcanic cliffs. They emerged into a large open area, most of which was desolate. The peak of Gemspar Mountain loomed over them like a constant threat, yet among this desolation, next to the entrance to a cave in the side of the mountain, was an expanse of grass, perhaps eighty feet across, with various fruiting bushes and a vegetable patch, all surrounded by a fence. It looked like the whole thing had been cut out of a different landscape and dropped here.

Alia saw the bemused looks and smiled.

"Welcome to my home," she said. "The cave is ancient,

but the garden is my own construction."

Tobias was obviously impressed. "Does it not drain you, to sustain this kind of green magic?"

She shook her head. "The only magic needed for the garden was for the transportation of soil, Tobias. It gets plenty of sun and water, all free."

With the horses tied up, she led them into the cave. It seemed extensive, going back into the rock of the mountain for at least a few hundred feet, before bending away out of sight, the true extent impossible to tell. Lamps were burning everywhere, keeping it bright. Simple shelves were filled with glass jars of various contents, some of which were rather grim. Patch made an effort not to look at them too closely.

Barver still pushed the Witch-puppet, and Alia pointed to a spot by one shelf. "Over there, if you don't mind," she said, and Barver did as instructed. "The birds and insects around here are my eyes and ears. It's easy to tell when there are intruders in my part of the forest. Not very common, these days. My reputation seems to be enough discouragement."

"Why do you have the puppet?" asked Barver. "Surely you can just…" He made a spell-casting motion with one hand.

Alia gave him a warm smile. "Magic is an effort. I save my powers for the work that interests me. Lately I've not had need for elaborate magical defences. *Witchy* there is rather effective at chasing off strays. Also, she's considerable *fun*." She walked across to a large trunk and opened it up. It contained a vast number of little glass vials and bottles. "This is research," she said. "Out here, I refine my skills in peace." She gave Tobias a long, pointed glare. "In *peace*, Tobias. I wanted to be left alone, and never see any of you again. Why have you broken your word?"

Patch looked from Alia to Tobias and back again, feeling a very definite chill in the air.

"I kept my word," said Tobias. "Until I had no choice."

"And now you're here," she said. "Seeking help from the all-terrible Witch, even though I swore I would *kill* you if you came. *Any* of you."

Patch frowned, wondering who exactly Alia meant by "any of you". He shared a worried look with Wren and Barver.

Alia caught the look on Patch's face. She narrowed her eyes at him, making Patch's knees suddenly feel very wobbly. "Do I disappoint?" she said to him. "Did you want to see the old Witch, the *mad* Witch? I can pretend to be like that, if you want. I can be what the Council thought I was. A seeker of unnatural power, dabbling in things no Piper should touch! Things that even Casimir feared!" She clenched her fists and turned towards the cave entrance. As she went, the lamps within the cave dimmed as one.

Patch felt Wren's claws grip tightly to his coat, and he found himself putting his own hand on Barver for support.

Outside the cave, the moonlit sky was clear. Alia raised her arms, and clouds seemed to congeal out of the heavens.

"Power without limit!" cried Alia, and the clouds began to move in a slow spiral. Lightning flashed within them. "Unconstrained! Terrifying!" she cried, before shouting out a long series of incomprehensible words, each spoken with unmistakable rage. Lightning flared like none of them had ever seen before – tinged purple and red, it spread out in shapes like claws, bathing the whole forest in irate light.

She lowered her arms. Gradually, the lightning faded, and the clouds vanished. The lamps within the cave grew bright once more. She turned to Tobias and heaved a deep sigh. "Is that *fear* I see in your eyes?" she said to him. "I don't know what hurts me more. That you broke your word, or that you kept it for so long. That you really believed I could hurt *you*, of all people. You really did fear me."

Tobias suddenly looked rather fragile. "I kept my vow," he said. "I left you alone. But not because I feared you. I did it because you *asked* me to." She said nothing in reply, only looked at him with sadness. Tobias put his hand on her shoulder. "It's…it's good to see you again."

Alia seemed dazed for a moment. Then she stepped away, letting his hand fall from her. "I half-expected a visit from someone," she said. "Given what happened at Tiviscan."

"You heard about the attack?" said Tobias.

She nodded. "A little bird told me. I'm not surprised Drevis didn't come. I *might* have killed him."

"It was the Council who expelled you, Alia, and that was before Drevis was one of them. He was always on your side. And while Casimir was your greatest champion, don't forget that Rundel was also outspoken in your defence."

"Ah," she said. "Rundel." She let out a long sigh. "I *suppose* I can't let the old goat die, if I can help it. Back to the business in hand, then. Tell me what happened."

Tobias nodded. "His Apprentice brought him to me, close to death. My strongest healing Songs have kept him alive, but are unable to deal with the poison." He went to the cave entrance, where his horse was tied, and fetched the jar containing the metal box. "Here," he said, handing her the jar. "*This* is how it was inflicted."

Alia held the jar up. "*Enigma enicatus*," she said.

Tobias nodded. "A death puzzle. Rundel said if we identify its targets, we might identify the attacker."

"An *enigma enicatus* is a booby-trapped magical device," said Alia. "Difficult to make." She opened the jar and passed her hand over the top, back and forth. "Mmm. The *style* of the spells within it is unusual. You should take this to Ural. It's a very *engineered* form of sorcery. It'd be right up his alley. He might recognize the style, and point you to its creator. He knows much more about the Sorcerers of the world than I do." Tobias looked immediately wary. "Good Lord, Tobias, what is it?"

"Ural is dead," said Tobias. "Bludgeoned, without witnesses to what happened. Rundel was called to investigate, and was poisoned by the box when he picked it up."

Alia was stunned. "Ural Casimir, dead?" She closed her eyes, visibly distressed by the news. After a moment she opened her eyes again, and Patch could see they were wet. "Come," she said, venturing to a table beside her trunk of potions. "We must investigate the box."

The others followed, but Patch found himself frozen for a moment, distracted by a sudden realization. He'd thought the name Ural was familiar, and now he knew why. It was Ural *Casimir*, the Sorcerer Engineer. One of the Eight!

And there was something else he'd thought of, something that was surely impossible, but which made him look at Tobias and Alia with fresh eyes.

Wren jabbed his cheek. *Snap out of it*, she signed. *They're waiting for us.*

He nodded without a word, and went to join them.

Alia handed out pieces of rag to Tobias, Madder and Patch, and took one herself. "Each of you must spit in your rag," she said, and as they did she went to a corner where a hunk of cured meat sat. She cut some pieces from the meat and returned. "You first," she said to Patch. She took his rag, and wiped his spit over the surface of one piece of meat. Then, using a pair of tongs, she thrust the meat into the jar and pressed it against the box. Nothing happened. "Now you," she said to Madder. She repeated the process, and again there was no reaction.

"Can you be sure this works, Alia?" said Tobias.

"Hush!" she said. She took the rag from Tobias and wiped it over the third piece of meat. This time, when she pressed it to the box there was an audible *click*. She pulled the tongs away just in time to see a small needle disappear back into the metal surface. Black liquid dripped from the meat. She gave Tobias a dark look, and then tried her own spit with the last piece. Again, the click, and the meat was injected with poison. "As I feared," she said. "The targets include Rundel and the two of us. I give you one guess who else might be a target."

"Let's not get ahead of ourselves," said Tobias, giving Patch and the others a wary look. Alia saw the expression on his face and nodded. To Patch, the meaning was obvious: let's not talk in front of *them*. His suspicions grew almost to the point of bursting out of him, but he held his tongue.

"Now to identify what the substance is," said Alia. "Give me a moment." She took samples of the black poison from the pieces of meat, then added various liquids from vials she took down from the nearest shelf. A few minutes later, she nodded with satisfaction. "Moon-rot," she said. "A nasty fungus, but the effect has been enhanced with sorcery as you suspected. No wonder your Song couldn't quite deal with it." She hunted through the vials in her trunk and selected one containing a bright purple liquid. "Aha!" she announced, standing up. "This should do it." She took a long metal rod and touched it to the black poison, then swirled the rod in the purple liquid. The colour immediately changed to green. "This must remain absolutely still for at least eight hours," she said, placing the vial in a tiny stand on the table. "By then it will have transmuted fully, and Rundel's cure will be complete. I'll come with you to Marwheel long enough to administer it, Tobias, not a moment longer. He'll remain unconscious for a week, perhaps two, but he should live."

"Thank you, Alia," said Tobias. Brother Madder offered out the pouch of money he'd reclaimed from the brigand leader.

"No, no," said Alia. "Keep it. You have need of it, I know, running your infirmary. You've been treating a firefoot outbreak recently, haven't you? And doing a fine job, too."

"You know about that?" said Tobias.

Alia grinned. "Oh yes, I've kept my eye on you, Palafox."

That was it – Patch couldn't hold it in any more. "Palafox!" he barked. "I knew it! I *knew* it!"

"Oh," said Alia, wide-eyed. "Damn."

Barver and Wren were staring at Patch. *You knew what?* signed Wren.

"*Palafox, Corrigan, Kellenfas, Stone...*" recited Patch. "*Casimir, Hinkelman, Drevis and Throne.*" Barver and Wren gave him bemused looks, but Tobias and Alia were watching him warily. "The names of the Eight," said Patch. "Kellenfas, Hinkelman and Throne died in the quest. Of the survivors, we have Drevis, now a Lord of the Pipers' Council. We have Stone, now a Virtus in the Custodian Elite. The other three sought new lives, away from the fame that their quest had brought. First, Casimir, the Sorcerer Engineer. Who does that leave?"

"Palafox and Corrigan," said Barver. "What are you saying?" He looked to Wren, and Wren shook her head and shrugged.

Patch heaved a sigh. "You two should have paid more attention to the tales of the Eight! Don't you know their first names?"

"Mmm," said Barver. "The stories only mention them once, but I *think* I do. Let's see...Palafox's name was T—" His mouth dropped open and he stared at Tobias. Then he stared at Alia. Then he fainted, crushing a chair.

Wren was staring too. *No way*, she signed.

Patch gestured to Tobias. "Tobias Palafox, Hero of the Battle Elite." He gestured to Alia. "Alia Corrigan, the Great Piper of Shielding Songs!"

And Rundel Stone's dead friend— signed Wren.

Patch nodded. "—was Ural Casimir, the Sorcerer Engineer."

Barver was back on his feet, looking groggy.

Patch looked at Tobias and Alia. *"That's* why you're all old friends," he said. "You were all members of the Eight. And someone's trying to kill you!"

Barver fainted again, narrowly missing a table.

"We don't know that for certain," said Tobias.

"I think it's clear!" scoffed Alia. "Someone finally decided to get rid of us, the last of the Eight. We ruffled too many feathers in our quest, and stepped on too many toes!"

"We did make enemies," said Tobias, sounding oddly proud.

Alia nodded. "We did," she said. She looked at Patch and frowned. "And now you know our secret. You must choose: swear to tell no one, or die in *terrible pain.*"

"The first one," said Patch quickly; Wren gave an emphatic nod.

"A good choice," said Alia. She nudged Barver with her foot, but he didn't stir. "That goes for you too," she said. "Unconsciousness is no excuse." Finally she turned to Brother Madder. "And what about you?"

Madder smiled. "I'm an old friend of Tobias, ma'am," he said. "I knew him before the Eight set off on their quest.

I've never betrayed his secret. And if I can be open, while Tobias has never told me the Witch's true identity, I'd come to that conclusion some years ago."

"Really?" said Alia, her eyes narrowing.

"Indeed," said Madder. "Whenever Tobias had a little too much brandy, and someone mentioned the Witch of Gemspar Mountain, or the name of Alia Corrigan, it was never long until Tobias spoke of a mysterious lost love, his voice filled with longing and sorrow. But you can trust me to keep it to myself, ma'am."

Tobias's cheeks were reddening.

Alia blinked for a moment, then coughed. "Well then," she said, and took a deep breath. Once she'd composed herself, she rubbed her hands together with purpose. "Glad that's all settled. We'll start out for Marwheel when Rundel's potion is ready, but in the meantime we have a certain curse to deal with! I must prepare!" She looked at Wren. "It's your turn, little one. Don't think I forgot you!"

Wren started to tremble. Patch rubbed the top of her head to reassure her.

"Have faith!" said Alia. "Ural Casimir saw that I had even more potential as a Sorcerer than as a Piper. Oh, *Ural*...how can you be gone?" She looked up to the moon, tears in her eyes. She wiped them away. "He believed in me. It was my destiny. Even though the Council declared me a witch and cast me out, I don't regret it one bit."

237

"Can we do anything to help you get ready?" said Patch.

Alia nodded. "We need a large fire, as big as you can make it. Take lamps into the forest, all of you, and fetch as much wood as you can. I'll start my preparations." She went further back inside the cave, where the shelves were laden with books, and began to consult her texts.

Patch and Wren looked at Barver, who was still out cold.

Leave me on the table next to him, signed Wren, and Patch did, taking a lamp and following Tobias and Madder outside.

After a minute or so, Barver's eyes opened. He sat up suddenly in near-panic. "Someone's killing the Eight!" he said. "One by one!" He blinked and looked around. "Where did everyone go?"

Wren gave him an affectionate smile. *Welcome back, big fella*, she signed. *Now go and get me some firewood!*

21

Awkward Truths

There was plenty of dry wood among the creepy gnarled trees in Alia's part of the forest. Barver's contribution to the wood gathering dwarfed that of anyone else, which was no surprise given that he could carry half a dozen actual *tree trunks* on each trip. It wasn't long before they'd assembled the bonfire a safe distance from the cave entrance and Alia's garden. The wood took flame readily, and soon the bonfire was well ablaze.

Alia came out of the cave carrying a small leather pouch, paper and some thin pieces of charcoal. She got everyone to sit facing the fire, then stepped closer to it and spoke a few garbled words. Taking a handful of some kind of powder from her pouch, she cried out in a high-pitched warbling voice and threw the powder at the flames.

There was a vast plume of yellow smoke, alive with sparks.

Alia walked to where Patch sat, with Wren on his shoulder as usual. The others were a few feet behind them, watching with interest. "Right!" said Alia, looking at Patch. She set down the paper and gripped a piece of charcoal. "I need background on Wren, please. You're her friend. You can speak this—" She waved her hands around madly.

"Merisax hand speech," said Patch.

"Oh yes!" said Alia. "That's it! I never quite got around to learning it. Go ahead, then. Ask her how this curse came about. I'll take notes." She was poised with her charcoal on the page.

"Oh, she's told me the story a few times now," said Patch. "She's the daughter of a wealthy nobleman, and last summer she was kidnapped by a Sorcerer and forced to work as a maid in his castle. She tried to escape, and *blam*!"

"Rat curse!" said Alia.

Patch and Wren both nodded.

"Where was this castle?" said Alia. "What was the Sorcerer's name?"

Patch looked to Wren, who'd never told him those details. She signed, and he translated. "The village of Axlebury," he said. "The Sorcerer's name is Underath."

"Okay," said Alia, writing it down. "What we must do is look for a chink in the construction of the curse. If we find something to pick at, we can try and build a *counter*-curse. We may be able to shatter the curse outright, but I make no guarantees. Building a spell, a hex, a curse – these are similar to layering the parts of a Piper's Song. Building a counter-spell requires those layers to be understood, to allow them to be cancelled out. First I need something of yours, little rat. Hair and nail." She produced a pair of sharp scissors, and Wren flinched. "Don't worry, I won't take much." Patch held Wren gently as Alia snipped a tiny bit of fur from her back. "Now, your paw." Wren held her paw out, trembling, and Alia cut the very tip from one claw. She put the clippings into a small square of paper, then folded it into a little parcel. "That'll do," said Alia. She handed the parcel to Wren. "You must throw it into the flames!"

Patch stood and carried Wren as close to the fire as the fierce heat would allow. She threw the parcel, but it fell short.

"I've got it," said Patch. He set Wren down and stepped forward; braving the severe heat he grabbed the little parcel and went to throw it into the fire himself.

"Wait, she's the one who has to—" started Alia, but Patch had already let go and the paper was in flames. Alia shook her head as Patch came back with Wren and sat down. "Oh, fine. Ignore me, I'm just the expert." The fire erupted into more smoke, white this time, the sparks filling the cloud with an astonishing range of colours. Alia smiled.

241

"Oooh, hang on! We've got lucky!" She gripped her piece of charcoal, ready to take notes, then turned to the others behind them, who were whispering. "Shush!" she said. "It's starting!"

Everyone looked on in awe as the coloured sparks in the fire began to gather into something recognizable.

A tiny run-down cottage in the midst of rolling fields.

"Wren!" came a voice, and Patch almost *jumped*. But the voice was from the fire, booming loud; suddenly a woman's face appeared, kind and concerned. "Where are you going, young lady?"

And there she was, a girl of thirteen – Wren, as she used to be. Earnest and smiling, she wore a long skirt, which was a little threadbare, striped with rings of red and white. Patch looked at the red-ringed tail of his rat friend and knew it was no coincidence.

"Mum," said Wren. "The time's come for me to get work. I know how hard things are for you and Dad, and I'm an extra mouth to feed. I have a plan, and I won't be talked out of it!"

Wren's mother hugged her. "How I wish it wasn't so," she said. "Don't be gone too long."

"Six months at most," said Wren. "I'll save as much of my pay as I can!"

The smoke from the fire darkened.

Patch gave Wren – the *rat* Wren, on his shoulder – a pointed look. "Daughter of a wealthy nobleman?" he whispered. She was staring at the fire, looking mortified.

"Shhhh!" hissed Alia. "We'll miss something!"

The smoke lit up again, to show human-Wren walking through the countryside, a determined expression on her face. In the distance was a castle – far smaller than Tiviscan Castle, but impressive all the same. The viewpoint changed, and now Wren was at the castle door, knocking.

A weary-looking middle-aged man, dressed in an elaborate robe, opened the door and peeked out. "Yes?" he said.

"You are Underath, the Sorcerer?" said Wren.

"I am."

"Sir, I was hoping to offer my services as a maid."

Underath looked astonished. "I've been seeking staff here for twenty years. Nobody's ever come before."

"I'm here," said Wren. "Do you wish to hire me? Yes or no?"

"Yes," said Underath. "But be prepared! Of the hundred rooms in the castle I use only four. Those four are filthy with use, and the rest are filthy with neglect! Pick any bedroom you choose; keep yourself to yourself. The kitchen is always well stocked. Can you cook?"

"I can."

Underath seemed elated at the idea. "Good, for I cannot! I've been living on salted meats and cheese and bread and wine. Cook whatever you will, and I'll be grateful to end the monotony. Come!"

The view changed again. They now stood on a high wall that ran round a courtyard, in the middle of which was a large dark-grey griffin. It looked up at the two humans with a wary eye.

"That is Alkeran," said Underath. "The courtyard is his, and his alone. Do not speak to him. He is quick to anger." They re-entered the castle, coming to a room where shelves of books filled the walls, potions and their ingredients cluttered tables, and sheets of paper littered the floor. "Here is my study. Keep the dust to a minimum, and tidy my papers. Beyond that, touch nothing."

Wren bent down and picked up some pages, looking at them with fascination. "Should I keep your writings ordered somehow, sire?" she said. "These notes are on necromancy, while these are on the history of prophecy."

"You can read?" said Underath.

"My parents taught me."

"How quaint to teach a girl something so useless to her! Just tidy the papers into one neat pile."

Wren betrayed no emotion, save for a brief narrowing of her eyes. She nodded, and looked with interest at the bookshelves, reaching out to them.

"Do not touch the books!" warned Underath.

"As you wish, sire," said Wren.

(The smoke of the fire weakened, to disappointed sounds from those watching. Alia reached for her pouch and threw another handful of powder into the flames. The smoke billowed up again, and the images began to re-form.)

The days passed. Wren, wearing the simple clothes of a maid, entered rooms filled with dust and spiderwebs, and she cleaned them; she cooked, she ate, she slept.

One day she went to Underath's study to retrieve his dinner plates. She heard snoring. Underath was asleep in his bedroom.

Cautiously she went to his desk. A great leather-bound volume of magic was lying open. She began to read it, concentrating hard. Then a light of understanding filled her eyes.

Again and again, as she collected the dishes from Underath's evening meal, she listened for the snoring and read what she could. At one point, deep in thought, she reached out to a spoon without touching it. She read aloud from the book and the spoon wobbled. A smile of utter delight crossed her face.

Day after day, she read; day after day, she could do more. She lit a candle without using a flame; she repaired a broken plate with words alone.

"Sire?" she said, as she brought Underath lunch one

day. "I have heard it said that Sorcerers often take on an apprentice, yet I know that you never have. Will you ever do so?"

"Perhaps," said Underath. "Young men of talent are rare, though. Ah, lunch! Good." He started to eat. "Actually, I have something to tell you. I'll be gone for a week. I shall ride Alkeran to a distant land, so you shall be alone. You have nothing to fear in this place, and I shall see you soon."

When she returned to her room, Wren cheered. A week to study freely!

Once Underath had left on his journey, she began to scrutinize his most precious books late into the night. In her room, she stood before an old ragged mirror: "Sire? And what if *I* was to ask...to be your apprentice?" She closed her eyes. "You can do this, Wren, you can ask him when he's back."

Finally, a shadow in the sky announced the return of the griffin, and of Underath. She went to greet him. The door to the courtyard opened, and standing beside Underath was a woman of cold beauty. When the woman laid eyes on Wren her smile contained nothing but malice.

"I have news, maid!" said Underath. "I am newly married! This is my wife. I have sought a companion even longer than I had sought a servant – a wife wise enough to keep within touching distance of my *superior* intelligence. I shall have no more need of a maid after today, but I will pay you well for the work you have done these last few weeks." He tossed a pouch of coins to her.

Crestfallen, Wren still had the courage to speak. "I was...I was going to ask to be your apprentice."

Underath laughed. His wife raised a sinister eyebrow. "You?" said Underath. "A girl?" He patted his wife's head, as if she was a pet. "It's not even right for a *woman* to be a Sorcerer, let alone a simple *girl*! Now run along and prepare a celebration meal for us!"

She did as she was asked. When she brought the first tray of food to the study, Underath guided her through to another room, one that used to be empty but which had been transformed into a dining room. An impressive table was laid out with plates and cutlery.

"See how I've been making changes to the castle already?" said Underath. "Nothing is too good for my beautiful wife!" He saw the food Wren carried – a wonderful-looking pie, bread, and soup. He smiled. "Thank you, maid. I know you're disappointed, but I wish you well, in all you do."

"I'll bring your best wines for the meal," said Wren. "And I've made some desserts, too."

She brought the rest of the food and drink to the dining room. Underath's wife was there, smiling her malicious smile.

"There's no need for you to tidy after, maid," said

Underath. "I grant you the night off, to let you gather your things ready to leave at dawn."

But that was not Wren's plan.

She returned later and, as she'd hoped, there was snoring from Underath's bedroom. This was, of course, why she'd made her meal with such care. They had eaten well, and now they would sleep well, too.

Silently she went into the study and chose four of Underath's books on sorcery, smaller ones that she could carry more easily. She crept out of the castle into the gloom of dusk, dressed in the red-ringed skirt she'd worn when she first arrived.

She froze when a voice spoke up behind her.

"If I'd not seen it with my own eyes, I wouldn't have believed it," said Underath. "You were right, wife!"

Wren spun round. Underath was standing there, his wife by his side.

"I told you she couldn't be trusted!" said the woman. "Look! Look what she takes from you!"

Wren hung her head, angry and ashamed. She dropped the books and the pouch of coins at her feet. "Keep your books. Keep your money. I can become a Sorcerer! I've always known it! I only ever came here because I wanted to learn!"

Underath shook his head. "I thought you were loyal," he said, obviously hurt. "Go. *Go*."

"This is betrayal, my love!" said his wife. "She's the lowest kind of vermin! A *rat*! Why not make sure she never forgets it, dearest?" Grinning with malice, she placed her hand on her husband's arm.

Underath's expression was one of sorrow and regret, but it changed: oh so slowly, it changed. His eyes hardened, and he took on a look of spite and rage.

He muttered some words and began to wave his hands. A purple glow appeared round the tips of his fingers. He cried out, his arms pointing straight at Wren. The purple glow became impossibly bright and hurtled towards the girl, exploding around her.

The light faded, and when it was gone there was only a rat with a red-ringed tail. It squeaked in terror as it ran off into the trees, chased by the cruel laughter of the Sorcerer and his bride.

The sparks subsided. The smoke from the bonfire was now just ordinary smoke.

Wren hung her head. The silence was uncomfortable.

Eventually Alia cleared her throat. "Ahem," she said. "Yes. Um. There are details that don't *quite* match the account you gave, Patch."

"Don't I know it," said Patch, glum. He turned to Wren. "Kidnapped, were you? Wealthy parents, eh?"

Wren looked tearful. *I was desperate for your help in Patterfall*, she signed. *It seemed like such a little lie.*

Patch shook his head. "And you tried to steal his magical texts?" said Patch. "I can't believe this."

Wren gave him a defiant stare. *What?* she signed. *Are you upset that I can't reward you for your help? Is that why you became my friend? For the money?*

Patch was dumbstruck by the accusation. "Well!" he said. "Well, then...then I..." He felt very angry indeed, but he had a sudden fear that, perhaps somewhere deep down, he was guilty as charged. He hoped not.

"Enough!" said Barver. "You would risk your lives to save each other! Here we are, on the cusp of a cure for Wren, and you squabble over things that *don't really matter*!"

Long seconds passed before Wren and Patch found they could bear to look at each other.

"Sorry," muttered Patch. "I just thought you'd be more honest with me than that. *Friends don't have secrets*, isn't that what you said?"

There was a sudden *crump* from the fire. Everyone backed away as flames grew again, and colourful sparks exploded outwards with a loud bang.

"Something more for us to see!" said Alia. "Shush! *Shush!*"

The images in the fire resolved themselves, along with

250

the sound of rock grinding against rock, and the cracking of masonry.

Patch's face filled the image in the smoke, coughing as the dust of the attack on Tiviscan Castle filled his cell.

"Uh oh," said the real Patch, looking at the features of his past-self looming above him.

Alia seemed confused for a moment, but then she looked at Patch and mimed throwing the parcel into the flame. "A little of *you* has crept into the spell, it seems," she said. "Looks like you were a prisoner somewhere. Wait a moment…is that Tiviscan dungeon? It is! You're a *criminal*?"

"It's fine, Alia," said Tobias. "He—"

"You knew?" she said.

"I did. There's nothing to worry about, we just—"

Suddenly Tobias stopped talking. He stared at the fire, as did Alia.

As did all of them.

"Aye!" came a voice.

There in the smoke's magical images, the prisoner in the Iron Mask lay, his injuries obvious. His hands came up and tore at the mask, which swung open and fell to the floor.

"Aye…" said the thin-faced man, coughing up blood as past-Patch drew closer. "Aye…am…I…am…" The man swallowed and took a breath. "I am not the Piper of Hamelyn."

Then the dragons came. The man was taken, the expression on his face one of simple relief. He was thrown into the circle of fire the dragons made for him, and he perished.

With perfect timing, the images died and the smoke retreated. The bonfire's centre collapsed in on itself.

Everyone was staring at Patch, even Wren. *Especially* Wren.

Patch coughed. "Um," he said. "Ah. Yes. Didn't I mention that bit?"

22

THE CHILDREN

You accused me *of dishonesty, eh?* signed Wren. *Take a look at yourself, you big dolt!* She hopped off his shoulder and went over to Barver, who was glaring at Patch.

Tobias seemed stunned. "You told nobody about this?" he said. "Even when you found out that Alia and I were part of the Eight, you still said nothing?"

Patch looked around at all the accusing eyes. "What *should* I have done? I'm supposed to be in the dungeons until I die. You want me to start blabbing about the Hamelyn Piper's last words, and get thrown back into a cell? I'm happier not doing that, thank you!" He folded his arms and scowled.

Alia, who'd been pacing furiously up and down, stopped and looked at Tobias. "The Mask was *off* him," she said. "He could say anything he wanted, and lie without restriction."

"You saw the same thing I saw," said Tobias. "You saw his eyes. Did it look like a lie?"

"Insane, then," snapped Alia. "He forgot what he was, perhaps. I don't *know*."

Tobias looked at her, a terrible doubt in his eyes. "Could we have imprisoned the wrong man?"

"Impossible!" said Alia. "We caught him with his Pipe, we knew the Songs he'd played! And the witnesses! The townsfolk of Hamelyn identified him, as did the child who was left behind—"

"The boy with the limp?" said Barver.

Alia gave a deep sigh. "That poor young soul." She clenched her fists. "You'd only need to see the look on that child's face to know we'd caught the right man."

"But his last words!" said Tobias, agitated. "He'd been trying to say that sentence, to deny he was the Piper of Hamelyn, for almost a decade!"

Alia put a hand on his shoulder. "You torture yourself for no reason, Tobias. Think back to the end of our quest. Think back!"

Tobias took a long slow breath, trying to settle himself. "We'd tracked the Hamelyn Piper down, in the Ice Fields near Port Hagen," he said. "He defended himself with a display of Dark Piping that was beyond anything I'd seen before."

Alia looked at him with an affection she'd not shown until now. "That was the day you got your scars. I thought I'd lost you—" She drifted to silence for a moment. "The Hamelyn Piper was caught in the same blast, yet he escaped uninjured."

"But we *had* hurt him," said Tobias. "When we found him again, he was dazed, bewildered. Barely able to speak. But the evidence was clear: he was the Hamelyn Piper." He nodded, the uncertainty gone from his face. "Whatever he said just before his death, it means nothing. We must listen only to the evidence, and the evidence speaks with one voice. It was him!"

Patch was trying hard to believe that the prisoner's last words had meant nothing, but he was finding it difficult. There was something else worrying him, though – something Alia had mentioned. "Wait," he said. "You said you got his Pipe when you caught him, and you knew what Songs he'd played. In all the stories I heard of the Eight, the Pipe had been destroyed, so the history of its Songs was lost. Which is the truth?"

Alia and Tobias shared a long look.

"She was, um, *mistaken*," said Tobias.

Alia frowned at him. "The Hamelyn Piper is dead," she said. "Perhaps the time for secrecy has passed."

"Alia," said Tobias, in a cautioning tone. "We *both* took a vow."

Alia looked to the ground, thinking. At last she shook her head. "We found the Pipe," she said to Patch. "And it told us what had happened to the children."

Barver, Patch and Wren looked at Alia, open-mouthed with shock.

Patch eventually managed to speak. "You know what happened to them—?"

"The Hamelyn Piper had *tried* to destroy his Pipe before he was caught," said Alia. "There were only fragments left. Rundel Stone attempted to extract the history of the Pipe's Songs from those fragments, even though we all thought it was impossible. But he found two Songs of immense power. One had been played on the night the human children disappeared. The other was played after the dragon children were taken. I saw Rundel's face crumple as he found out the truth. I watched as his heart grew cold and bitter. Hope had left him."

Barver was staring at her. "What happened to the children?" he said. "What happened?"

"Don't, Alia," said Tobias. "Please."

Alia ignored him. "Both were Songs of execution, old Songs that were once used to carry out death sentences. For the dragon children, it was the Song of Endless Sleep. This slows the breathing of the target until they fall unconscious and die. For the human children, it was the Song of Dispersal. The children of Hamelyn were obliterated, their flesh and bones scattered like dust across the skies."

Barver gasped. "And the Pipers' Council have known this all along?"

Alia nodded. "Yes. And the dragon authorities, too."

Patch shook his head. "But the Mask was going to force the Hamelyn Piper to answer that question! If they already knew the answer, what was the point?"

"The Mask's question wasn't about the fate of the children," said Alia. "We already knew their fate. It was about why he had done it, these senseless acts, these atrocities... *Why?* To get that answer, the Hamelyn Piper had to live – yet if the world knew the children were dead, his execution would have been impossible to stop! Then, the question of *why* could never be answered. So the Council ordered the fate of the children to be kept secret. The Dragon Triumvirate were reluctant to agree, and brought us to the brink of war, but they did agree in the end."

"And now it is over, at last," said Tobias. "The Triumvirate must have decided that no answer would ever come, and when the opportunity arose they made their move and killed the Hamelyn Piper. Whatever the Council does in retaliation for the attack on Tiviscan, they'll be secretly relieved that their most hated prisoner is dead."

"Even so," said Patch. "With his final words the Hamelyn Piper denied his guilt. Surely you must tell the Pipers' Council about this?"

"I will tell Rundel, and let him decide what to do," said Tobias.

"But you can't tell him about me!" said Patch. "Right now I'm listed among the dead. If he found out I'm alive, it would condemn me to a life of being hunted!"

"I'll not mention you," said Tobias. "It seems fair that we keep your secret, if you keep ours. I'll just say Alia conjured a way to see the Hamelyn Piper's final moments, and she told me what she'd heard."

"You think you could fool Rundel so easily?" said Alia. "Such magic needs a willing witness, and he'll want to know who that witness was."

"I'll tell him you have invented a new magic that needs no witness," said Tobias.

"He'll not believe you," said Alia.

Tobias thought for a moment. "He'll believe it if *you* tell him," he said.

Alia looked at him with a raised eyebrow. "You want me to wait around until Rundel wakens and speak to him? Just to keep this lad from the dungeons? Not likely! I have better things to do!" But the faces around her – Barver, Wren and Patch himself – were looking at her with the pleading expressions normally found on cold kittens or hungry puppies. She glared back at them, defiant at first, but her defiance gradually ebbed away. "*Oh very well!*" she snapped.

Tobias nodded. "It's decided, then. We'll let Rundel choose what to do, when he awakens."

The word "awakens" made Patch think of sleep; he couldn't hold back a yawn, and the yawn spread to Wren, and then Barver.

"The night is deep," said Alia, looking up to the moon. "Sleep, everyone. Especially you, Wren." She bent down and gathered the pieces of paper she'd brought with her, which were covered now in circles and arrows and hastily scribbled words. "I have my notes to study, to seek a flaw in Underath's curse. I will see you at dawn!"

23

THE CURE

They slept near the embers of the bonfire. When dawn came, Alia woke them with a shout before walking off, a large earthenware jar in her arms.

Wren stretched and rubbed her eyes, but Patch knew she hadn't slept much. Neither had he.

Beside them, Barver was still snoring. Patch nudged him until he sat up with a start, one eye still shut. "How *dare* it be morning," muttered Barver.

Tell me about it, signed Wren. She looked over to where Alia stood, some distance from them, pouring salt from the large jar to create various shapes on the ground.

"She must have found a way to help you, Wren," said Patch.

I'm scared to ask, signed Wren.

They all watched Alia prepare, and at last she came over to them. "I'm ready," she said. "Wren, I'd hoped to be able to shatter the curse once and for all, but I fear it was too well constructed. Instead, I offer you this." She held up her hand, and in her fingers was a bracelet with intensely blue beads. "I did find a slight flaw in the curse, one that will let you be shielded from its power temporarily. This bracelet will give a few days at a time of human form. It's the best I can do." She put the bracelet around Wren's midriff. "Sadly it's not just a case of putting the bracelet on. It must be bonded to what is called your 'morphic countenance'. The process is painful." She looked at Barver and Patch with narrowed eyes. "And the two of *you* must not interfere, under any circumstances! It would put your friend in great danger. Do I make myself clear?"

They both nodded; Alia's stern gaze was enough to make anyone terrified of disobeying her.

"Make sure they do as they're told, Tobias," said Alia.

Patch felt almost sick with fear for Wren, yet he could do nothing but watch as Alia took his friend over to the salt symbols and set her down in the centre. She poured more salt from the jar, forming an outer circle thirty feet across. The circle complete, Alia stepped inside and began to speak. Patch couldn't place the language, a harsh and guttural tongue, all phlegm and spit. Her words turned into a chant.

"*Ree tee ko pak!*" she cried. "*Thagh pak skarra tak!*"

She raised her arms straight up as the chant grew in volume. A continuous low rumble began, and Patch could see the air within the circle shimmer.

Wren squeaked, and scratched at the bead bracelet with her hind legs, clearly in discomfort.

"*Ree tee ko pak!*" cried Alia. "*Thagh pak skarra tak!*" Her arms swept down suddenly, open palms held out to Wren. The air above the salt circle seemed to have texture now, moving like oil spilled in water. Patch looked to Barver, both of them deeply uneasy. The low rumble grew ever louder.

Wren shrieked, twisting in agony on the ground. Smoke started to rise where the beads touched her fur.

Patch stepped forward.

"We can't interfere!" said Barver, but Patch ignored him and went even closer. He moved around the outside of the circle. There was heat coming from it now, and the light within seemed to redden suddenly. Alia's chant continued louder and louder, and Patch saw her face…

He ran and fetched his Pipe from his bag. As he rushed back, Tobias stood in his way.

"You heard her," said Tobias. "Interfering could harm Wren!"

Patch pointed into the circle. "*Something's wrong!* Look at Alia, Tobias! Look at her *eyes*!"

Tobias looked. "Dear God," he said, backing off.

Alia's face was a grinning mask and her eyes were glowing red. Her chant took on an edge of madness – laughter burst from her mouth after every few words, a terrible insane *cackle*.

Wren was screaming now, writhing in pain, smoke pouring from her fur. Everyone was frozen, staring as the light within the circle darkened, until only the red glow from Alia's eyes remained.

"She'll be killed!" said Patch. He got as close as he could to the circle and stretched his foot out to the textured air. As he'd expected, the air formed a barrier. He looked at the swirling patterns directly above the salt and remembered how Alia had described the intricate layers of a Sorcerer's work, and how it was not so different from the layers of a Song.

He started to play the same counter-Song he'd played to save Wren back in Patterfall. To his amazement, he could see patterns forming on the barrier, patterns that changed as he played. He tried to create something that matched the shapes already there, hoping it would somehow negate them. Again and again, he tweaked what he was playing and observed how the patterns altered, and suddenly he struck lucky – a tiny gap seemed to open up, and widen. He intensified his playing, then reached out his hand. It *was* a gap, a break in the barrier wide enough for him to fit through, if he dived! He steeled himself and made the attempt, passing through the gap and landing hard inside the circle. He looked back at the barrier and saw the gap closing over. The noise was overwhelming, as if he was in the centre of a howling storm, Alia's yelling and Wren's screams only just audible. Wind whipped the black earth into his face, and he could barely see.

He tried to move towards Wren, but it felt like moving through deep mud. Then Alia's face leered at him, inches away. From this close, her eyes were even more terrifying – Patch could see a fire within, churning and flaring up.

"The deed is done, Brightwater!" she cried, cackling. "Look! The bracelet is bonded to her! She changes!"

"Wren!" he yelled. His friend's body was surrounded in smoke. "*Wren!*" He made to go to her, but Alia's hand gripped his shoulder.

"Leave her be, boy. Let me take a look at *you*!" Patch trembled with fear as Alia examined him from head to toe, those fiery eyes emitting a fierce heat. Loud as the winds around them were, Patch could hear her perfectly, as if she was speaking directly into his mind.

"I see you!" she said. "Your past! Your future! I see Tiviscan Castle!"

"That's in my past," cried Patch. "*Absolutely* my past."

"Perhaps!" she said. "Know this: should you ever return to Tiviscan, there will be a heavy price to pay! And what else do I see –" she studied him again, her grip on his shoulder painful now – "I see betrayal!"

"Betrayal…?"

"Yes, betrayal! The words come to me now, the *betraying* words. Listen and remember! The words I say next, Brightwater, burn them into your memory. There will come a time when you hear these words! A mouth that speaks them is a traitorous mouth, and will betray you to that which you fear most! When you hear them spoken, get away as quickly as you can! *Run!*"

Her frightening grin faded and she closed her glowing eyes. The wind dropped as she spoke in a gentle sing-song voice: "They thought they had us. But we're almost clear. Just the ridge to go. What's wrong with you? What's wrong?" Her eyes opened again and she stared at him. "An odd set of words, don't you think?" she said. Her voice shifted in tone, as if she was having a conversation with herself. "I agree, very odd! What say you, Patch? The lad's gone so very pale. The day's been quite a strain, I imagine."

She let him go and began to cackle once more as the howling wind returned. Patch fell to his knees, bewildered by what she'd said. Suddenly a hot blast of air hit him hard, flinging him backwards out of the circle.

There was silence.

He sat upright as a shadow fell across him. It was Alia, offering him a hand up. Her smile was utterly normal now, as were her eyes.

"That's got a bit of a kick, hasn't it?" said Alia as she

helped Patch to his feet. She dusted herself off, seeming rather high-spirited.

Patch looked to the salt circle. All signs of the barrier had vanished, and a dense mist was starting to dissipate. In the middle lay Wren: human, wearing the clothes they'd seen her wear as she'd tried to flee from Underath.

"It worked…" Patch said.

"It did," said Alia. "She'll be fine in a minute or two. I said you could trust me."

"Ye-ess," said Patch, not *quite* over how things had gone. "It was the glowing eyes and the insane laughter that were worrying me."

"Glowing eyes again, eh?" said Alia. She gave him an apologetic smile. "I lose track of things when it gets intense, so I can't remember what happens. Sorry if I scared you. I'll admit it gives me the heebie-jeebies, but that's just how it works." She frowned, as if remembering something. Then she whispered: "You tried to break into the circle, didn't you—?" She leaned closer, squinting a bit as she looked at him. Her eyes widened suddenly. "You *did* break in! Fascinating! And very *very* stupid of you."

"I was worried something had gone wrong," he said. "Sorry."

"Incredible that you managed it at all! But the *problems* it could have caused… For you, mainly. I didn't hurt you, did I? Or predict the day of your death, anything like that?"

"Um, what do you mean?" said Patch.

"You know. A prophecy. A warning. That kind of thing. I was really on form in there, I can tell you."

Patch thought of her prediction of betrayal, unsure what to tell her. "You really don't know what you did?"

"Not a clue. It often gets a bit intense, but that was a doozy."

"So…would giving me a prophecy be bad?"

"They're dangerous things, prophecies," she said. "Never straightforward. Tend to cause endless trouble." He was about to tell her the truth, when she added: "And I'd be absolutely *riddled* with guilt if I had, that's all."

"Ah," said Patch. It struck him that she didn't really need to know. Given that she'd been helping Wren, surely he could save her from her own guilt? "In that case, no. You didn't."

Alia smiled with relief. "Thank goodness for that."

In the centre of the circle, Wren was starting to sit up. Everyone turned to her.

"Hold on," said Alia. "Let her get her bearings."

Barver came to stand beside Patch, and they watched as Wren looked around her, nervous and confused. She scratched her nose, and then she stared at her hand for a good minute or so, bewildered.

Gradually, her wary expression was broken by a smile that grew and grew until, grinning broadly, she leaped to her feet. "Ha!" she cried. She jumped on the spot, then jumped again, laughing. She started to run, and hop, and leap, speeding around the salt circle and the ashes of the previous night's bonfire.

Suddenly her smile fell away. She looked down at herself, and the smile returned. "Phew!" she said. "Fully clothed!" She punched the air. "I was worried about that." She saw Patch and Barver, and her mouth opened in a look of utter delight. She ran to Patch and gave him a hug, then switched to hugging Barver. Then she hugged Alia, and Tobias, before hurtling over to Madder and giving him a hug too, whooping and laughing as she went.

At last, thoroughly exhausted, she returned to where Alia was watching her with amusement.

"Happy?" said Alia.

Wren nodded rapidly. "What a result!" For the first time, she noticed that the beaded bracelet was now on her left wrist. "How does it work, then?"

"When the beads are all blue, concentrate, wish it, and you'll become human for a while. Once invoked, you will remain human until the power in the bracelet runs its course. When that happens, make sure you're somewhere safe, as you'll become a rat again! Then you must wait until the power of the beads has returned before you can be human once more. The time will vary – days, at least. You'll know when it's ready."

Wren nodded, and took a closer look at the bracelet.

"A warning," said Alia. "Do not remove it, or allow it to be removed. The spell would break, and the only flaw in the curse would be closed. You'd be a rat, immediately, and no amount of magic would shield you in future."

"Understood," said Wren.

"See the colour fading on one bead?" said Alia. "Each bead changes to white in turn. When all have changed, you become a rat again. As I said, make sure you're somewhere safe when that happens."

"And will it always hurt so much?" asked Wren.

"Yes," said Alia. "Becoming human and becoming rat, both will hurt."

"Every time?"

"Every time."

Wren let out a deep sigh, and nodded. "Alia, is there any chance I might find a proper cure?"

"This is the best I can do." Alia looked to the ground for a moment, visibly upset that she had failed to do more. "At this point, only one other option remains."

Wren's eyes lit up. "Really? What?"

"Seek Underath," said Alia. "As the one who cursed you, he'll know exactly how the curse was constructed. He might agree to undo it himself."

Wren looked incredulous. "Isn't it just a *teensy* bit unlikely he'd help?"

Alia nodded. "He did seem the unforgiving type, I agree. But I'd suggest flattery. Tell him how *amazingly well-made* the curse was, and how only a *wonderfully clever* Sorcerer could unpick it. You never know, he might say yes. Assuming he doesn't just kill you."

Wren despaired for a moment, but suddenly she smiled again. "Oh, I think he'll be only too willing to help! He'll know he has no choice when he sees what powerful allies I've brought with me! The greatest Piper in the world, and the most fearsome beast you'll ever meet!"

She threw her arms out dramatically and gestured towards Patch and Barver, who instinctively looked behind them to see what Wren was talking about. It took a few seconds before they realized she'd meant *them*.

"Ah," said Patch.

"Um," said Barver.

Wren clapped, grinning. "Glad you're aboard!" she said. "Underath won't know what's hit him!"

24
AXLEBURY

Alia spent the next hour checking Wren for possible problems with the spell that had been cast, using an elaborate range of tests that included burning hairs plucked from Wren's head, and making her balance pine cones on her elbow.

In the meantime, Patch found a blank sheet of paper and a piece of charcoal on one of the tables in Alia's cave, and wrote down the words she had spoken in the circle of salt.

The prophecy.

They thought they had us. But we're almost clear. Just the ridge to go. What's wrong with you? What's wrong?

He stared at the words he'd written. Someone would speak those words, someone who would betray Patch to whatever he feared most, and Patch would have to flee at once. Alia had mentioned how prophecies could cause trouble, and he had to agree – he was already worrying about it.

He began to fold the paper up nervously, as if it was dangerous.

"What do you have there?" came a voice.

Startled, Patch turned to see Barver. "Nothing," he said, putting the paper into his pocket.

Barver nodded to the cave entrance, where Alia was now getting Wren to hop for as long as possible. "Wren's serious, you know," he said, keeping his voice low. "About confronting Underath."

"I don't think that would end well," said Patch. "From what we saw in the fire, didn't you get the feeling his *wife* was the scary one?"

"Perhaps, but if I can speak with Alkeran, his griffin, I may be able to learn our best course of action. There might be something we could offer, in exchange for help. You know, something valuable. And magical…"

Patch stared at him. "You mean the *Mask*?"

"I notice you still haven't mentioned it to Tobias or Alia."

"Of course not!" said Patch. "It's valuable! And essential to my future, since Wren's parents aren't *quite* as rich as she'd suggested, and are actually very, very *poor*. The Mask is the only thing of value I possess."

"So you won't part with it, even to help Wren?"

Patch grumbled to himself for a moment, his teeth firmly clamped together. "Okay, okay. If the Mask will buy Underath's help, then…fine."

Barver patted him on the back. "You have very high principles," he said. "You should be proud."

"Proud and poor," muttered Patch.

As they left Gemspar, Wren rode with Patch, and Alia with Tobias. Patch found himself half-wishing for bandits to attack again, just to see how the Witch of Gemspar Mountain dealt with them. *Spectacularly*, he reckoned, but in the end the journey was uneventful.

When they reached the Abbey, Patch dismounted and led the horse to the gate, with Wren still in the saddle.

Erner Whitlock hurried out to greet them, in his black-and-purple Custodian robes.

Patch was pleased to see his friend, and they gave each other a hearty hug. "Shouldn't you be arresting me?" Patch said quietly. "Before I run away again?"

"Why would I arrest you, Henry Smith?" said Erner with a wink. "How did it go?" Patch smiled and nodded to the rider on the horse, and Erner grinned. "Wren? Is that you?"

Wren jumped down from the horse, and hugged Erner. "It's me! The less ratty version."

"You're cured then?" said Erner.

"Sort of," she said. "It's temporary, but I hope to remedy that soon enough."

Tobias and Alia joined them. "We have the medicine to heal Rundel," said Tobias. "How is he faring?"

"No deterioration," said Erner. "Your healing Song has been doing its job."

"Good, good," said Tobias.

"What are your plans?" Erner said to Patch. "Will you stay a while at the Abbey?"

"When Rundel Stone wakes, I want to be as far away as possible," said Patch. "The sooner we leave, the better."

"Do you know what you're going to do?" said Erner.

"I'm not decided yet," said Patch. "But a new life in the Eastern Seas is an option."

Erner looked anxious. "A dangerous place, my friend."

"He'll be fine," said Barver. "I'll look after him."

"I'm sure you can do that very well," said Erner.

"We have some errands to run first," said Barver. "The letter," he added, looking at Patch – his mother's last wishes.

"And I need to see Underath," said Wren. "The Sorcerer who cursed me. It seems he's now the only one who can fully undo his work, so I have no choice but to face him! I've vowed not to return home until I'm cured, and I intend to keep that vow."

Erner was horrified. "That sounds far too risky, Wren!" he said. "Please reconsider! If only I could go with you, but it's not Custodian business. Even the most *stupid* Sorcerer would think twice before incurring the wrath of the Custodians by attacking someone under their protection."

"If I might suggest something?" said Alia. She gave Erner a quick handshake. "Pleased to meet you. I'm Alia. Magic expert, friend of Tobias, long story." She held up the little jar with the death puzzle inside. "The box which poisoned Rundel has an unusual magical style. I studied Underath's curse and noticed similarities. Not quite the same, so I doubt Underath created the box, but he might have suggestions as to who *did*. It's a starting point if you wish to find the culprit. So if you, as a Custodian Piper—"

"*Apprentice* Custodian," corrected Erner.

"Indeed, but it means that going with them to Underath *would* be on official Custodian business. Just an idea." She smiled, looking rather pleased with herself.

Erner grinned. "And a very *sensible* idea," he said. "It would mean a great deal to me, to be able to help my friends. I'll gather my things and return shortly."

As Erner headed back through the gate, Tobias stepped forward and shook the hands of Patch, Barver and Wren in turn. "Now we must get inside and minister to Rundel," he said. "Good luck with the journeys ahead, all of you!"

Madder bade farewell too, then he and Tobias led the horses into the Abbey grounds.

"I'll follow in a moment," said Alia. She turned to Wren. "You went to Underath to become a Sorcerer. How long have you known that was what you wanted?"

"I think I've always known it," said Wren.

Alia nodded. "Watching you in Underath's castle as you learned the basics of sorcery from his books, I saw your potential clear as day. I could understand if your brush with magic has put you off, but in a year or so it's quite possible that I would consider taking on an apprentice…"

"Really?" said Wren, excited.

"Someone like me," said Alia, wistful. "Eager to study hard. Dedicated and obedient."

Wren's excitement seemed to drain away entirely. "Oh," she said. "I thought you meant me."

Patch put an encouraging hand on her shoulder. "She *does* actually mean you, Wren."

Alia smiled. "Perhaps I should reconsider?"

"No!" said Wren. "I can be all those things. Absolutely!"

Alia nodded. "Well, if you do decide that sorcery is still your future… come and find me."

Once Alia had left, they sat on the grass by the road as they waited for Erner to return. Wren's attention was suddenly diverted as a large beetle struggled through the grass near her feet. "Ooh!" she said, picking it up and biting into the juicy abdomen. "Blaaargh!" she cried, spitting it out. "That's disgusting!"

Patch shrugged. "It's always been disgusting, Wren."

"As a rat those things are delicious," she said. "But as a human..." She spat again, and scrunched up her face. "Yuck! That's going to linger." She gathered herself for yet another spit.

Erner reappeared at the gate. He was leading three horses, and Brother Duffle walked beside him.

"I've commandeered Rundel Stone's horse for the trip," said Erner. "And I borrowed a third from the Abbey. It will speed up our journey." He handed one set of reins to Wren.

"Brother Duffle!" said Barver. "I'm glad you came to bid farewell!"

"You left this item in the pigsties," said Duffle, handing something to Patch.

Barver and Wren saw it and grinned. "Fox and Owls!" they both declared. Patch put it into his bag.

Brother Duffle gave Barver a serious look. "Now," he said, holding up a small glass jar. "An ointment for your shoulders and wing joints. Apply generously as required." He handed the jar to Barver, who placed it in one of his harness packs. "How about trying a few flaps to see how you look?"

"Okay," said Barver. "I'll try." He stepped away to give himself space, and then started to flap his wings – very gently at first, but giving a couple of really strong beats at the end. "Feels good."

"Everything looks fine," said Duffle. "You're almost there. Be careful though! Promise me not to overdo things! And can I say, it's been an absolute honour healing you."

"The honour was mine," said Barver, shaking Brother Duffle's hand. "And I promise to take things slowly."

They arrived in Axlebury three days after setting off from the Abbey. Wren was keen to reach Underath before changing back into a rat, so she could let the Sorcerer know exactly what she thought of him. As such, she'd been eager to push on at every opportunity. It had meant taking only a few hours of sleep each night, and Patch was exhausted by the time they rode into the village.

Axlebury was busy, an early market drawing traders and shoppers in the central square. Barver attracted plenty of interest on their arrival, but his cheery greetings were enough to settle the nerves of the wary villagers.

"That's Fendscouth Tor," said Wren, pointing to a large craggy hill some distance away. "Underath's castle is on the far side." All but one of the beads on her bracelet was entirely white now, and even that last bead had only the barest amount of colour left. "Oh hell's *bells*," she said. "I'm almost out of time."

Barver took a gentle hold of her hand, and looked closely at the bracelet. "You could change at any moment," he said. "I'm afraid we must wait here until it's happened. Underath will have to make do with *our* sharp tongues, instead."

Wren muttered to herself, but Patch caught Barver's eye – they both knew it was better this way, as Wren would accept Barver and Erner taking the lead when they reached Underath's castle.

Barver reached for his money-purse. "That inn over there," he said, squinting to read its sign. "The Old Raven. I'll get rooms for each of you, and a stable stall for me. We should rest for the night, and see the Sorcerer tomorrow. And, right now, it'll be somewhere private for Wren to, um, change." As he spoke, he did some shoulder exercises that Brother Duffle had suggested. His flight muscles were almost back to normal, and once or twice on the journey he'd attempted flying for a few seconds at a time.

Wren nodded. "That'd be welcome, but I think two rooms are enough. I'll have changed back soon, and I won't need a bed. I'd also rather not be alone once it gets dark. I'll probably have nightmares about owls."

With the rooms arranged, Erner took the horses to the stables to tend to them. Wren went up to one of the rooms for privacy, and refused Patch's offer to stay with her, so Patch and Barver ordered some small ale and sat in anxious silence at the front of the inn, sipping their drinks as they worried about her and waited for Erner to come back.

After a while, Barver took something from his harness and looked at it warily.

"Is that your mum's letter?" asked Patch.

Barver gave a big sigh. "Yes. The one I'm to open when I reach my destination."

"You haven't been tempted to open it in advance, then?"

"Of *course* I've been tempted," said Barver. "But I won't. Her instructions were specific. I must go to the place she's described, any time after the Scale Moon, and only read the letter when I get there."

"The Scale Moon?"

"The next full moon marks a special day in the Dragon Calendar, a few days from now. My wings are ready, I think. As long as I can remember the higher air currents at this time of year, I can ride the winds. If I set off soon I'll arrive just as the Scale Moon rises."

"And would you have the strength for a passenger?"

Barver frowned. "I appreciate the offer," he said. "The thought of going alone is—" Patch thought he could see his friend's eyes tearing up a little. "But my mother's instructions are to open the letter in a dangerous place called the Sun Canyon, in the middle of a desolate, harsh desert known as the Dragon Wastes. Nobody lives there. Nobody even *goes* there."

"I still want to come," said Patch. "If you can carry me for the flight?"

Barver shifted his wings a little. "That won't be a problem," he said. "But it's not *you* I'm worried about."

Patch nodded. "Wren," he said. "The last thing she needs is danger. If Underath cures her then she'll be happy for us to take her to her parents, but if not…"

"Then she'll insist on going with us," said Barver. "In which case, I think you must stay here with her. There's enough of my mother's Vanishing Gift left for you to stay at the inn until I return."

"You'd have to sneak off without telling her," said Patch. "And I don't relish the look she'll give me when she realizes what's happened."

Barver laughed. "Wren is courageous, loyal and very stubborn. I can only *begin* to imagine her anger at us for being so protective."

"It's good that she means so much to you," said Patch.

"She does," said Barver. "She reminds me of someone, you see." He shook his head slowly, looking sorrowful. "I was a lonely soul as a child. As the only dracogriff, the other children both feared and mocked me. I had one great friend. My young cousin, Genasha. I'd known her from the

day she hatched. Independent, short tempered and rude!"
He grinned.

"That *does* sound like Wren," said Patch.

"And honest, and loyal, and funny. Yes, Wren reminds
me very much of Genasha." He fell silent for a moment.
"The year before I left for adventure in the Islands of
the Eastern Seas, Genasha died. Her blood thinned. It's a
common enough disease in dragon children, but most
recover. She did not." He closed his eyes. "My mother
behaved very oddly after Genasha's death. She never once
mentioned her name, and if I spoke of my cousin she would
become cold. It seemed as if her heart had turned to *ice*.
It was the breaking point for our relationship. Genasha's
death hit me very hard, but my mother didn't seem to care
at all. That's why I left home, and why I didn't speak to my
mother again."

They finished their ales in silence, and the innkeeper
came to fetch their empty tankards. "Another drink, lads?"
she asked.

From above them came an awful scream, which was
suddenly cut short and replaced by a few seconds of
squeaking. Then there was silence.

The innkeeper looked up to the window of one of the
rooms they'd rented. "That's your friend?" she said, eyes
wide with panic. "We must help!"

Patch's throat was dry, hearing such a horrible noise

coming from Wren. "I can assure you everything is fine," he said. "Our friend has...a severe terror of spiders." It was the best he could come up with on the spot. "She must have seen one."

"Oh!" said the innkeeper. "Fair enough. They do get very big in this old place."

"I hope Wren's okay," said Barver, once the innkeeper had left.

Patch nodded. "I'm thinking two things," he said. "The first is that we shouldn't wait until tomorrow. We need to get to Underath right away and free Wren from this curse, whatever it takes."

"Agreed!" said Barver. "What's the second thing?"

Patch shivered. "That I'll have to get rid of every spider in my room to have any chance of sleep tonight."

Patch left Barver and went up to check on Wren. He knocked gently and entered. Wren was on the bed, curled up. Patch sat next to her and she climbed onto his shoulder, still trembling. He could see markings in the fur running around her midriff, and pointed them out to her: a series of grey circles, one of which was slightly blue. The bracelet was *part* of her in rat form, he realized – when the circles all turned blue, she would be ready to change again. "Is there anything I can do to make you feel better?" he said.

Absolutely, signed Wren. *Let's go and see Underath, right now.*

Patch nodded. "I was thinking exactly the same thing," he said. "First though, I have a little job I need to do here." He took his Pipe out from his pocket. "Let's see how my new Pipe handles these critters!"

Critters? signed Wren.

"You'll see," said Patch. He stood and opened the door, and also the door to the second room they'd rented, across the corridor. He started to play. He built a gentle Dream, but it sounded very different to the one he'd made for the rats in Patterfall. The note lengths, for instance, were far shorter. His target, after all, was much smaller than a rat.

It was the money spiders who appeared first, dozens of the tiny dots coming out of the beams above them and drifting to the floor, where they formed a line. Then the larger ones peeked out, intrigued, perhaps ten or fifteen of them emerging from between floorboards. At last, the real *biggies* came out of hiding from under the bed and behind the few bits of rough furniture in the room. Patch's eyes went wide; Wren stared at them. There were only four, but four was more than enough when they were that size.

Patch changed the Song slightly, and the eager spiders traipsed across the corridor to the other room, where the Song made them think the juiciest of all the world's flies awaited them. Journey completed, Patch closed the other room's door and returned. "When we get back, we'll all spend the night in here, I think," he said.

I'm not good with spiders, signed Wren.

"Me neither," said Patch. "I pity whoever rents that room next."

25

Underath
the Sorcerer

With Wren on Patch's shoulder, they set off to Fendscouth Tor. They'd left the third horse – the one borrowed from the Abbey – back at the inn stables, getting a well-earned rest that Patch was quietly envious of.

The way was steep, through windswept scrubland. As they rounded the Tor, Underath's castle came into view, sitting on the edge of a forest that swept down towards a large lake.

"You two stay here," Erner told Wren and Patch. "This should be safe enough for you, while Barver and I speak to Underath, and see how things are."

Wren grumbled, but conceded that it was for the best.

Barver flexed his wings. "I think I'll try a bit of air time!" he said.

"Be careful, big fella," said Patch. "Are you sure you're ready?"

With a great leap and a huge grin, Barver took off. Patch watched with mixed feelings. It was a delight to see him enjoy himself so much, but being out of practice didn't lend itself to graceful flying. Soon, with a heavy landing, he was back on the ground.

"Feels good!" he said. He reached up and rubbed his shoulder.

Patch got off his horse and sat on a nearby granite outcrop. He was wearing his bag across one shoulder, eager to keep the Hamelyn's Mask close by rather than leave the bag tied to his saddle. Its value was too great – either Barver would manage to strike a bargain with Underath, with Wren's cure in exchange for the Mask, or the Mask would fetch a good price later and give Patch his chance at a new life.

Erner galloped towards the castle. Barver ran beside him, occasionally going airborne for a few seconds. At one point he veered off route and plunged down unnervingly before recovering.

Hmm, signed Wren. *I think I'll let Barver get the hang of flying again before I ask for a ride.*

With a while to wait, Patch reached into his pocket and unfolded the paper he'd written Alia's prophecy on. Wren stared at it.

I remember hearing those words! she signed. *I thought I dreamed it!*

"Alia spoke them in the circle of salt. She couldn't remember much and was worried she'd given me some kind of prophecy. She seemed so anxious about it, I didn't have the heart to tell her that she'd done exactly that. A prophecy that someone would betray us, but that we could recognize them by the words they would speak." He read the words aloud: "*They thought they had us. But we're almost clear. Just the ridge to go. What's wrong with you? What's wrong?*" He shook his head. "'Get away when you hear the words,' Alia said, 'as quickly as you can. *Run!*'"

Wren nodded. *I heard her*, she signed. *Then she spoke in a curious way, right?*

"Indeed," said Patch, thinking back. "Although pretty much *everything* was curious at the time. Her glowing eyes, for a start." *An odd set of words, don't you think?* Alia had said, almost conversing with herself. *I agree, very odd! What say you, Patch? The lad's gone so very pale. The day's been quite a strain, I imagine.*

He shivered at the thought of the fiery red eyes.

The words on the paper seemed to taunt him. He groaned. "I wish she'd not said anything. I'll be listening out for it every day and it could be years before it happens. Decades, even."

So ignore it! signed Wren. *From what little I know,*

prophecy is usually more trouble than it's worth.

"Ignore it?" said Patch. "Easier said than done." He folded the paper up and returned it to his pocket.

After a while, they saw Barver flying back towards them. Below, Erner was galloping on his horse.

Wren frowned. *Are they running away from something?* she signed.

Patch made sure Wren was secure on his shoulder before he mounted his horse, ready to speed off if necessary.

"Wait there!" cried Erner. He pulled up in front of them as Barver landed heavily, out of breath. Erner's concerned expression wasn't encouraging. "You need to see this," he said.

They left the horses grazing outside the main gate of Underath's castle and approached the entrance.

"The doors lay slightly open when we arrived," said Erner. "I called out and got no response, so entered carefully." He pushed the doors wide to reveal an entry hall. It was chaos inside. Every piece of furniture was upended. Glass littered the ground, and the smell of stale wine and ale filled the air. "This is what I found. Everywhere I looked is the same."

Wren stared at the mess in horror. *We have to find Underath*, she signed.

"His griffin is not in the courtyard," said Barver.

"Whatever happened here, it was weeks ago," said Erner. "There's rotting food on a table upstairs. I found his study. All his books were gone. I suspect the Sorcerer has fled."

Barver squeezed through the entrance and looked around. "We should search the whole castle. If Underath has gone, there must be clues as to his whereabouts." He sniffed the air, and moved towards another set of doors, flinging them open. The courtyard lay beyond. He pointed to a stone building within it. "The griffin's stable," he said. "There may be things we can learn about Underath there."

Erner nodded. "Patch, stay with Barver. You two take this half of the courtyard, check the various doors and cellars. I'll take Wren and search the other half."

"Agreed," said Patch. Barver hurried across the courtyard towards the stable. Patch let Wren climb onto Erner's shoulder, then went after Barver, finding him inside the stable hunting through shelves of the griffin's belongings. "You see anything interesting here?"

"Plenty of books," said Barver. "Alkeran was an avid reader. Mostly tales of adventure, but some philosophy too. Wait, look!" He moved to one wall and lifted some kind of large *ring* from the floor.

Patch realized what it was: a locking collar, to which was attached a formidable iron chain. "Did Underath use that for his griffin?"

Barver shook his head. He raised the chain to show that it was short, and not fixed to anything. "Presumably all that remains of a much longer chain," he said. "No, Alkeran was not a prisoner here. Griffins and Sorcerers are a good fit for each other, Patch. Both prefer isolation, and they can provide one another with a degree of safety. Alkeran and Underath are colleagues – perhaps even friends. The rust on this collar suggests it has not been in use for many years, yet Alkeran keeps it in his home. Interesting."

Patch nodded. "I'll start searching in the courtyard. I'll call if I find something." He left the stable and went to a nearby hatchway in the side of the castle. He opened it up, and there was coal inside. He looked to the stable again and saw a chimney, so the coal was presumably for the griffin's fireplace. Across the way, he could see Erner and Wren getting on with their search.

The courtyard had been out of bounds for Wren while she'd been living in the castle, so there was little advice she could offer Erner. They came to a row of doors, and Erner tried the first. It was locked; Erner took out his Pipe and played a rapid high-pitched Song. The lock thudded open.

Wren applauded, impressed. *I've not seen Patch do that kind of thing,* she signed.

"Thanks," said Erner, bowing his head. He opened the

door and a terrible stench of rot came from within. Inside were barrels, from which liquid was seeping. He closed the door in a hurry.

These must be the food stores, said Wren. *Underath magically restocked the kitchen from them, and the stores were charmed to be cold. Not any more.*

Erner frowned and went to the next door. Again, it was locked; again, Erner played to unlock it. He opened the door and entered.

A yelp came from one corner, and Erner stepped to the side instinctively as something shot from the shadows and thudded into the door frame, a puff of some kind of powder coming from it when it hit. Wren looked to where the object had fallen – it was a small leather pouch. She looked over to the corner, and there, wearing his favoured elaborate robe, stood Underath, terrified. He carried a bag filled with bread. Wren clenched her paws into little angry fists at the sight of him. She noticed how scruffy he seemed, his face and robes grubby, the hair on his head uncombed. He had always prided himself on his clean-shaven face, but now a ragged beard had grown.

Underath was distraught. "A Custodian Piper! Forgive me, I thought you were a brigand come to murder me! You caught me by surprise!" At that moment, he noticed Wren on Erner's shoulder. His face fell. "Oh dear," he said. "It's you, um, maid-person."

Wren scowled the deepest scowl she'd ever managed.

"Her name is *Wren*," said Erner. "I assume you are Underath?"

The Sorcerer nodded.

Erner glanced down to the pouch that Underath had thrown. He gave the Sorcerer an angry glare. "A Kaposher Pouch, eh?" said Erner. "If you're going to use that, you can't afford to miss!"

Wren had read about Kaposher Dust in one of the many books she'd pored over in Underath's study. It was a sleeping powder, difficult to make and highly prized by thieves – throw a Kaposher Pouch at an unwary victim, and they would be rendered unconscious in moments by the dust that puffed out.

"I am Erner Whitlock," said Erner. "I represent the Pipers' Council in an important matter." He rummaged in his shoulder bag, then held up the jar containing the little box that had poisoned Rundel Stone. "We shall discuss Wren's situation in a moment. First, tell me everything you can about this."

Underath took it, wary. As he examined it through the glass, Erner reached into his bag and produced a cloth; keeping one eye on Underath, he gathered up the Kaposher Pouch in the cloth and placed it carefully in his bag. "In case you get any *ideas*," he said.

Underath waved dismissively. "I have others." He

removed the lid of the jar and sniffed. After a moment, his eyes widened. "Oh no, this is a very nasty little thing. A death puzzle. Quite a complicated one."

"And did *you* make it?" said Erner.

"Absolutely not!" said Underath, sounding offended. He replaced the jar's lid and passed it back. "I don't make such weaponry. It's clumsy and brutal."

"I'm assured your style of magic is very similar," said Erner. "And remember, Sorcerer. I am here on Council business. I could make life difficult for you if you don't help."

"Make life difficult for me?" said Underath, with a sneer. "As if it's not hard enough already!" He glared at Erner, but soon bowed his head. "Very well. Look to the far north. Near Ygginbrucket, where a Master once lived. I was his pupil, and this *death puzzle* has his hallmarks. Hence the similarity to my magical style."

"The Master's name?"

"Sagharros. Died fifteen years ago. This box is of recent construction, so it definitely wasn't him. It may have been made by another of his students."

"And you're sure the box has nothing to do with you?"

"I swear it!"

"Mmm…" said Erner, stroking his chin. "Perhaps I will trust you more, once you undo the cruel curse you set on my friend here."

Underath looked back at them, pale. "I can't, I'm afraid," he said. "I'm somewhat indisposed. I have no magic to spare."

"We saw the state of your castle," said Erner. "What happened here?"

Underath scowled. "My *wife* happened," he said, venom in his voice. "She's long gone now. She took my griffin and left!" He looked at Wren. "Did you notice anything odd about her? For example, did I mention her name at any point?"

Wren thought for a moment. She shook her head.

"There's a reason for that," said Underath. "I don't *know* her name. Isn't that strange? I know *nothing* about her. I don't think I ever did. There I was, off on a trip somewhere, and the next thing I know I'm married, and *happy*, and not thinking straight, with no memory of how it happened."

Erner raised an eyebrow. "Did you drink much wine on this trip of yours, by any chance?"

Underath looked at him with scorn. "If only it was so simple! That woman hexed me! I still don't know how she did it, but she got the better of Underath. *She stole my heart.*" He sagged, shaking his head in misery.

"Pull yourself together!" said Erner. "So you lost out in love! You must still make amends to Wren!"

"That's *not* what I mean," said Underath. He reached

to his robe and unbuttoned it at the front. "She *stole* my *heart*," he said. He pulled his robe apart and exposed his chest. "Literally."

Erner and Wren gasped. In the middle of Underath's chest was a big hole, charred around the edges. "Nasty!" said Erner. The hole wasn't empty, though. "Is that…is that a *shoe*?"

"Yes," said Underath, seething. "She took my heart and thought me dead, but I had a little life left in me, and magic enough to keep death at bay. The shoe was a hasty replacement. All I had handy, really." He looked down bitterly at the hole in his chest, with its oddly pulsating shoe. "It takes every scrap of magic I have merely to keep going day by day. Slowly, the wound will close and the shoe will transform into a new heart, but it will take a year, perhaps longer."

"So you're refusing to undo Wren's curse?" said Erner.

"Look at me," said Underath. "I'm a wretch. I haven't the power to craft the undoing of a curse. Especially such a *fine* curse." He moved towards them, and reached out to Wren. She squeaked, and gnashed her teeth at him. "The circle around your waist… I see someone's had a go at fixing you already. Some kind of morphic deflector, I'm guessing. Interesting work, but not really a long-term solution." He looked up, a sly smile on his face. "There is one way I could help, however. For a price."

296

"What price did you have in mind?" said Erner, wary.

"My griffin," said Underath. "Get me my griffin back."

"If your griffin was happy to leave with your wife, then it's not for me to interfere."

"Happy?" said Underath. "*Happy?* Alkeran was her target all along. She told me as I lay there with my life's blood draining away. 'It was your griffin I wanted, Underath, not you!' For what purpose she wanted him I do not know, but that's why she took my heart – there is an old, dark spell to give control over a griffin. A spell that requires the heart of a friend, kept in a box and tied around Alkeran's neck…" There was a look of genuine loss in Underath's expression, a look that Wren had never seen or expected to see on the Sorcerer's face. In all her time in this castle, she'd never known that Alkeran was anything more to the man than just a handy means of transport. "He's a troubled soul," said Underath. "Nightmares plague him, of a time long ago when he was held captive. He's never told me more than that, but it's easy to see his pain, and his fear. I promised to keep him safe and I've failed him. So remove my heart from around his neck and free him. Bring my heart to me, and I can quickly regain my powers, but you must bring my *griffin* back too if you want me to create a cure."

Erner looked to Wren. "Can we trust him?" he said.

Does it matter? she signed, disheartened. *He obviously hasn't the strength to cure me, and we're not going to be able to bring back his griffin. I'm doomed!*

"Nonsense," Erner told her. He turned to Underath. "Do you have any idea where your wife may have gone?"

Underath frowned. "None, I'm afraid," he said. "Now if you don't mind, I'd like to gather some food and get back into hiding."

"Hiding?" said Erner. "Hiding from what?"

"From the mercenaries, of course!"

Erner's face fell. "What mercenaries?"

"Nastiest bunch of hired soldiers I've ever laid eyes on," said Underath. "My wife had some kind of deal with them. Gave them the castle when she left. They've made a terrible mess of the place. Didn't you notice them?"

Erner and Wren stared at him.

Patch searched a room storing equipment for horses – saddles, martingales, bridles. It looked as though no one had been in there for decades. He came out and walked over to the largest of the doors on this side of the courtyard, and as he reached out to open it something ripped through the air. It pierced the sleeve of his shirt and the strap of his shouldered bag, pinning him to the door.

A crossbow bolt. He stared at it, gobsmacked.

"Aw, look at that," came a voice from behind him. "See, your aim's way off!"

Patch turned his head as he desperately pulled his arm, and saw a mean-looking pair of men clad in well-worn leather armour. One of them smiled, showing off a mouthful of broken teeth. "We'll be with you in a jiffy, mate," he said to Patch, leering. He turned to his colleague. "Come on, get that reloaded."

"I'm harmless!" said Patch. "Just looking for Underath, that's all!"

"The old Sorcerer? He's dead, mate. Like you'll be in a second. This is our castle now. You're trespassing!"

Patch yelped and pulled as hard as he could, but he couldn't free himself.

"I can't get the bolt in," complained the man with the crossbow. "Why do they make these things so hard to reload?"

His colleague scowled. "You need to pull that lever back more." There was an audible clunk as the mechanism fell into place. "There you go!"

"Ta!" said the mercenary. He turned to Patch, who was still frantically trying to get free. "Right then, just you hold still while I murder you."

Patch whimpered and closed his eyes. A moment later the unmistakable sound of roaring flame filled the air, accompanied by hearty screams. When Patch looked again he saw two smouldering corpses on the ground. Behind them, Barver was grinning.

"That was a bit brutal, wasn't it?" said Patch.

Barver shrugged. "They caught me in a bad mood," he said.

"Don't worry, Wren," said Erner. "Patch will be safe. He's with Barver." He turned back to Underath. "We didn't come across anyone in the castle. How many mercenaries are there?"

"A hundred, maybe. They have dogs with them."

"Dogs?"

"You know," said Underath. "The big ones mercenaries love so much. War dogs."

"War dogs," said Erner, looking anxious.

Is that a problem? signed Wren.

Erner looked to the door. "We have to warn them."

At that moment, they heard a roar of fire, and screams. Erner ran out into the courtyard, Wren clinging tightly to his shoulder. Behind him, Underath hurried to the door and locked it, his muffled voice coming through the thick wood. "Good luck with that!" he said.

✦   ✦   ✦

Barver came over to Patch and pulled the crossbow bolt out, freeing him.

"Thanks," said Patch. "That was a close one!"

The door the bolt had lodged in now started to swing open very slowly. The smile on Patch's face crumpled as he saw what lay in the large room beyond.

A long table, filled with bottles of ale and rounds of cheese, surrounded by benches on which dozens and dozens of unconscious mercenaries were slumped.

One of them snorted and opened his eyes. "Wha—?" he said. He looked at Patch. He looked at Barver. Then he looked at the smouldering corpses of his colleagues. "Awaken, lads!" he yelled. "There's trouble!"

Patch backed away as the mercenaries began to stir. He reached for his Pipe. He could try some battle Songs and take out a few of them, he knew.

"Oh don't worry," said Barver. "I can handle this lot!"

Then the growling started.

From the shadows within the room, two vast dogs emerged, almost as tall as the men around them. Their grey skin looked as tough as leather and much of it was without fur, giving them the appearance of being riddled with mange. Saliva was starting to drip from the mouths of both dogs. Their teeth were horribly long.

Barver was staring fearfully at them. As Patch watched

the massive dogs approach he knew the odds were firmly in the mercenaries' favour.

War dogs hadn't actually been bred for war, originally. It had been for *hunting*, and the prey they'd been bred to hunt gave them their other name.

"*Dragonhounds*," said Patch. He heard a shout and turned to see Erner running across the courtyard.

"Time to fly," said Barver. "Quit fiddling with that Pipe and get on my back! I'll grab Erner and Wren on the wing."

"Are you sure you can carry us all?"

Barver frowned. "We're just about to find out," he said.

Patch jumped on and held tight to the straps of Barver's battle harness. Barver launched himself into the air, straining hard to get speed. Ahead of them, Erner braced himself, arms raised. Barver grabbed him around the midriff and gained height immediately, setting Erner on his back.

"Where's Wren?" cried Patch, and then he saw her head poking out from Erner's robe. He took her and set her by Barver's neck, where a notch in the harness would give her some protection. She put her arms round a strap and held tight.

The dragonhounds prowled in the courtyard, and the mercenaries readied their bows. A bolt shot past them, and Barver attempted to get higher. Up they went, until they could get over the castle wall to the forest beyond, but below them the mercenaries opened another gate and allowed the hounds out.

"Tenacious, aren't they?" said Erner.

"We, um, killed two of their colleagues," said Patch. "I guess it annoyed them."

"Ah," said Erner. "I suppose it would."

"Where should I head for?" panted Barver.

Wren started to sign frantically, and Patch relayed the message. "See the lake in the forest?" he said, pointing. "If we fly over it, a large gorge lies on the other side of a ridge. They won't be able to cross it."

Soon they were flying just over the treetops, but the hounds were closing fast. If the dogs got ahead, it would only take them two leaps up a tree and Barver would be within reach.

"Go higher, Barver!" yelled Patch.

"I'm trying!" yelled Barver.

Erner took out his Pipe and tied his bag to Barver's harness. "Patch, we should ready some defences! If the hounds jump for us, a Push Song should be enough to deflect them! Hook your feet under the harness like this."

Patch nodded and watched Erner slide each foot under parts of Barver's harness straps. He tied his own bag to Barver and did the same as Erner with his feet. It was uncomfortable, but it gave him both hands free to Pipe. He set about building a Push Song, a simple defensive force that was the first battle Song any Piper learned.

Barver roared and picked up the pace, his great wings straining. On his back, everyone was watching as the hounds narrowed the gap, those frothing jaws even more horrible from such a short distance, the snarls terrifyingly near.

Then they were over water. Barver roared again, this time in triumph. Wren cheered and Patch laughed with relief. The hounds barked with rage for a moment before pounding along the side of the lake, but by now they were so far back Barver could just keep his current speed.

At the far end of the lake the forest rose sharply. "That must be the ridge," cried Erner. "Safety lies on the other side!"

"You hear that, Barver?" said Patch. "Head over that ridge, and you've saved us all!" He looked back and grinned at Erner. They both put their Pipes back in their pockets and unhooked their feet, holding on with their hands again.

"They thought they had us," said Erner. "But we're almost clear! Just the ridge to go!"

Patch froze, his blood turning to ice as Erner's words sank in. The words of the prophecy.

They thought they had us. But we're almost clear. Just the ridge to go. What's wrong with you? What's wrong?

He looked to Wren. She had one paw over her mouth, horrified. She shook her head slowly, back and forth.

Patch could hear Alia's warning: *There will come a time when you hear these words! A mouth that speaks them is a traitorous mouth, and will betray you to that which you fear most! When you hear them spoken, get away as quickly as you can! Run!*

It can't be, thought Patch. *It can't be.*

A moment of hope came to him: Erner hadn't said *all* of it, not yet.

"What's wrong with you?" said Erner, baffled.

Patch shook his head, not wanting his friend to say anything else; not wanting him to complete the prediction.

"What's *wrong*?" said Erner.

It was done. The traitor Alia had warned them of was Erner, however much Patch wanted to deny it. A terrible emptiness filled his heart as he realized what he had to do. Erner was watching him with utter confusion.

"I can't do it," said Patch, his vision blurred with sudden tears. "I *can't*." But he had no choice. "I'm sorry," he said, desolate. He gave Erner a sudden shove, sending his friend flying off Barver's back and into the lake below.

26

STILL NOT
QUITE DEAD

Barver started to circle back. "What happened?" he yelled.

"Keep going!" shouted Patch.

"We can't go without him!" said Barver.

"*Leave him!*"

Barver turned his head to look directly at Patch, and he saw that Patch meant it, even if he didn't understand. He faced front and, jaws clenched, turned towards the far shore of the lake and the ridge beyond it, flying harder than he'd ever done before.

Patch looked at Wren, clinging to Barver's harness. She was glaring at him, eyes wet, shaking her head and trembling, but there was nothing he could say to her. He glanced back and saw Erner swimming towards the lake shore.

There was movement just inside the trees. The dragonhounds had made up most of the ground they'd lost.

"They're closing on us," said Patch.

"I know!" cried Barver.

"You need to go higher!"

"I *know!*"

It would be tight. If they were going to beat the hounds to the ridge, it wasn't going to be by much.

"I can't get the height," wailed Barver.

"You can do it!" said Patch.

Wren squeaked at him. *Your Pipe!* she signed. *Get ready to hit those dogs with something!*

Patch took out his Pipe and hooked his feet under Barver's straps again. He started to build another Push.

They reached the shore. The hounds were heading for the peak of the ridge. Barver was almost screaming now, putting all his might into squeezing out that last drop of height and speed. Wren and Patch watched the hounds.

The ridge: closer, closer.

The hounds: gaining, gaining.

The Push was ready. Patch held it, seeing the hounds get slightly ahead, watching them bound up the elm trees in front of them, and then...

Barver saw them leap, and swung right. One dragonhound had managed to jump higher than the other, and it was almost on top of Patch when he loosed the Push.

The Song hit the beast hard enough to stall its trajectory, and it fell just under Barver, howling as it flailed with its claws and plummeted out of harm's way.

Breathless, Patch turned to see what had happened to the second hound. His heart sank – it had found purchase. Its jaws were clamped around Barver's neck, and it was shaking its head violently to work its teeth under the scales. Its back legs were fending off Barver's arms, stopping him wrenching the hound away. Blood was already flowing. Barver roared with pain, but he was managing to stay in the air.

The trees vanished under them. Suddenly they were past the ridge and over a deep gorge. Patch raised his Pipe again, but he wasn't sure what he could use without risking Barver too. He decided to try something more direct: beside him, tied safely to Barver's harness, was his bag. He undid the fastening strap and took out his knife, putting his Pipe inside before fastening it again.

"Hold on tight," he told Wren. He unhooked his feet from Barver's straps and lunged past her, gripping Barver's harness as he swung the knife at full stretch, thrusting it deep into the dragonhound's paw. The blade went through until it scraped Barver's scales.

The dragonhound yelped. Livid, it pulled its jaws from Barver's throat and snapped towards Patch, snarling with rage, gobbets of bloody froth flying from its slavering mouth.

It was the respite Barver needed. He pulled higher just in time and they reached the other side of the gorge, skimming the treetops. As Barver gained a little more height, the hound clamped its jaws around his throat again and they veered suddenly to one side.

Patch's grip wasn't quite enough. He slipped forward and the hound swiped at him with its injured paw. The claws caught on Patch's shoulder and yanked hard.

Patch fell. Above, he saw that the dragonhound still had its grip on Barver's throat. Wren, barely managing to cling on, stared forlornly after him, just as they had watched Erner plunge barely a minute before.

He braced himself, but the first branch he hit took all the wind from him and knocked the knife from his hand. He knew there would be plenty of other painful branches before he reached the ground.

Patch stood as quickly as his shaky legs and rattled head would allow. He was in agony from head to toe, but nothing seemed broken; without the branches to slow his fall, he would certainly have fared much worse.

Although he'd been preoccupied with plummeting, he was certain he'd heard a crash nearby. He reckoned the battle in the air had lasted only a few more seconds after he'd left it.

Ahead, the tops of the trees had been broken here and there. He feared terribly for Wren and Barver. There was no noise, not even birdsong. Aware of every breath, every step, every crunch of leaf and snap of stick underfoot, he started to walk.

The treetops showed more and more signs of damage as he went. Then, there it was: a massive oak, once tall and proud, had been ripped apart by a great impact. The top third of the trunk had fallen to the ground, and the next third had been shattered. At the base, covered in broken branches and blood, was the still figure of Barver.

Patch remembered the first time he and Wren had met their friend, and how they'd assumed the dracogriff was dead, but this was different. The wounds on his neck glistened with fresh blood, and his head was twisted at an angle that filled Patch with dismay.

Yet the greatest fear of all struck him when he noticed one other detail.

The dragonhound was nowhere to be seen.

Suddenly Patch realized that his own breathing sounded horribly *loud*. He held his breath and listened; the only thing he could make out was his heartbeat. Something small hit him on the head. He looked up and saw nothing, but another object came out of nowhere and got him square on the nose. This time he saw it hit the ground: an acorn.

"Wren?" he whispered, squinting to see if there was any

sign of movement above him. He raised his voice a little. "*Wren?*"

He heard a distinct squeaking from above and peered harder, shading his eyes from the sun that was coming through the leaves. Nothing there…nothing *there*…

There! He could just about see Wren on a high branch, waving frantically.

"It's all right, I see you!" he said. His reassurance did nothing to calm her down. "I'm okay! A little bruised and battered, but—" He stopped, sensing something. Wren's squeaking grew even more urgent, and he realized that what he'd taken as *waving* was actually *pointing*.

A little whimper came from his throat when he heard the sound of the dragonhound's harsh panting behind him. He turned his head to see.

It was ten feet away, its muzzle soaked in Barver's blood. There was red on its flanks from open cuts. He turned fully to face the massive beast, its head higher than Patch's own. A vicious growl started up in the creature's throat as it edged closer to him.

He felt oddly *calm* as he watched slobber drip from the jowls of the massive dog. Its eyes narrowed, and the growl became even more sinister. The animal was preparing to devour him. The calmness he felt was the expectation of death.

He hardly noticed the high-pitched squeal from above,

even as the squeal grew louder and louder, nearer and nearer...

As one, Patch and the hound looked up to see a small shadow falling from the sky. Wren flopped onto the confused dragonhound's head and clamped her teeth deep into the fleshiest part of its ear.

The hound let loose a terrible yowl and shook its head this way and that with greater and greater violence, trying to dislodge the insolent rat. Wren's grip was firm, however, all four little claws clinging to the beast's sparse fur, her mouth dripping with the hound's blood just as the hound's had dripped with Barver's.

Back and forth the hound swung its head, yelping and angry, gnashing at the air. Patch backed away and watched in awe. The hound moved closer to the nearest tree and swung its head hard at the trunk, trying to catch Wren in the middle, but Wren was too quick, jumping to the other side of the head just in time. Without her tooth-hold on the ear, though, she was struggling to keep hold of the animal's fur.

The hound sensed she was in trouble and quickly spun for another attempt at crushing her against the tree. With a howl it smashed its head at the trunk once more.

Patch closed his eyes, unable to look, but when he opened them again he couldn't understand what he was seeing. The hound was motionless, its head pressed against the tree trunk, while Wren was on the back of its neck jumping up and down with her arms in the air.

Celebrating.

Then he saw: jutting from the beast's neck was the sharp end of a broken branch, still attached to the trunk. Blood started to gush from the wound. The hound gasped, and its legs buckled, but it remained skewered to the tree. A final sigh came from the dragonhound as it died. Wren took a well-deserved bow, and Patch applauded the monster-killer rat. *Nobody messes with Wren!* she signed, before her triumphant expression turned to concern. *Patch, you're bleeding!*

"I'm fine," he said, but the encounter with the hound had made him forget the all-over pain he'd been feeling after the fall. His shoulder was the worst. Wren was right, he saw – there was blood seeping through his shirt. He put his hand to his shoulder blade and felt where the dragonhound's claw had caught him. He pulled his hand back and saw the bright scarlet that covered it.

He wasn't good with blood at the best of times, but when it was his *own*, he was absolutely useless. "Oh," he said, and fell away in a dead faint.

Patch came round with Wren on his chest, squeaking at him.

Get up, she signed. *We need to check on the big guy.*

As he sat upright, she climbed up to his uninjured shoulder. He stood and started walking towards Barver's motionless form, and each step felt like the ringing of a death knell. He could see the fear on Wren's face, too.

Please let him be okay, she signed. Patch didn't even attempt to reassure her. Things were bleak, and he didn't think there was any chance at all that...

Barver sat up with a start and raised his arms defensively. "Yaar!" he yelled, his eyes still half-closed. "Where are you, foul creature?"

Wren squeaked with relief.

"Hello there!" shouted Patch. "We thought you were a certain goner this time!"

Barver blinked. "Where is it?" he said. His eyes settled on the dragonhound's corpse. He flinched, then realized that the beast was dead. "Wow. How did that happen?"

"Wren killed it," said Patch.

A slow grin spread across Barver's face. He looked at Wren, and she told him the story of the dragonhound's death. *All hounds shall tremble when they hear me squeak!* she signed.

Barver let out a delighted laugh. "I'll make a legend out of you, Wren!" he said. He stretched, turning his head from side to side; a great crack came from his neck joints, making both Patch and Wren wince. The blood on Barver's neck looked appalling.

"Hold on, Barver," cried Patch. "You should lie still for a while yet. You're badly injured!"

"What, this?" said Barver, gesturing to the wounds. "This is nothing. Looks much worse than it is, believe me." He turned to the massive tree he'd collided with, and whistled. "Now *that's* impressive! Luckily my head took the full force of the impact."

There was no answer to that.

315

27

THE DRAGON WASTES

It seemed somehow wrong to Patch. There he sat, while Barver – covered in a ridiculous amount of his own blood – treated the gouge on Patch's shoulder, using the ointment Brother Duffle had given him.

"I can't believe that jar survived," said Patch, as Barver packed the ointment away again.

Barver smiled. "I'm very careful." Patch couldn't help but look at the smashed oak beside them. Barver ran his hands over his own blood-soaked neck and winced.

"How is it?" said Patch.

"It smarts a little," said Barver. "But I heal quickly. My wings and shoulders have always been the exception. If the hound had gone for those instead of my throat, it would have been a very different result." He stretched out his wings and gave them an experimental flap. "They seem fine," he said. His expression grew serious. Patch could see something in his eyes – a question that he'd known was coming. "I think it's time you told me," said Barver, grim. "What happened with Erner?"

With a heavy heart, Patch explained about Alia's prophecy. Wren sat next to him, gloomy and silent.

"A tragic thing," said Barver when Patch finished. "I always thought I had a good sense of people. On our journey from the Abbey I had no such inklings about Erner. Still, you two knew him far better than I did. Could the prophecy have been wrong?"

It was very specific, signed Wren. *Every word he spoke was as Alia predicted.*

"And his betrayal, Patch?" said Barver. "What could that have been? Would he have sent you back to the dungeons, did you think?"

"I didn't have *time* to think," said Patch. "In my mind I could just hear Alia's instruction to get away as fast as possible. Now that it's done, I don't know if it was the right thing." He hung his head. "It certainly doesn't *feel* like it." In his mind, he could see Erner swimming to the shore, and wondered if his Pipe had been lost as he fell. If so, he'd surely been captured by the mercenaries; what fate lay ahead for him?

"We must move on," said Barver. "We can fret about

317

such things later, but first we must decide on our plans. What are we going to do now?"

Wren explained everything that had happened when she and Erner had seen Underath.

"Then our course is clear," said Barver. "I pledge myself to bring Underath's griffin home. And you, Patch? Will you join me?"

"Of course," said Patch.

I'm grateful, signed Wren. *But not until you've completed your mother's last request, Barver. I know how heavily that weighs on you. And then we must rest, for several days at least, before we set off to find the griffin.*

"It might be longer than a few days," said Patch. "We'll need time to prepare. And more money." He reached into his bag – still tied to Barver's harness – and took out the Mask. "Should we head to the Islands, Barver? We'll arrange to sell this as soon as possible."

"And so a plan emerges," said Barver. "To the Dragon Wastes for my mother's last wish, and then on to the Islands of the Eastern Seas. Sell the Mask, cure Wren, and have adventures along the way!"

"Some *safer* adventures would be appreciated," said Patch.

Barver grinned. "Understood! I'm sure we can manage that."

Wren suddenly scampered up to Barver's neck and gave him a hug.

Thank you! she signed. *I thought you two were going to take me to my parents and make me stay behind!*

"Leave you behind?" said Barver. "Unthinkable!"

Patch nodded, putting the Mask back in his bag, and as he did he noted Erner's bag was still tied beside it. He could hardly even *look* at it. They had left Erner behind, and the thought made him feel sick. Never again.

"We stay together," he said, "whatever happens."

The flight to the Dragon Wastes was a revelation. Without the need to race ahead of certain death, Barver could take his time, making use of rising heat and wind coming off hills to maintain his height. The speeds they reached seemed impossible to Patch, travelling in a single day what might have taken months on foot. By nightfall they had landed at the coast, overlooking the sea from a high cliff.

The sea crossing would be the most dangerous part of the journey, a hundred miles without a place to land. With the sun setting behind them, the darkening waters ahead looked ominous.

They camped, and foraged some berries before the last of the light had gone.

Patch and Wren were anxious as they set off over the sea the next morning, but the weather stayed calm and the air was warm. For hours they soared, and at last the land came into sight. Vast cliffs rose out of the water, the rock a mixture of oranges and reds.

"The Dragon Wastes!" announced Barver. "Rock and desert, a bleak wilderness. We fly on until we see the Hands of the Gods. There, we'll stop and locate the Sun Canyon." He was in his element, relishing the updraughts as he glided effortlessly above the dramatic and barren terrain. Soon, shapes rose on the horizon: features that dwarfed everything else in the landscape.

The Hands of the Gods.

Patch was awestruck. It was a formation of rock stacks, but even at this distance it was clear that they were immense. There were six wide stacks; on each, a further five stacks climbed high and ended in what seemed to be impossible curls and points.

Six hands, each with five fingers that ended in a *claw*.

"Impressive, aren't they?" cried Barver over the noise of the wind. "Tradition holds that the gods were once defeated by the great Lords of the Night Kingdoms, who turned them to stone. They reached to the sky as they died. They came back from the dead, of course, and had their vengeance. My mother taught me that the stones are a natural formation, worn down by ancient seas, but looking at them in person I can understand believing the old tale. We land on the highest claw!"

"Uh...on *top* of it?" said Patch, terrified; it seemed such a delicately balanced thing, but as they flew nearer he could see that there was no need for fear. The tip of the claw was at least a hundred feet across, and had stood solid for untold centuries.

Barver roared in glee as he touched down on the rock. "Feel free to dismount," he said, but he said it playfully.

No chance, signed Wren.

Patch was in complete agreement. Solid as the rock was, the sheer height was terrifying and the wind gusted hard. In the circumstances, the edge of the claw could never really be far enough away for his liking. "I think we'll stay on your back," he said. "If you don't mind."

Barver smiled. "Not at all." He broke out some of his rations and offered them around, little flecks of dried meat that had a strong fishy odour. Patch and Wren were reluctant at first, but it tasted rather like mackerel. They drank from their waterskins, and it was several minutes before Barver spoke again. "The Sun Canyon should be visible from here. It's almost as impressive in size as the Hands, but it's still very far away."

Wren was already squinting into the distance. *What does it look like?* she signed.

"It's a huge circle," said Barver. "With additional smaller canyons feeding into it like the rays of the sun." He strained to see, and at last pointed. "I have it! Are you both secure?"

Wren and Patch made sure of their grips. "We're good," said Patch. Barver ran to the edge of the great claw and leaped.

They landed where the instructions from Barver's mother indicated: at the northernmost point within the Sun Canyon.

Patch climbed down onto the brutal heat of the sandy ground, and Wren got onto his shoulder. "So what next?"

"My mother's instructions say that there is a triangular rock. We dig under the rock until we find something, and then I am to read the sealed letter." They glanced around, and Barver's eyes settled on a chunk of stone five feet high, a rough triangle. "You two had better get back," he said, as he leaned down and took the strain. With a roar of effort he flipped the stone over. He reached to his side pack and untied a short-handled shovel, offering it to Patch.

"Me?" said Patch.

"I…I don't know what's there," said Barver. "I could damage it."

Patch and Wren shared a look, but they said nothing. They were both thinking the same thing, though – Barver was wary of what he might find. Patch took the shovel and made a start, Wren standing nearby in the shade of a rock.

It wasn't easy work, as the sides of the hole kept collapsing. Once he was down three feet or so, the hole kept its shape. Patch stepped down into it and got on with the digging, as the pile of excavated sandy earth grew behind him.

Four feet down. Five.

Then he saw something.

He lifted out a tiny black pebble and held it up to the light, his eyes wide. "Volcanic glass," he said, looking at it in awe. "It could even be *obsidiac*. Black diamond." He set it on the side of the hole and continued to dig. "We could sell that, too."

"We'll do no such thing," said Barver. "Be very careful with it! We must return it to the soil when we've finished."

Wren scoffed. *You shouldn't be so superstitious,* she signed.

"I can't help it, Wren," he replied. "From an early age, they drill into dragon children that taking black diamond is a terrible crime."

Patch dug a little more. "Oh, hang on, I've got something else." It took him a few moments to free his new find from the dirt, then he lifted it up. It was a large shiny black chunk as big as his hand, very like the pebble he'd found before. "There's our answer," he said. "It can't be obsidiac. As far as I know, the biggest piece ever found was about the size of a chicken egg. This *must* be plain old volcanic glass, nothing more."

Barver stared anxiously at the black lump. "Is there a way to be certain?"

"Perhaps," said Patch. "They say it can make a Pipe sing by itself, but that could just be a myth. Give me my Pipe from my bag, would you?" Barver reached into Patch's bag and pulled out the Pipe, tossing it over. Patch brought the lump closer and closer to his Pipe until they were less than an inch apart. He shook his head. "See?" he said. "Nothing." But then he caught a slight whisper. He let them *touch*.

A sudden explosion of noise came from the instrument, deafening him – he dropped his Pipe and tossed the lump to the side, but the Pipe played on, intricate layers that he recognized from the Songs he'd already played on it.

The sounds faded. He looked up at Barver and Wren. "I, um, think that was a definite reaction," he said.

Barver was horrified. "My mother has led us to a stash of black diamond?" he said. "What was she thinking?"

"Well," said Patch, continuing to dig. "There's one way to find out. Read the—"

Suddenly he yelped and scrambled out of the hole. Wren held her hands to her mouth in shock.

"What is it?" said Barver.

"Nothing," said Patch. "A…an insect startled me. Read the letter."

"An insect?" said Barver. He started to walk towards the pit.

"No!" yelled Patch, moving towards him to intercept. "*Read the letter.*"

Barver frowned. He was reluctant but stayed where he was. He opened the letter from his mother and read aloud.

My Dearest Barver,

This is the hardest letter I have ever had to write. I love you, my son, and yet I drove you away. I drove you away to save you.

I owe you an explanation. Where else to begin, but with the Hamelyn Piper? That evil man rots in the dungeons of Tiviscan Castle, yet for me that wasn't enough. My need to understand his crimes became an obsession.

The question gnawed at my soul: why would anyone kidnap children, human and dragon, never to be seen again? There was never an answer that made sense to me.

And then, the year before you left, I discovered something. I may yet be proved wrong, but if I am right then there is one simple fact that outweighs all else:

I finally have the answer I sought. I know why the Hamelyn Piper did what he did.

Barver stopped and looked up from the letter, his eyes wet. "What have you seen?" he asked. "What's in the pit?" Patch said nothing.

Go on, signed Wren. *Read it all.*

Barver looked back to the letter and continued:

One year after the Hamelyn Piper was captured, a novice scholar arrived at our home and asked that I follow him. I left you sleeping, my son, and did as the novice asked, for there was something in his eyes that told me that it was important, and that questions would have to wait.

He brought me to a cave outside the city, and within the cave was an old dragon, eyes clouded by sheer age. The old dragon sent his novice outside to wait.

"You are Lykeffa Knopferkerkle," the old dragon said to me. "An advisor to the Dragon Triumvirate."

"I am."

"You saved us from launching a war against the humans, after the Hamelyn Piper. You worked with Lord Drevis of the Eight, and secured peace."

"I did. Who are you?"

"My name doesn't matter. I am a scholar, and I had to meet you in secret to tell you something. It is a burden I would pass to you, for I can do nothing more about it. You are familiar with the Order of the Skull?"

"A little," I answered.

Barver stopped again. "The Order of the Skull," he said.

"The religious sect of dragons who deal with the burial of the dead."

"Yes," said Patch. "There are no graves in dragon culture, are there? The bodies are taken away and buried in secret."

Barver nodded and continued to read.

"The Order is based around a holy work, called the Book of Lost Names," said the old scholar. He produced a copy from beside him. "The rules for where burials may take place are specified in a single passage here: Chapter 4, verse 18." He opened the book and recited the passage. "The dry lands are not to be used for the rituals of burial. Only where plants may grow, and the earth is rich. In the dry lands, where heat is master, it is not just the dust of the ages that is left. There is also the shadow of memory; and for a child, this will be all there is." The scholar closed the book. "You see, burials must happen in fertile places, never in desert. Do you understand why?"

I shook my head. "I don't understand that part. What does 'shadow of memory' mean?"

The old scholar smiled sadly. "It means grief. The Order of the Skull believes that if they follow the rules in this ancient book, then the grief suffered by the relatives of the dead dragon will be lessened. If they break those rules, then the grief will be even worse, especially if it is a child who has died." He held up the holy book.

"But this is a translation," he said. "The ancient language the book was first written in is my area of expertise. Years ago, I realized that the translation 'shadow of memory' could be wrong. I kept my silence, however. I always thought it best that nobody knew."

I stared at the scholar. "Explain yourself," I urged. "What does nobody know?"

"The ancient word here translated as 'shadow' was more commonly used to mean 'dark', or 'black'. The ancient word here translated as 'memory' was more commonly used for 'unbreakable', or 'diamond'. Black diamond, Lykeffa."

"I do not understand," I told him.

"In the dry lands, where heat is master, it is not just the dust of the ages that is left. There is also black diamond; and for a child, this will be all there is." The scholar shook his head. "Don't you see? This text was never about grief. It was a warning. And it explains why the Hamelyn Piper took the dragon children!"

"Scholar," I told him. "I'm sorry, I don't understand what you're saying!"

The scholar had spoken with a quiet voice up to then. Suddenly, he shouted: "Black diamond is the bones of the dead!"

It seemed to Patch that the air had been sucked from

around them; breathing seemed more difficult, as the weight of the words settled. All this, and Barver had yet to see what Patch had uncovered at the bottom of the pit he'd dug.

I fell silent, shocked.

"This passage tells us what happens if a dragon is buried in desert," said the scholar. "Some small part of its bones will darken, and form black diamond. I believe this is why the Order of the Skull was created thousands of years ago, even before we first encountered humans – to ensure dragons are buried in ways that will not create black diamond, and so not create such terrible power to be misused. Yet the truth has been forgotten! 'And for a child, this will be all there is!' You see? The bones of a child, buried in desert! Pure black diamond! The dragon children were what he was after all along!"

"This is impossible," I told him. "What proof do you have?"

"Proof?" he said. "None! And now I am too old to do anything except pass the burden to you. Before the End of the Skies comes!"

The End of the Skies, my son. The old legend in which the earth gives up a vast store of black diamond, and all life is destroyed in the chaos that follows.

I left the old scholar in that cave and hurried home.

I was eager to forget what I'd learned, but again and again I would ask myself: why would anyone kidnap a hundred dragon children, never to be seen again?

And now the answer came: the bones of those children, buried in desert, will turn into the most dangerous magical substance that exists, in a quantity nobody ever imagined possible.

Yet why did the Hamelyn Piper take the human children? That I don't know, but I can guess. A war with the humans would have been unavoidable if only dragon children had gone.

I thought about what I should do. Without proof, this was just the ravings of a mad old scholar. Yet to prove it would need me to take a terrible risk. If I was discovered, it would mean shame, imprisonment, even death – and perhaps not just my own. You too would be at risk, simply for being my son.

I drove you away to save you from that. To save you from having to see your mother brought down; to save you from suffering the same fate.

And so, I sought the proof.

Seven years ago, when your cousin Genasha died and the Order of the Skull took her, I followed them, and watched as they buried her. When they left I committed an unforgiveable crime.

I stole the body from its resting place.

But I had to know.

Each year I have visited the site where you now stand, and so far no changes have occurred, but now illness has taken me. Soon it will be time to check again, and thereafter to return each year; this is what I ask of you.

I hope for all our sakes that the old scholar's fears were misplaced. I hope no change ever happens to those bones.

But if the worst comes to pass, you must find the bones of the stolen children and destroy them! You will need help, but the truth of black diamond must remain secret except to those who can be trusted completely.

I do not know how my dragon colleagues would react, so you must seek out Lord Drevis, the human I trust above any other. By capturing the Hamelyn Piper, the Eight saved us from far more than they ever knew. Imagine such evil power in the hands of so evil a man!

I love you. I wished to spare you this, but in the end it is a burden I must pass on. I know you have the strength to see it through.

You are all that stands against the End of the Skies.

Forgive me,

Your mother,

Lykeffa Knopferkerkle

Barver let the letter fall to the ground. He looked up at Patch and Wren, tears flowing down his pain-stricken face.

"What's in the pit?" he said. Patch could only shake his head, lost for what to say. "*What's in the pit?*" cried Barver.

At last the dracogriff moved slowly around Patch, and stood over the hole in the sand.

He kneeled and looked inside. There was the pebble of black diamond Patch had first found, and the larger chunk that had brought the reaction in the Pipe.

And beside them, beginning to blacken, was the skull of a dragon child.

28

RETURN TO TIVISCAN

Barver let out a terrible roar of despair.

"*Genasha!*" he yelled. "How could my mother do this to you? *How could she do this?*" He plunged his hands into the pile of sandy earth beside the pit and started to push it all back into the hole, covering the horrors within.

Patch grabbed Wren and quickly moved away to give Barver room to vent his anger.

The letter from Barver's mother was on the ground nearby; Barver glared at it, then let loose with a burst of flame, incinerating it. He flung his head back, the flames still coming.

Patch and Wren looked on, almost *fearful*, unsure if Barver was even aware of their presence.

When the flames stopped, Barver sobbed. He replaced

the triangular rock over Genasha's grave, then looked at his friends, heartbroken. "Genasha died holding my hand," he said. "When the Order of the Skull came to take her, it almost destroyed me. My mother made her excuses and left, telling Genasha's parents there was work to attend to…" He paused, then screwed up his face in disgust. "I tried to hate her, you know, for being so cold about Genasha's death. Eventually I left and didn't contact her again. I tried to hate her. And now…" He closed his eyes. "You should have told me, mother. You should have let me help you."

"She was protecting you," said Patch. "She hoped she was wrong about all this."

"But she wasn't wrong," said Barver. "My mother did what she knew was right, even though it caused such pain. She sacrificed everything in her quest for the truth – a truth that we are the first to really *know*. Somewhere in the world, in a dry and remote place, one hundred dragon children lie buried. And for what? For obsidiac. For black diamond. For power." He clenched his fists, visibly fighting his anger. At last he sagged, looking to his friends as he wiped away his tears.

We must do as your mother said, signed Wren. *Tell Lord Drevis.*

"Yes," said Barver. "My mother vouched for him, and that's good enough for me. But nobody else. The secret of black diamond cannot get beyond those we can trust."

Patch nodded. "Maybe Tobias and Alia would also be—"

"Nobody else!" said Barver. "Think, Patch! Can't you already *hear* the words, even from those we respect, those who mean well? 'We should take the black diamond and use it for good,' they would say. Tobias, perhaps, or Alia. Or Rundel Stone. That's a road to infighting, and the certain abuse of the black diamond's power. Not to mention war with the dragons—"

Patch thought about it, unsure – *couldn't* the obsidiac be harnessed for good? The dragons wouldn't have to know about it, and...

He shook his head, horrified by how easily his thoughts had taken that path. "You're right, Barver," he said. "The temptation would be there. It would always be a problem."

Barver nodded. "Some of Genasha's bones have already completed the change, and the rest is turning dark. It could be years before the bones of the stolen children have all transformed, or it might already have happened. Finding it will be a challenge! Still, the better it was hidden, the safer it remains, as it's unlikely to be *stumbled* upon. With the Hamelyn Piper dead, nobody knows where it is."

"If he truly *is* dead," said Patch.

"Enough of that!" said Barver. He sounded tired. "Tobias and Alia were certain of it. You're just tormenting yourself! The bones of the dragon children must be found

and destroyed. We go to Lord Drevis at once. Agreed?"
He looked to Wren.

Agreed, she signed. *Tiviscan it is, but I'll have to be the one who goes to meet Drevis.*

Patch heaved a sigh, and nodded. "True," he said. "I'd probably be recognized and arrested before I could even *see* Drevis, and Barver would cause utter panic. How long do you think it'll be before you can change into human form?"

Wren looked down at the circles in her fur, over half of them blue now. *A couple more days, maybe.*

"There is one more thing," said Patch. "Alia warned me there would be a heavy price to pay for returning to Tiviscan. That might not just mean *me*. We could all be in danger. Are you both absolutely sure you want to do this?"

Wren stood proudly on her back legs and solemnly quoted Barver's mother. *You are all that stands against the End of the Skies!* she signed. *I think that has to be more important than our safety.*

They landed well before dawn in forested hills over a mile away from Tiviscan, after two days of almost non-stop flight. Barver's shoulders had started to cause him discomfort, but with the help of Duffle's ointment he'd kept going.

During their journey, almost all of the bead-like markings on Wren's fur had become blue again. It wouldn't be long before she could change into human form; then she would set off to Tiviscan Castle and contact Lord Drevis.

In the meantime, they rested. Barver was exhausted, and fell asleep within minutes of landing. He was restless as he slept, muttering Genasha's name often, and calling for his mother. Patch took his little tent from his bag and set it up for himself and Wren, and soon they were asleep too.

When Wren awoke, she roused Patch and showed him that her band of markings was completely blue. Patch sat up and stretched. He looked outside the tent, and reckoned it was mid-morning. They'd had three or four hours of sleep at the most, and could have done with far more, but they had a job to do.

Soon they were all up and ready. They looked at each other, wary of how important their task was.

"We should get on with it," said Barver.

Wren nodded. *Time to change!* she signed. *Back in a minute.* She scampered off into the privacy of the trees. There was a blood-curdling shriek, and a few moments later Wren reappeared in human form, brushing down her clothes and looking somewhat flustered.

"Right," she said. "So *that* still hurts."

"How bad was it?" asked Patch.

"Like being turned inside out while somebody hits you with a mountain," she said. "Here I go, then. Wait here for my return, hopefully with Lord Drevis by my side. Wish me luck!"

They muttered a reluctant farewell, and as she went they found it very hard not to follow.

Wren walked through the forest and joined the road to Tiviscan. She could see the Castle ahead; wooden scaffolds encased the lower walls and the cliff face, as the work to repair the damage from the dragon attack continued.

For mid-morning, the town seemed empty and subdued. When she reached the main Castle gate, there was almost nobody around, and it set her nerves on edge. The gate itself was shut, so she knocked at the guard door.

The wooden flap in the door opened, and a Piper in Custodian uniform looked out at her.

"Yes?" he said, sounding fed up. He looked Wren up and down. "What is it, young peasant?"

Wren glanced down at herself, and had to admit she was a bit grubby. "I'll give you that one," she muttered under her breath. "But don't push your luck."

"I didn't quite catch that," said the Custodian.

"I have an important message to deliver to Lord Drevis," said Wren.

The Custodian frowned. He turned his head behind him. "Hey!" he called. "Dana! Get over here and listen to this!" He turned back to Wren, and she really didn't appreciate the dismissive look on his face. Another Custodian joined him – a woman, looking just as dismissive as he did.

"What's up, Klaus?" asked Dana.

Klaus smirked. "This... *person* wants to give Lord Drevis an important message." The two Pipers looked at each other for a moment, then turned to Wren and burst into laughter.

Wren felt a nugget of anger building inside her. She glared at them. "I mean it," she said. "It's important."

When the laughter faded, the woman sighed. "Lord Drevis is attending the Convocation, girl. He should be back here this evening. Who shall I say is asking after him?"

"My name is Wren Cobble," she said. "What did you say he's attending? A Convoc-what?"

The Pipers smirked, and Wren's nugget of anger grew. "A Convocation, girl," said Dana. "A gathering of the greatest Pipers in the lands!"

"Okay," said Wren. "Can you just point out where the Convocation is happening, so I can go and find Lord Drevis?"

Klaus shook his head. "Honestly, child. Just get yourself off home. We don't have time for games."

"I warn you!" said Wren. "This is of the *utmost* importance!"

The smiles vanished. The Pipers both narrowed their

eyes. "*Listen*, you insolent little pig," said Dana. "Run along, if you know what's good for you. Understand?" She shut the flap.

Wren seethed for a moment, then stepped forward and knocked repeatedly. This time, it wasn't just the flap that opened – it was the whole guard door. Wren took a few wary steps back, as both Pipers came out. They didn't seem at all friendly.

"That's *it*," said Dana. "You're coming with us. A night in the cells will teach you to show respect to your betters."

Wren let out a huge sigh. "You really did ask for this," she said. In her right hand were half a dozen daisy chains. She calmly threw one at each Piper, as they watched her with bemused scorn.

She'd made several stops as she'd come through the forest, so that she could gather and prepare a selection of useful flowers and plants. Underath's books had many complicated spells, far beyond her understanding, but she'd memorized a few humble little enchantments.

With the daisy chains, she'd tried a simple cooperation spell. She wasn't entirely sure it would work, but she kept her fingers crossed. As long as the targets didn't regard her as much of a threat, and so had their guard down, she reckoned she had a good chance.

Klaus bent down and picked up a daisy chain; so did Dana.

340

"What's this?" said Klaus, wide-eyed. His voice was oddly sing-song, like a dreamy child.

Dana grinned at her daisies. "Pretty!" she said.

Wren smiled. Her spell had certainly done *something*. "So, where is the Convocation taking place?"

The two Pipers nodded, their grins not slipping for a moment.

"In the Monash Hollow," said Dana. "The Council members are all there, as are most of the Elite Pipers from the Castle and many more who have travelled far." She waggled her finger at Wren. "Not us though. *We're* not there. We're *here*."

"It's not fair!" said Klaus. "A big party to celebrate the Death of the Hamelyn Piper, and we're missing it all! I mean, we've been helping out with preparations all week, but do we get to enjoy it?"

Dana shook her head. "Nuh uh!"

"Feasts and dancing!" said Klaus. "Games and challenges! And we have to stay here and watch the Castle." He frowned in a way that a grumpy five-year-old would have been proud of. "We're missing all the fun!"

Dana stuck out her lower lip and nodded. "Yuh huh!"

"Fair enough," said Wren. She was done here. She turned round and started to walk off.

"Hold up!" said Dana. She looked at Klaus. "Weren't we going to chuck her in a cell?"

The two Pipers blinked and shook their heads as if they had water in their ears. The spell was slipping, and *rapidly*. Wren delved into a pocket where she'd put some little bunches of clover stalks that she'd bewitched for an emergency. Quick as a flash, she snapped a bunch in two. "I can go about my business!" she said. "You should go and have some tea now!"

Dana nodded. "You can go about your business. We should go and have some tea now."

Wren felt a surge of pride at how well that one had gone, but Klaus was scowling at her.

"Hang about!" he said. "Is she...is she using *witchcraft*?"

Dana scoffed. "What, a good-for-nothing ruffian like that? Get a grip, Klaus!" They both shared a laugh, and then looked around with surprise. Wren, it seemed, had vanished.

"Where'd she go?" said Klaus.

"Fast runner," shrugged Dana. "Good riddance to her." She walked back through the guard door.

"I don't remember there being a tree out here..." said Klaus. He moved towards the tree for a closer look.

Wren felt like a bit of a fool, standing there with her arms stretched out to her sides as the Custodian Piper peered at her. The tree-glamour was the only magical disguise she'd managed to learn in all her time poring over Underath's books, and while the birds had always been fooled by it, she felt a huge relief that it had worked on the Piper too.

She felt something land on her arm.

"Ooh!" said Klaus. "A woodpecker!"

Wren gulped.

"Come on, Klaus," called Dana. "Your turn to make the tea."

"Yeah, okay," said Klaus, and off he went into the Castle, closing the guard door behind him.

Very carefully, Wren turned her head and stared at the bird. "Really?" she said.

The woodpecker blinked. For a moment it looked confused, and then, decidedly embarrassed, it flew away in shame.

29

DARK INSTRUMENTS

Wren returned quickly to Barver and Patch, and told them about the Convocation. She was still rather cross about the way she'd been treated by the two Custodians, but she didn't mention it; nor did she say anything about the spells she'd cast. Tempting as it was to boast, she wanted to keep that kind of thing quiet for now.

Barver wasn't exactly impressed by the news. "Pah!" he said. "A celebration of the Hamelyn Piper's death is hardly a strong message of anger to send to the dragons, is it? They badly damage the Castle, and what's the response? 'You did a terrible thing, dragons, but also we're really happy about it thanks.'"

Patch nodded. "They clearly *are* happy about it," he said. "A Convocation is rare. There's an annual Spring

Festival held in Monash Hollow, but turning it into a Convocation makes it a much larger affair – with the greatest Pipers from near and far, not just ordinary Pipers and trainees."

"Well, that's where Lord Drevis is," said Wren. She looked at Patch. "Lead the way!"

Monash Hollow was a wide circular area of grassland to the east of Tiviscan, surrounded by woods. Barver, Patch and Wren took position on a neighbouring hill, giving them a good view of the Hollow that let them appreciate how big it was – at least half a mile across.

Even so, every part of it was covered in tents and people. There were plenty of non-Pipers at the Convocation, including people running food and clothing stalls. It was no wonder Tiviscan had seemed so quiet; most of the population were here, either making a little money out of the huge event or simply enjoying the spectacle.

The sounds that reached them contained celebration and excitement and – naturally enough – music. Patch could hear the playing of the Garland Reel, a traditional spring melody that accompanied the Garland Dance. He spotted those who were dancing, and smiled as he watched. The Garland Dance was essentially a *game* – pairs faced each other holding hands, dancing quickly sideways in a long line, and at different cues in the music the pairs had to change what steps they were doing. Those who got it wrong had to leave the dance, and as the music sped up the changes grew more frequent until only two dancers remained.

In the middle of the Hollow was a series of temporary structures, including a vast and impressive stage, which had been decorated as a towering mock-up of Tiviscan Castle made of painted cloth and scaffolding. It must have been at least a hundred feet high.

"Wow," said Wren. "Whoever did that has put in a *lot* of effort."

Patch looked at the throng, astonished by the sheer number of people. With a slight tremble he imagined how bad the toilet pits would be by the end of the day. "I loved the Spring Festival each year," he said. "But they were nothing compared to this! Look at how many Elite Pipers are attending! Such an opportunity for them to pass on their knowledge and experience. See that side?" He pointed to a fenced-off area where sheep grazed. "The Drover and Arable Elite are demonstrating their farming skills there. And if you look to the left –" there was a wide expanse of ground that had been churned up into crater-pocked mud – "the Battle Elite are showing off what they can do." He thought back to his own battle training. He'd learned that what generals most valued was anything that boosted morale or – when a fight was at risk of being lost – gave the fighters a frenzied bloodlust. Patch had hated those lessons. The role of the Battle Elite in war typically meant treating soldiers as nothing more than weapons: using Songs to stop them caring about their own lives. Yet he'd been fascinated by Songs like the Push, and its close relatives – blasts of destructive force could be launched with incredible precision by the best of the Battle Elite. Patch had never quite mastered the *precision* side of it, but the destruction part was fun, when lives weren't being threatened. "Whatever Song you can think of, somewhere out there will be a place for interested Pipers to learn more."

"What's the massive pretend Castle for?" asked Barver.

"Spring Festival always has a central stage for a tournament," said Patch. "I imagine the Convocation Tournament will be even *more* thrilling, given how many Elite are present. I mean, they've really pulled out all the stops with that stage, haven't they? Look at the size of it!"

"A thrilling tournament?" said Wren. "What kind of things do they do?"

"Lots of contests to pit the best against the best," said Patch. "For Custodians it might be chasing someone over obstacles, say. It can get very exciting."

There were Pipers on the stage as they spoke, but little movement. "They're not *doing* very much," said Barver, frowning.

Patch squinted until he recognized the uniform. "They're

Arable Elite," he said. "It could be a race to see who gets some seeds to germinate and sprout first, or who can get water to flow uphill the fastest."

The three of them watched intently. After a few minutes without any activity to speak of, a whistle blew and one Piper celebrated by leaping up and down.

"Germination race, probably," said Patch.

Wren shook her head in disbelief. "Gripping entertainment," she said. "*Gripping.*" Then she set off to find Lord Drevis.

When she emerged from the trees at the edge of the Hollow, Wren was half-expecting to be stopped and questioned by some more surly Custodians. Instead, the people were friendly and smiling, enjoying their day.

She headed for the mock castle stage first, thinking that perhaps the Council would be near the centre of the action. The stage itself was empty at that moment, so she went round towards the rear to see if she could spot anyone important-looking. She was sure she could hear activity going on further within the structure, and took a closer look at one of the large sheets hanging down around the exterior – canvas, it seemed, painted to resemble castle stonework. She was about to have a peek behind it when a hand grabbed her shoulder and firmly turned her round.

A large man was giving her a very disapproving glare.

"No access," said the man, his voice oddly emotionless. "Go."

"Oh, I was just—" started Wren, but the man clearly wasn't going to take any nonsense.

"Go," he said again, in that same impassive way. Wren noticed that his eyes didn't seem to carry any emotion either – not anger, or annoyance. Not even boredom.

"Go," said the man once more, giving her a shove.

"Okay, okay," said Wren. "No need for that. I'm going."

She thought about trying another part of the stage area, but there were other men around, dressed almost identically to the one who'd shoved her. Instead, she headed out into the crowd, passing a woman selling iced buns.

"Pay him no mind, my sweet," said the woman, smiling.

"You saw?" said Wren.

The woman nodded. "They've been helping set all this up, but they're not the friendliest souls. I suppose they just don't want anyone messing about near their centrepiece! Think of the work it took!" The woman looked up at the mock castle looming high over them.

Wren's gaze followed. "I suppose you're right," she said.

"Here," said the woman, handing her one of her iced buns. "No charge! You deserve some kindness after that."

Wren grinned and thanked her. She ate her bun, glancing around the Hollow, looking for any sign of the Council.

At last she saw a group of Custodian Pipers emerge from a particularly impressive tent. They were followed by five overly serious-looking men and women in robes that must have weighed a ton. As they neared the stage, she could see their faces clearly, and recognized them from Patch's trial. The Piper's Council! Her opportunity to speak to Lord Drevis would come soon enough.

Once they reached the stage, the Custodian Pipers and the Council members walked up some steps at the side. Wren watched from a little way back as the Custodians held up their hands, signalling for quiet. When the general hubbub had settled down, a Custodian spoke up with a loud, clear voice. "Ladies and Gentlemen, and Pipers in Attendance!" he called. "The Lords and Ladies of the Council will hereby make an announcement regarding the events to be held this evening! I give you Lord Drevis!"

There was a round of respectful applause. Lord Drevis stepped forward and addressed the crowd. "Welcome to you all! Today is the day that we shall celebrate an end to the saga of the Hamelyn Piper. It is with delight that I announce that tonight's feast shall be followed by a spectacle of fireworks and wonders arranged by the Battle Pipers of Kintner!" There was a great cheer from the crowd. Drevis settled them down with several waves of his hand. "Those yet to lodge their horses in the stables at Tiviscan please be sure to do so in advance of the display. Also –"

Drevis pulled out a sheet of paper and looked through it – "I've been asked to…to—"

He drifted off into silence. Wren frowned, puzzled.

There was a very low droning sound in the air, which varied rapidly as if an insect was attempting to fly into her ear. Wren looked around, expecting to see a swarm of bees or something similar nearby, but there was nothing.

Instead, she noticed curious behaviour in those standing near her. Slowly, everyone bowed their heads in silence, including Drevis and the others on the stage. The low droning grew louder and more rhythmic, and a melody began to take shape. Wren could see that it wasn't just those nearby who were affected. Within the vast Hollow, every single person was now standing utterly still, head bowed.

She looked to the person next to her, a Piper with a blue and grey uniform; she took the woman by the shoulder and shook her vigorously. "Wake up!" hissed Wren. The Piper didn't open her eyes. Worse, she felt stiff as a corpse, muscles locked in place.

This wasn't good.

Suddenly, the people gathered round the stage began to stride backwards in unison. Wren did the same, not wanting to be left standing alone. When they all stopped, the ground around the base of the stage was empty.

A group of men, dressed just like the one who had

shoved her earlier, spread out along the back of the stage, then reached up into the cloth drapes beside them and seemed to *pull* on something. The meticulously crafted mock castle began to come apart. Painted canvas fell away from the wooden scaffolds, and then those scaffolds fell away too, landing on the newly vacated ground.

What Wren saw being revealed underneath – something that had been hidden there all this time – made her tremble with a fear that was almost overwhelming.

Where the mock castle had stood was a curious collection of huge cylindrical shapes. The tallest and widest of them, in the middle of the structure, was a hundred feet high and four feet wide; the cylinders became ever smaller out to each side.

It was a *Pipe Organ*, and each of the Pipes was deep black in colour.

Wren stared at it, open-mouthed. The sound was coming from those Pipes.

On the stage, one final canvas sheet was pulled away to reveal a figure wearing a long hooded robe, sitting at a multi-tiered panel of keyboards and pedals that would have been more at home in one of the great cathedrals. Hands and feet started to fly up and down the keys and levers, and the low droning sound grew more and more complex, with higher notes added now, to create intricate melodies.

The hooded figure stood and walked to the centre of the

stage to take a bow, and even though the keys of the organ weren't being played, the music kept going – just as it did whenever Patch paused while playing his Pipe.

Wren looked around at the silent people and felt a deep chill as she realized what was going on. She tried hard not to react – drawing attention to herself could be disastrous.

"Time to go," she muttered. She backed away one slow step at a time. When she felt that she was at a safe enough distance from the stage, she made for the trees as fast as she could.

Once in the woods she ran, plunging blindly through bushes. When something loomed up just ahead of her, she screamed.

It was Barver. "Are you okay?" he said, looking just as panicked as she felt.

Barver was alone. "Where's Patch?" she asked.

"He fell into some kind of trance," he said. "I could hear those odd sounds, so I moved him down the other side of the hill until they faded. He went limp and collapsed. Then I came to find you." There was dread all over Barver's face. "What's happening, Wren?"

"Didn't you see it?" she said. "It was hidden underneath the fake castle."

"I left our vantage point to get Patch to safety," he said. "*What* was hidden?"

She told him.

They found Patch where Barver had left him, sitting behind an outcrop of rock. He was rubbing his head and moaning. Wren kneeled beside him. "Patch!" she said. "Snap out of it! We need you!"

Patch looked at her, finding it hard to focus. "Did I fall?" he said. "I don't—" He flung a hand to his mouth in shock: while they were far enough away for the organ music to have lost its power over him, it was still audible and he was able to pick out some of the familiar rhythms and melodies that lay within the intricate sounds. "Oh. Oh no."

"It's a Pipe Organ!" cried Wren. "The Pipes are vast, and they're dark black, Patch! The black diamond, the bones of the dragon children! It's already been harvested, and turned into a huge Pipe Organ! Everyone in the Hollow is under its spell!"

Patch stared at her, despairing. "An obsidiac Pipe Organ?" he said.

"Exactly!" said Wren. "There was someone at the keys, and surely there's only one person it could be!"

Patch shook his head, dreading what she would say.

"It's the *true* Hamelyn Piper!" cried Wren. "It must be!"

Patch wanted to run away, to just leave and not return, but he forced himself to take a deep breath. He slapped the side of his head quite hard. "Think!" he said to himself.

"Think!" He looked at Barver. "You're immune to the Song being played?"

"I seem to be," said Barver.

"It may be human-targeted, then," said Patch. "But why is Wren unaffected?"

She shrugged and held up her wrist, waggling her bracelet. "I guess I'm technically still a rat," she said. "With modifications."

Patch thought for a moment. "In that case, this is going to be up to you two," he said. "I can't get closer to the music or I'll be just as useless as everyone else in the Hollow."

"So what do we do?" said Wren.

"I'll fly down and incinerate him," said Barver.

Wren smiled. "I like that idea."

"No," said Patch. "He'll be ready to defend himself. The moment he saw you, he'd knock you out of the sky. Probably kill you in the process."

Barver tutted. "This is *me* we're talking about."

"Please, Barver," said Patch. "That Pipe Organ could have incredible power. It'd be like the Battle Pipes at Tiviscan, but ten thousand times stronger."

Another sound joined that of the organ music. *Voices.* "Go and take a look, Wren," said Patch. "Tell us what's happening."

She hurried up the hill and returned a minute later. "Some of the crowd are standing in rows and columns, like soldiers," she said. "They're moving suddenly every few seconds – both arms up, then to the sides, then down. They keep shouting every time they move, something I couldn't make out. The rest of the people are at the edges of the Hollow, standing motionless with their heads bowed."

Patch listened carefully to the music. He could feel it *pull* on his mind, but he knew he was just beyond its range. "Like soldiers—" he said, an idea forming. "Does the Pipe Organ look like it could be moved around easily?"

"Not a chance," said Wren. "It's just as big as the castle mock-up."

Patch frowned. "Then he needs an army. Unthinking, and controlled utterly by him. But the control would have to continue even after the Piping stopped, or they could never *go* anywhere."

"Is that possible?" said Barver.

"The permanent domination of the mind of another person," mused Patch. "A Song of absolute control, of *puppetry*. Making someone a mindless slave! That kind of thing isn't *supposed* to be possible."

"Wait!" said Wren. "A man stopped me going too close to the back of the stage, and I swear he was in some kind of trance. There was something *wrong* about him. Apparently he and others like him helped build the stage in the first place."

"Puppets!" said Barver. "It would make sense for the

Hamelyn Piper to recruit some before he came here, to help him prepare."

"Then such a Song must be possible after all," said Patch. "And he's attempting to enslave everyone in the Hollow, all at once!"

"Not everyone," said Wren. "Half of the people had taken themselves to the Hollow's edge."

"Did you notice a difference between them?" said Barver. "Those at the edges, and those being controlled?"

Wren thought for a moment. "Pipers!" she said. "It was the ordinary people at the edges, Pipers in the centre!"

"An army of Pipers," said Patch, dread filling him. "And among them the best of the Elite…"

Wren's eyes widened. "And surely he would arm them all with obsidiac Pipes!" she said.

"They'd be invincible," said Barver.

Patch listened to the Song again. Parts of it seemed familiar enough – he thought he could unpick those aspects if he had a chance. "He's gradually taking them over," he said. "How long it requires I don't know, but if he succeeds then silencing the organ won't be enough. They'll already be his soldiers."

"So we strike now, before it's too late!" said Barver. "Let me toast his noggin!"

Patch shook his head. "No incinerating unless absolutely necessary," he said, to Barver's disappointment. "The very *minds* of his victims could be at terrible risk if the Song simply collapses! We need a way to disable the Hamelyn Piper safely. Knock him unconscious, maybe, so I can get down there and try to reverse the Song."

The three of them thought in silence.

"I've got it!" cried Wren. She went to Barver's side and delved into Erner's bag, pulling out a cloth and carefully unwrapping something.

A leather pouch.

"This might be just what we need," she said. "Kaposher Dust. Underath had it."

"Ah!" said Barver, nodding. He took the pouch from Wren, feeling its weight. "I can throw the pouch at the Hamelyn Piper if I get close enough, but it's a risk. As long as it still has potency there's plenty here, but Kaposher goes stale easily."

"We should test it," said Patch, taking it from Barver. He reached to the ground beside him and picked up an acorn. With extreme care he untied the mouth of the pouch, then dipped the acorn inside and tied the pouch shut again. He tossed the acorn high into the branches of a nearby tree.

They waited.

They heard a squeak and a squirrel dropped out of the leaves, falling like a stone. It was out cold.

Satisfied, Patch gave the pouch to Wren. "You'll both have to do this," he said. "Barver, you must focus on flying.

Wren, you open the pouch up fully and throw it. Don't breathe the dust, whatever you do."

"And how do we get close, if he'll swat me like a fly?" asked Barver.

"I'll try to draw his attention," said Patch. "But I can't promise much, from so far way." He reached into his bag for his Pipe, but his fingers touched something else. He pulled out the Hamelyn Piper's Mask and unfolded it.

"If only we could slap *that* thing on him!" said Barver.

"Would it work?" said Patch. "Casimir built the Mask to block Songs passing through it, purely to stop the Hamelyn Piper lip-playing his way to freedom. It wouldn't prevent him playing that organ."

There was a thought buzzing in his head, however. He thought back to the stories of the Eight, as his own words echoed around his mind: *this was designed to block Songs passing through it.*

But that wasn't quite true – it wouldn't let Songs *leave*. The Songs of another could still affect the prisoner while he wore the Mask, so that the Pipers guarding him could use whatever was needed to restrain him.

It was a one-way barrier to the magic of music.

Patch folded the Mask, then unfolded it again. The action was smooth and took very little pressure. Fold; unfold.

He did it once more, but this time he twisted it in a

slightly different way, and the Mask was inverted when it opened. The curious markings in the metal – those runes that Casimir himself had engraved and inlaid with obsidiac – were on the *outside* of the Mask now, not the inside.

Barver and Wren were staring at him.

"You don't think—?" said Wren.

"It's worth a try," said Patch. He raised the Mask to his own head and put it on. He had an immediate sense of claustrophobia. With the Mask's latch broken he had to keep it closed with one hand. He strode towards the hilltop, Barver and Wren following. As he walked the music grew louder, but he could already feel the difference.

The Obsidiac Organ was having no effect; the Mask was protecting him.

"Do you have twine, Barver?" said Patch.

Barver nodded and produced some from his side pack. "Hold still," he said, and gently secured the front of the Mask.

Patch was the Piper in the Iron Mask, now.

He took his Pipe from his bag. "But can I Pipe while wearing it?" he said. "I'm going to play you some courage. Tell me if it works."

He began to create the Song of Courage; as he played, Barver and Wren straightened up and thrust out their chins, looking to the sky, determined and fearless. Yet for once, Patch himself didn't get any benefit from his Song.

"It's *definitely* working," said Wren.

"Good," said Patch. "I'll be your distraction. I'll hit him with everything I've got. It should give you a window of opportunity. But whatever happens once the Kaposher is thrown, get out of there as fast as you can and leave this place! Don't wait to check he's unconscious, just go! Get back to Marwheel Abbey: to Tobias and Alia, and Rundel Stone. Make sure the world knows what's happening here!" Barver and Wren both shifted uneasily, saying nothing; Patch hoped their courage wasn't about to override common sense. "Do you understand? Whatever happens, get away from here as fast as you can!"

Wren frowned. "But what if you—?"

"Swear it!" cried Patch. "Even if I get into trouble, there's to be no *rescuing* of any kind!" He fixed his gaze on them both. Eventually they nodded.

"I swear," mumbled Barver.

"Me too," said Wren, reluctantly.

"When the Hamelyn Piper is unconscious I'll tie him up and put the Mask on him," said Patch, taking the rest of Barver's twine. "Then I'll see if I can use the Organ and reverse the Song's effects. Now go! Hide at the rear of the Hollow, then wait for my signal. The Pipe Organ itself should give you some cover as you fly at him."

"What's your signal going to be?" asked Wren.

Patch grinned through the Iron Mask. "Chaos!"

30

THE SONG OF THE HAMELYN PIPER

Patch watched from the edge of the Hollow.

The civilians were standing around the perimeter with their heads bowed, all but forgotten by the Hamelyn Piper, whose focus was entirely on his new army. Now that he was so close, Patch could make out what it was these "soldiers" were shouting each time they changed position: "We obey you, Lord!"

The Hamelyn Piper was sitting at the organ, his arms moving in a frenzy over the keys. Standing along the back of the stage were a dozen large men, identically dressed; Patch assumed they were the ones Wren had mentioned, the Puppets. The organ's Song kept growing in complexity, the movements of the sleeping army becoming more refined as the Song grew ever richer. The Hamelyn Piper's control of his victims was increasing.

Patch gripped his Pipe. The Iron Mask felt more uncomfortable every second, making it hard for him to concentrate. He thought of that poor innocent prisoner, who had worn it for almost a decade, and scolded himself. He needed to ignore the Mask and focus!

His plan was simple enough. He'd promised chaos, and if there was one Song that had caused chaos in his own life, surely it had to be the Dance. And while the Hamelyn Piper had an army, Patch realized he could have one too – the unconscious civilians were no longer the target of the organ Piping. If Patch could reach them with the Dance, then delivering the chaos he'd promised would be within his grasp!

The Dance was a flexible Song; that was how Patch had been able to match it to the reels and jigs he'd taught the various bands he'd played with, after fleeing Tiviscan. Whatever the tune, he knew how to play the Dance underneath it. If it was a familiar tune for a well-known dance, those caught in the spell would perform the moves that the tune required.

He watched carefully as the Pipers in the Hollow repeated their movements again and again. A plan had taken shape in his mind.

He put his Pipe to his lips and started to play, hoping he was too far from the stage for the Hamelyn Piper to notice anything amiss. The feet of the civilians nearest to him began to tap out the rhythm he played. As expected, none of the Pipers were responding – they were lost to the Song of the Pipe Organ.

He risked playing a little louder to draw in more civilians, and then he moved along the perimeter of the Hollow. The civilians followed behind him in a line, like sleepwalkers, taking rhythmic steps with their heads still bowed. Each had a dreamy smile on their lips as, deep in their slumber, they enjoyed their dancing.

With perhaps two hundred recruits gathered, Patch turned and walked into the Hollow. He led his followers along the space between two columns of Pipers, who continued to follow their commands, oblivious to Patch and the civilians. When he was halfway to the Pipe Organ he changed his Song to include the melody of something everyone would know.

The Garland Reel.

At once, the civilians did as the reel required. They paired up and faced one another, two lines of dancers just fitting into the gap between the columns of Pipers.

Patch paid close attention to the sequence of movements the Pipers were following. It included a section where they raised one leg, balanced on it for a few seconds, then lowered it, before doing the same with the other leg.

Timing would be everything. He waited for that first

leg-raise to happen again, and when it did he played the musical cue for the dancers to separate and take three quick steps backwards. The civilians did just that, but now they bumped hard into Pipers who were all standing precariously on one leg.

Here it was: Patch's attempt at chaos. He could hardly bear to watch in case his idea simply fizzled out, but the line of Pipers teetered back and toppled – right into the next line, who also fell.

And the next.

And the *next*.

Patch couldn't contain his glee as the wave of toppling Pipers spread out and kept on going. The Pipers let out grunts and yelps as they fell, still trying to perform the movements that the Organ was commanding them to do. Unable to stand up again, they twitched their limbs and shouted, "We obey you, Lord!"

By the time the toppling petered out, a third of those in the Hollow lay on the ground flapping like landed fish. At the centre of the confusion, Patch let out a triumphant shout, laughing as hard as he could. He saw the Hamelyn Piper suddenly freeze, hands stopping above the Organ keys.

He had finally noticed.

The Hamelyn Piper jumped up from his seat and strode to the edge of the stage, his mouth gaping open. The toppling had failed before reaching those closest to him, and as the music continued to play within the Pipe Organ they kept on with their bizarre drill. "Who dares to defy me?" he shouted. "*Who dares to defy me?*"

"I do!" yelled Patch. He raised his Pipe and started to build another Song – a Push, just to rile the man even more. He launched it and for once his aim was good enough to knock the Hamelyn Piper off his feet, even from such a distance.

The man was stunned for a moment, but snapped out of it and pulled a dark Pipe from his belt, quickly weaving notes together, taking Patch by surprise with the speed and strength of the result. A pocket of air shot from the Pipe straight at Patch, sending him flying before he could move out of the way. Winded, he quickly picked himself up off the ground.

The Hamelyn Piper roared in anger and started to build another attack; Patch was building one too. They launched simultaneously and the two Songs hurtled towards each other. At the midpoint the Songs collided, and a deafening thunderclap echoed around the Hollow. The two Pipers set about forming yet another attack.

Suddenly Patch saw Barver closing in fast from behind the Organ. If the Hamelyn Piper hadn't been focusing on Patch, Barver would have been the target of those powerful Songs, but instead he and Wren had a clear run. It was only as Barver flew over the tops of the organ Pipes that the

Hamelyn Piper saw him, and by then it was too late.

The open pouch of Kaposher hurtled down towards him and exploded. A cloud of dust obscured the man, and some of the Pipers closest to the stage collapsed as the Kaposher reached them.

Barver and Wren saw Patch and started to head towards him.

"Go!" shouted Patch, waving at them to leave the Hollow. "*Go, now!*" He looked at the huge cloud of Kaposher obscuring the stage. The way that the pouch had *exploded* left Patch feeling very uneasy indeed. "*Get out of here!*"

They seemed to get the message, and began to turn.

Then Patch felt the cold edge of a knife at his throat, and a strong grip on his arm; his Pipe was wrenched from his hand. He didn't dare move, but he could see the sleeve of the arm holding him, with the colours of a Custodian's uniform.

The Hamelyn Piper's voice boomed through the air. "You fly *anywhere*, dragon, and he dies!"

A swirl of air began to spin on the stage, taking the dust cloud higher and higher until it dispersed. The Hamelyn Piper was standing there, the hood of his robe still hiding most of his face, but not his malicious grin. He was surrounded by a shimmer of air, the telltale sign of the protective shield he'd managed to create. The shimmer faded as the short-lived barrier vanished.

All around the Hollow, fallen Pipers were recovering and rising to their feet.

"Let him go or I will *burn* you," shouted Barver, maintaining his height.

"My *soldier* will slit his throat if you make any such attempt," cried the Hamelyn Piper. He waved a hand in a carefree gesture. "By all means try!"

Barver scowled but did nothing. On his back, Wren glared at the man.

The Hamelyn Piper gestured to his "soldier". Patch was pushed towards the stage and forced up onto it. He saw the members of the Council standing on the grass nearby, their faces blank.

"Now isn't *this* interesting," said the Hamelyn Piper. He pulled back his hood, and ran his fingers over the Mask covering Patch's face.

With the man's hood down, for the first time Patch got a good look at him, and all he could do was stare. Terrible scars covered his face, long healed-over but deep. The man's right ear was ragged, half-gone. But that wasn't why Patch stared.

He'd seen that face before, without the scars, but filthy and bearded. "My God," he said. "You…you look exactly like him."

"What are you babbling about?" said the man, raising an eyebrow.

"The prisoner in the Iron Mask."

The man's eyes narrowed for a moment, and then he smiled. "Oh, very good! *Very* good. You do seem to know a lot, don't you? And you have his Mask. However did you come by it? I thought it hadn't been found. I must try not to kill you, so you can tell me all about it later!" He looked more closely at the Mask, and his smile became a sneer. "Ah, I see what you did! Inside out, I'm impressed! Very clever. I wonder if Casimir originally made it that way, as a device for his own protection?" He looked around at his soldiers, only half of whom had managed to stand again. The rest were lying still. "You're little more than a *boy*, and look at all the trouble you've caused me. That will take time to fix." He shot Patch a look of sheer malice. "His Pipe if you please!" he ordered, and the Custodian – the *soldier* – holding Patch handed it over. "Beautifully made," he said, studying it. "The glaze is unusual." He raised it to his nose and sniffed. "Not sure what it's made of, but look at mine!" He held his own Pipe up for Patch to see. "Obsidiac glaze, of exceptional thickness and quality. Better than yours, lad." He put his own Pipe away, and gripped Patch's with both hands. "Shame," he said, snapping it in two and tossing the pieces to one side.

Patch felt as if he'd been punched in the stomach. He'd been getting to *like* that Pipe.

"I suppose you must be a trainee, studying at Tiviscan,"

said the Hamelyn Piper. "Imagine! Tiviscan's last hope, a child!" He leaned close to Patch, leering at him. "I know a way to deal with children, lad." Patch squirmed in the grip of the soldier holding him, and the Hamelyn Piper backed away. "But yes, of *course* the prisoner looked like me," he said, smiling. "Our mother would have been *so* disappointed by what I did to him."

"Your own brother?" said Patch.

"My twin, no less! It was always my plan to have him punished in my place. I played a Song of Forgetting and Piped away his memories, then kept him safe in a secret location. All I had to do was lead the authorities to him when the time was right! But the Eight made everything *so* much more difficult. They kept closing in on me, hundreds of miles away from where I was keeping my brother. It was tiresome! They almost got me, too. Left me with *this*." He ran his fingers over the scars on his face. "A present from the Eight. I've wanted to repay the favour all these years, but I had to be patient and not draw their attention. And what patience I have shown! Then some idiot started messing around, playing illegal Songs and making everyone worry about Dark Pipers. I'd intended to put my plans into action *next* year, but I decided to bring everything forward. Rundel Stone had started to ask awkward questions! I couldn't take the risk that he'd stumble onto something, or get the other remaining members of the Eight involved."

Patch gulped. The idiot messing around and playing illegal Songs had been *him*.

"Why are you doing this?" said Patch.

"To rule! This world needs a ruler who's truly worthy of the responsibility."

"And that's you?"

"Of course! There are so very *few* people deserving of power. The rest –" he looked out across the Hollow, at all the people under his control – "cattle. *Sheep*." He leaned close again, and smiled. "Now, I *could* tear that mask from you and make you just another of my soldiers, but I wouldn't want you to miss the rest of the performance. I think you'll appreciate it. Right now, they obey my will for as long as the Song plays, but when I am done they will be mine *for ever*."

Patch saw the fearful look on Barver's face, and on Wren's. They had to escape, he knew, escape and warn the world – and Patch had an idea, a way he could help them do it.

"I have one question," said Patch. He made sure he sounded absolutely defeated. "Did you ever think of your brother, condemned in the dungeon?" His voice grew quieter with every word, and the Hamelyn Piper drew closer to hear better. "Did you ever think about what he suffered?" whispered Patch. "Have you no *compassion*?"

The Hamelyn Piper put his lips right up to Patch's ear. "No!" he snarled with glee.

His glee was short-lived. Patch turned quickly and flung his head forward with as much strength as he could muster, catching the Hamelyn Piper on the nose with the full force of the blow. There was a satisfying crunch as the metal Mask hit home. The Hamelyn Piper fell to his knees with a howl, his hands covering his face, blood pouring out between his fingers.

At once, Patch flung his head backwards, connecting hard with the soldier holding him; the soldier's grip weakened and Patch tore free. He ran towards the rear of the stage where the Organ Pipes loomed high above him.

"Get him!" screamed the Hamelyn Piper, and more of his soldiers – the Puppets – strode with terrible purpose towards Patch. The Hamelyn Piper brought his obsidiac Pipe to his lips and began to play a Song that Patch recognized at once. A battle Song, and a powerful one – it wouldn't take long to complete, but Patch realized it wasn't going to be aimed at *him*: the Hamelyn Piper had turned to face Barver and Wren.

"Barver!" Patch yelled. "Do as you swore! Get out of here!"

He could see the hestitation on Barver's face, but there was no other choice. The dracogriff flew hard; seconds later the Song was launched, catching Barver a glancing blow. He tumbled; Wren only just managed to stay on, but Barver kept them airborne.

The soldiers were closing in on Patch, and only one route was left: onto the very Pipes of the Organ itself. He leaped high and got his fingers on the edge of the smallest Pipe, pulling himself out of reach just in time. His pursuers hoisted one of their number up after him. He backed away, climbing the taller Pipes as he went; ahead, he could see more soldiers climbing the smallest Pipes on the other side of the Organ.

On the stage below, the Hamelyn Piper was working on another battle Song to throw at Barver, but after a few seconds he stopped. "No, no," he said. "That's boring. I've got a much better idea, and I do love a challenge!" He put his Pipe away and hurried to his keyboards. He sat and rubbed his hands to warm them. "Let me see..." he said, and he feverishly worked the keys and pedals, adding more layers to the Song.

Barver and Wren were halfway to the edge of the Hollow.

The Hamelyn Piper turned to look at them and frowned. "Nothing?" he said, disappointed. "Mmm. That really should have worked on a dragon. Hang on! Were those feathers I saw? Was that some kind of beak? A griffin?"

He played a slight variation on what he'd added before, then stopped and frowned again. Barver was at the edge of the Hollow now. They were almost free!

The Hamelyn Piper grinned. "Of course!" he said. "How stupid of me!" He looked up to where Patch was scrambling to ever-higher Pipes, always just out of reach of his pursuers. "Taking control of a mind is so much easier one-to-one," he called. "Even if the target is a dracogriff!" He began to play again, laughing as he did.

Dismayed, Patch watched as Barver turned and started to fly back, helpless against the power of the obsidiac Pipe Organ. Patch felt a hand grab at his ankle, and he kicked it away, almost losing his balance. There was only one Pipe left to climb now – the largest of them all. He had little strength remaining in his arms, but he hauled himself up. This last organ Pipe was four feet across. He could feel the deep notes reverberate in his *bones*. Its edge was only a few inches thick and he struggled to stand, almost toppling into the gaping hole at its centre.

Barver reached the stage, level in height with Patch. The dracogriff's eyes were blank; on his back, Wren pleaded with him. "*Barver!*" she cried. "It's *me! Please!*"

She met Patch's eyes and shook her head in despair.

The Hamelyn Piper smiled at Patch, then looked to Barver. "Let's deal with your rider first!" he said. "Fly until you are above the rocks over there. Drop your rider onto them from a *great* height. Then come back here and eat your friend."

"NO!" shouted Wren. She tried to jump from Barver, but he grabbed her by the arm and held her dangling under him as he flew off.

The Hamelyn Piper looked to Patch's pursuers. "Leave him where he is," he instructed. "Let him watch his friend die."

Patch looked on in horror. Barver flew away from the Hollow until he was directly above a wide rocky outcrop. Up, up he went, a hundred feet higher, two hundred, three, all the while ignoring Wren's screams.

At last he stopped climbing. He held Wren up in front of him and looked at her.

Wren was distraught, tears flooding down her cheeks. She could see no emotion in his eyes, only cold obedience.

"Please," she said. "Barver—"

He dropped her to a certain death below, then turned back to kill Patch.

31

A Heavy Price

Wren screamed as she fell. Above her she saw Barver flying off, and she knew his target was Patch. She wondered if her dracogriff friend was still conscious of what was happening. If so, he would be suffering horribly.

She tumbled down through the air. She could see the rocks below her as she hurtled towards them, and she knew what she had to do.

Wren reached to her wrist and took hold of the bracelet that let her take human form. Alia's words of warning echoed in her head: *Do not remove it... You'd be a rat, immediately, and no amount of magic would shield you in future.*

She pulled hard, and the bracelet came apart. The beads scattered in the air, becoming ash. Pain coursed through her body as she changed – immediately, and for evermore – into a rat.

At this size, she was safe. She could fall from any height, and the air would slow her down, cushion her.

Wren Cobble, *rat*, flopped onto the rocks and looked across to the Hollow. Barver had almost reached Patch. She closed her eyes, unable to watch.

Patch saw her change, and understood at once what she'd done. Tears poured down his cheeks, knowing what it had cost her.

Get away from here, Wren, he thought. She was the only one who could warn the rest of the world now.

Barver would be on him in moments. Below, the Hamelyn Piper's laugh became ever more insane as Barver approached his target. There was nothing he could do, except stand and wait for the end to come, keeping his footing on the vast organ Pipe and its gaping core.

The *Pipe.*

Patch gasped as the thought came to him. He shook his head, angry with himself for not thinking of it sooner.

Taking a deep breath, he lifted up his right foot and gathered all the courage he had. He stepped forward into empty space and fell, plunging into the darkness of the Pipe's interior. It grew narrower lower down, jamming him inside; the sense of claustrophobia was unbearable.

He could hear the Hamelyn Piper's laugh falter, hear him scream at Barver to stop. But it was far too late.

Barver would seek his prey, whatever it took.

Patch closed his eyes. A moment later, everything exploded around him.

32

AFTERMATH

Patch opened his eyes and found himself looking straight at the face of a rat: Wren was sitting on the Mask peering into an eyehole.

Get up! she signed, and moved off him.

He sat up slowly. Pieces of debris fell from him – smashed organ Pipes and chunks of wood. He groaned, every part of him in pain. His lip felt swollen, and he had cuts and bruises aplenty. He started to work at the twine securing the Mask, eager to get out of it, but Barver had tied it too well.

Any bones broken? signed Wren. She was perched on a large section of smashed Pipe, a few feet away.

"I don't think so," said Patch. He looked right at her, and felt tearful. "I saw you fall," he said. "I know what you had to do. I'm so sorry…"

Yeah, signed Wren. She pointed to the markings around her midriff. The pattern of beads was still there, but they were all solid black now. *Being a live rat is better than being a dead girl.*

Patch reached out his hand to her, and she ran to his shoulder.

He stood, and they looked around. Everywhere in Monash Hollow, people were on the ground, out cold. In places, some were stirring, or sitting up and holding their heads. The Council members were on the grass near the stage, starting to rouse themselves.

"How long have I been unconscious?" said Patch.

I got back here a few minutes ago, signed Wren. *It was a long way to run on little feet. Half an hour maybe? I thought you were never going to wake up.*

Just in front of them a large pile of debris suddenly rose up, startling them both. A very familiar head emerged from underneath.

"What happened?" said Barver, blinking. "Why is everything blurry?"

"You ploughed head-first into the organ Pipes," said Patch. "Don't you remember anything?"

Barver frowned. He stood up, the debris falling away from him. "The last I remember I was escaping with Wren on my back!" he said. "And then I—" His mouth opened wide with horror. Huge tears welled up in his eyes.

"*Wren!*" he wailed. "*No! I killed her!*"

"It's okay!" said Patch. "She's here!"

"I can't see properly," said Barver, sniffling. "Talk to me, Wren! Let me hear your voice!"

Wren squeaked.

"She's a rat again," said Patch. "She had to break her bracelet and change back to survive the fall."

"But that means she'll never be able to change again!" said Barver, blinking away his tears. "We'll find a way, Wren. We'll find that griffin, and—" He was cut off by a shout from nearby.

"We have been attacked!" came the shout. "Get the rest of the Council back to the tent!"

Patch looked across and saw a group of Custodians; standing among them was Lord Drevis, who suddenly pointed right at Patch. "He wears the Mask of the Hamelyn Piper! Seize him!"

The Custodians ran directly at Patch. He held his arms in the air. "Hold on!" he said. "I'm not—" One of the Custodians tackled him; they hit the ground together, and the Mask popped open and came off. The Custodian pinned him down, but the relief of being out of the Mask was immense. Then Patch realized Lord Drevis was looming over him, staring.

"Good God," said Drevis. "Patch Brightwater. What have you done? Explain what happened here!"

"You were under a controlling Song, Lord," said Patch.

"Everyone was! Try hard, and you'll be able to remember!"

Lord Drevis glared at him, but then his glare faded. "There was another man—" he said. He looked around at the debris. "He played a vast Pipe Organ. He tried to seize everyone's minds! You fought him!"

"That's it!" said Patch. "It's coming back to you!"

"He was—" started Drevis, but then his eyes went wide. "No. *No*." Drevis looked horrified. "Let him up," he ordered, and the Custodian released Patch and pulled him back to his feet. "I remember it now," said Drevis. "The Hamelyn Piper. How is that possible?"

"The prisoner in Tiviscan was his brother, Lord," said Patch. "He'd tricked you into imprisoning his twin, all those years ago."

"An innocent man," said Drevis, stunned. "I condemned an innocent man. Is the true villain dead?"

"He was at the keys when the organ was destroyed," said Patch. "He must have been crushed."

"Clear this area!" yelled Drevis. "Find the corpse! *Now!*"

They watched as the Custodian Pipers worked to clear the debris. Patch felt a dread building deep within him. As each piece of shattered Pipe and broken timber was thrown to the side, his dread grew.

When the stage was cleared, no sign of the Hamelyn Piper – and no sign of his Puppets – had been found.

They had vanished.

Lord Drevis ordered that the search be widened. He looked at the Mask he now held, then turned to Patch. "You were thought to have died when the dragons attacked," he said. "Instead, the chaos gave you the chance to escape. But why take the Mask?"

Patch shrugged. "I honestly don't know. But I'm glad I did."

Drevis folded it, inverting it again. "It protected you," he said. "Smart lad. And it's lucky for us that you came back to Tiviscan. Now, there's much you have to explain to the Council. Come with me."

Patch looked across to Barver and Wren, who were clearly anxious. He signed to them: *Wait here.* Then he followed Drevis, who led him across the Hollow to a sumptuous tent where two Custodians stood guard outside.

Drevis held the tent flap open for Patch. Inside, the other four members of the Council sat on wooden stools around a central table. Each of them bore scratches that showed how near the stage they had been when Barver had destroyed the Pipe Organ. Some held small glasses filled with a brown liquid that Patch suspected was brandy; he could see more than one hand trembling a little.

Patch stayed by the tent entrance, but Drevis strode over to the others.

"Your memories have returned?" Drevis asked them.

"More or less," said Lord Cobb. "Imagine, all this time. An innocent man in the dungeons!"

Drevis said nothing, but Patch knew the comment must have pained him.

"Those Pipes were obsidiac glazed," said Lady Winkless.

"Impossible!" cried Lord Pewter.

"No, no, he's correct," said Lady Rumsey. She held a fragment up. "I've yet to do the sums, but the glaze is thick. There must have been a vast store! Goodness knows how he got all that obsidiac."

Patch kept silent – he would tell Lord Drevis what he knew about the source of the black diamond, nobody else.

"Wherever it came from, it's ours now," said Lord Cobb. "It's a source of unspeakable power, and it will be researched. I'll put our top people on to it!"

"The dragons may have something to say about that," said Lord Drevis.

"Let them," said Cobb. "One thing's for certain, that amount of obsidiac will be very handy in rebuilding the Castle defences."

Patch had listened to this madness long enough. "You must destroy every fragment!" he cried.

Lord Cobb frowned. "Who's this? We're discussing sensitive Council business! This is no place for a boy!"

Drevis gestured for Patch to come closer, and Patch saw Lord Pewter sit up sharply, eyes wide.

"This is Patch Brightwater," said Drevis. "*This* is who was wearing the Mask, and fought the Hamelyn Piper."

"Brightwater?" said Lady Rumsey, peering at Patch. "Didn't we lock him up?"

"We did," said Drevis. "He was in the cell next to the Hamelyn Piper – well, the Piper's *brother*, as we now know. Brightwater was presumed dead after the dragon attack."

"Well then, there's only one course of action!" said Lady Rumsey. "Guard!" One of the Custodians entered the tent. "Throw this criminal in a cell at once."

"What are you doing?" said Lord Pewter.

"The law demands it!" Lady Rumsey replied.

"Enough!" said Drevis. "He saved us all. I believe a suitable reward is appropriate for his courage." On the table in front of him was a small chest, which he opened. He took out paper and a quill, and wrote for a few moments. When he was done, he stood and showed what he'd written to each member of the Council. "Any objections?" he said. There were none, although Lady Rumsey looked slightly peeved. "Good."

Drevis passed the paper to Patch, and Patch read it.

It was a pardon. It absolved him of all guilt, and meant he was free. Tears rolled down his cheeks, and he didn't care. He folded the pardon up and placed it in his pocket, his fingers brushing against another piece of paper – Alia's prophecy, and an unwelcome reminder of Erner. Even so, the joy and relief he felt at being pardoned was so strong he thought his legs might buckle.

"Wait!" cried Lord Pewter, rummaging in the chest where Drevis had found the paper. He took out a small block of wood and what looked like an ink pad. "It still needs stamping with the Council Seal to make it official."

Drevis smiled and held his hand out. "My mistake. Can I have it back for a moment, Patch?"

Patch reluctantly took the pardon out of his pocket and returned it, feeling like it would burst into flames or simply vanish, but it was stamped and back in his grasp within seconds.

Drevis smiled at him. "When this immediate chaos abates, we must talk more. I'd like to know just how a disgraced trainee saved Tiviscan, and the world."

"The Hamelyn Piper is still out there, Lord," said Patch. "The world isn't saved yet."

"You saved it for today, at least," said Drevis. "That's all a hero can ever do."

At that, the tent flap opened and an out-of-breath Custodian entered. "Lord Drevis, your presence is needed."

"Good," said Drevis. He looked to the Council. "The hunt for the Hamelyn Piper is being organized in the Castle as we speak, and I must oversee it."

"But there are things I must tell you—" said Patch.

"It will keep until later," said Drevis, and he left.

"I suppose we too should make our way to the Castle," said Lord Cobb. He stood slowly from his stool and began heading out.

"Oh please wait," said Lady Winkless. "I need to sit a moment longer. I'm too old to be in such a hurry."

"Indeed," said Lord Pewter. "Allow us to finish our brandies, at least."

"Oh very well," said Lord Cobb. He turned back to the table, then stopped, gesturing to something on the ground near Patch's feet. He looked at Patch. "Did you drop your pardon, lad?"

But Patch still had the pardon in his hand. He looked down and saw what Cobb meant, and realized at once what it was. He checked his pocket to be sure, and yes – the pocket was empty. When he'd removed the pardon to be stamped, the paper with Alia's prophecy had come out too and fallen to the ground.

Lord Cobb picked it up and unfolded it. Patch had a curious sense of unease.

"'They thought they had us'," Cobb read aloud, in a monotone voice. "'But we're almost clear. Just the ridge to go. What's wrong with you? What's wrong?'" Lord Cobb looked up from the paper. "An *odd* set of words, don't you think?" he said.

Patch felt every drop of blood drain from his face. He could hear Alia's voice in his mind, saying exactly the same thing: *An odd set of words, don't you think?*

"I agree," said Lady Winkless. "Very odd."

"What say you, Patch?" said Lord Pewter.

Patch stayed silent, too stunned to answer.

"The lad's gone so very pale," said Lady Rumsey. "The day's been *quite* a strain, I imagine!"

An odd set of words, don't you think? I agree, very odd. What say you, Patch? The lad's gone so very pale. The day's been quite a strain, I imagine.

The precise words Alia had spoken. Patch had thought that those words were mere ramblings, but instead they had simply been a continuation of the prophecy.

There will come a time when you hear these words, Alia had told him. *A mouth that speaks them is a traitorous mouth.*

This was the first time the words had been spoken in their entirety. *This* was the moment the prophecy had warned him of.

This moment, and no other.

He felt sick with guilt. Erner had never been a traitor. The *Council* were the ones who had spoken the words. *They* were the ones who would betray him to whatever he feared the most.

When Erner had said it, Patch had most feared returning to the dungeons, being put back into the Dark by Rundel Stone.

But now…

His mouth went dry as he thought about what he feared most now. It was the leering face of the Hamelyn Piper that came to mind.

He looked at the Council, trying hard to keep his emotions from showing.

Get away as quickly as you can, Alia had said. *Run!*

The Council were still awaiting an explanation of what was written on the piece of paper. "Just the words of a song I heard," said Patch. "I wrote them down. Odd words indeed. Now, if the Council will permit, I think I need to go and get some rest."

"Indeed!" said Lord Cobb. "We'll speak again later, as Lord Drevis said."

Patch managed to smile. He prayed that it seemed genuine, because at that moment he wanted to scream and run from the tent.

"Absolutely," he said, and left.

Somehow he kept that smile going all the way out of the Council tent and across the Hollow.

He reached his friends. Barver was lying face down on the grass, his wings outstretched and badly cut. Wren was perched on his snout. "Ah, there you are!" said Barver. "How did it go?"

"Um," said Patch. "Yes. It went...fine. I was pardoned.

Which was good." He coughed. "How's your eyesight? Still blurry? Can you fly, do you think?"

"Oh, my eyesight's recovered," said Barver. "But flying? I doubt it." He sat up and used his hand to lift one wing, then let it drop. It was completely limp. "Something's broken in there." He picked the tip up and bent it right back, making Patch and Wren wince. "It shouldn't be able to do that, either," he said, with a shrug.

"Perhaps we should, um, journey to Marwheel and call in on Brother Duffle to treat you?" said Patch. "Right now?"

"Oh, I'd rather rest for a few days," said Barver. "We all should! You seem agitated, Patch. Do you need to empty your bladder or something?"

Wren frowned with concern. *You do seem agitated,* she signed. *What's wrong?*

And even though there was nobody close enough to eavesdrop, Patch leaned over and whispered to them both, explaining what had just happened.

Barver stared at him. Wren stared too.

"Alia warned me that prophecies were dangerous things," said Patch, frowning. "Never straightforward, she said. Tend to cause endless trouble."

"She was certainly right about *that*," said Barver.

"So," said Patch. "Marwheel Abbey, anyone?"

Wren hopped from Barver's snout to Patch's shoulder. *We should leave at once, but how can we get away unseen?*

Patch nodded to the edge of the Hollow farthest from Tiviscan. "We can reach the Penance River from that side," he said. "If we can sneak into the trees, it's forest all the way."

"Avoid the roads," said Barver. "Good."

We've done it before, signed Wren.

"Are we sure about this, Patch?" said Barver. "The prophecy already led us astray once. You say the Council will betray us to the Hamelyn Piper, but how? And what about Lord Drevis? My mother trusted him."

Patch shook his head, uncertain. "Drevis left the tent before it happened. Perhaps he's trustworthy, perhaps not. That must be for Tobias, Alia and Rundel Stone to decide, when we tell them what's happened here. Let *them* deal with the Hamelyn Piper. We have our own business to attend to."

"Yes!" said Barver. "Our own business – to find Underath's griffin!"

Wren looked dejected. *Alia said breaking my bracelet would leave me permanently changed. Nothing can be done for me now.*

"What kind of talk is that?" scoffed Barver. "We'll find that griffin, Wren, and all will come good."

"There's something we have to do first," said Patch. He pictured Erner's shocked face as he'd fallen from Barver and into the lake below, swimming for shore to an uncertain future at the hands of those mercenaries. "We have a friend to rescue," he said. "Agreed?"

Agreed, signed Wren.

"Agreed," said Barver.

The Hollow itself was emptying, people going back to the town and Castle. Patch led the way to the far edge of the Hollow, and they waited. When they thought it would be safe, they walked into the cover of the trees.

Their departure went entirely unnoticed.

So it was that the three friends – Piper, dracogriff and rat – began the journey that would take them, eventually, back to Marwheel Abbey. Even after they reached the Penance River, each step they took was leaden, as they fretted about Erner, and the Council, and the Hamelyn Piper.

"Look at us," said Barver. "Together we saved the world, but we're weighed down by worries!"

You should play a Lift and lighten our mood, Patch, signed Wren. *Like you did to the little ant and the monks in Marwheel.*

"My new Pipe was destroyed," said Patch, thinking of the terrible feeling of loss he'd suffered when it happened. "I hope you can spare a few more feathers, Barver, when I make a new one?"

Barver nodded. "As many as you require."

Can't you play the Lift without a Pipe? signed Wren.

"I can try," said Patch. But his lip, injured when the Pipe Organ was destroyed, was too swollen. When he tried to whistle, all that came out were flubs and raspberries. "Sorry," he said.

"Never mind," said Barver. "Do you know the shanty 'Farewell the Winter's Frowning'? It's popular in the Islands."

"It's popular everywhere," said Patch. He cleared his throat and started to sing, his voice unsteady. *"Farewell the winter's frowning,"* he began. *"The sun's smile comes again."*

As Patch sang the rest of the verse, Barver sang too. Wren joined in with tuneful squeaks.

They gave voice to the lyrics of hope and renewal, and as they did their singing grew ever more heartfelt. Soon enough, hope had truly bloomed within them; they smiled and laughed once more. And all from a simple shanty.

For there is a truth, one that is all too easy to forget:

There is magic in music.

Listen...

Patch, Wren and Barver
will return for a second
spell-slinging, shape-shifting,
flame-throwing

SONGS OF MAGIC

adventure in 2019...

Check here for news:

@Usborne

@SethPatrickUK

@usborne_books

facebook.com/usbornepublishing

#ADarknessOfDragons

Acknowledgements

Patch, Wren and Barver have been waiting a very long time for me to tell their story. I thank them for their patience.

Thanks also to my agent, Luigi Bonomi, who encouraged me to follow my heart when I was dithering about what to work on next.

I'm indebted to Anne Finnis, Rebecca Hill and Sarah Stewart at Usborne for all their help and support in turning my early efforts into the finished work you have in your hands.

My final thanks, of course, go to my wife and children. Without you, there would be no music at all.

About the Author

S.A. Patrick was born in Belfast. When he was a child, he wanted to write video games, become an author, and have magical powers. The first two came true. If he does ever get magical powers, he hopes people like dragons and griffins because there'll suddenly be a *lot* of them around.

He has had four previous books published as Seth Patrick. *Songs of Magic: A Darkness of Dragons* is his first book for children.

Follow S.A. Patrick online

@SethPatrickUK

#ADarknessOfDragons